The
Legacy

A JOANNE KILBOURN MYSTERY

GAIL BOWEN

The Legacy

LIBRARY AND ARCHIVES CANADA CATALOGUING IN PUBLICATION

Title: The legacy / Gail Bowen.

Names: Bowen, Gail, 1942- author.

Series: Bowen, Gail, 1942- Joanne Kilbourn mysteries ; 22.

Description: Series statement: A Joanne Kilbourn mystery ; 22

Identifiers: Canadiana (print) 20230485901 | Canadiana (ebook) 202304859IX

ISBN 978-1-77041-746-5 (hardcover)
ISBN 978-1-77852-221-5 (ePub)
ISBN 978-1-77852-222-2 (PDF)
ISBN 978-1-77852-223-9 (Kindle)

Subjects: LCGFT: Detective and mystery fiction.

Classification: LCC PS8553.O8995 L44 2023 | DDC C813/.54—dc23

Published by ECW Press
665 Gerrard Street East
Toronto, Ontario, Canada M4M IY2
416-694-3348 / info@ecwpress.com

Cover design: Michel Vrana

This book is funded in part by the Government of Canada. *Ce livre est financé en partie par le gouvernement du Canada.* We acknowledge the support of the Canada Council for the Arts. *Nous remercions le Conseil des arts du Canada de son soutien.* We acknowledge the funding support of the Ontario Arts Council (OAC), an agency of the Government of Ontario. We also acknowledge the support of the Government of Ontario through the Ontario Book Publishing Tax Credit, and through Ontario Creates.

PRINTED AND BOUND IN CANADA

PRINTING: MARQUIS   5 4 3 2 1

CHARACTER GUIDE

JOANNE'S FAMILY

ZACK SHREVE: fifty-seven, Joanne's second husband of nine years. Once a hard-driving, hard-drinking paraplegic trial lawyer who lived like an eighteen-year-old with a death wish, he fell in love with Joanne and decided to clean up his act.

TAYLOR LOVE-SHREVE: twenty-two, a gifted visual artist. Joanne adopted four-year-old Taylor when her mother, Sally Love, Joanne's half-sister died. Lives with her childhood best friend, Gracie.

MIEKA KILBOURN-DOWHANUIK: thirty-six, Joanne's eldest daughter. Married to Charlie Dowhanuik (second husband). Mother to Madeleine (fourteen) and Lena (thirteen) from her first marriage and Desmond Zackary Dowhanuik (nearly two).

PETER "PETE" KILBOURN: thirty-four, Joanne's son, married to Maisie. Peter and Maisie have twin boys, Colin and Charlie (five).

ANGUS KILBOURN: thirty, Joanne's youngest son, engaged to Leah. He's a lawyer in the Calgary branch of Zack's law firm and a great admirer of his stepfather.

LEAH DRACHE: Angus's first love and fiancée. She's an MD, daughter of author Steven Brooks and niece to psychiatrists Reva and Mila Drache, who helped raise her.

CHARLIE DOWHANUIK (CHARLIE D): thirty-six, Mieka's husband. Host of the hugely successful radio show, *Charlie D in the Morning*. It's a mix of in-depth interviews, fun interviews, music and Charlie D's riffs on life.

MAISIE CRAWFORD: thirty-four, Joanne's daughter-in-law, married to Peter. One of Zack's law partners and a killer in the courtroom.

ESME, PANTERA (d.), AND SCOUT: Joanne and Zack's dogs.

GOLDIE: Charlie and Colin's new pup.

ASSOCIATES

NEIL McCALLUM: Bouvier dog breeder who has Down syndrome; owns an acreage east of Regina where he lives and operates with his mother, Margaret. A former friend of Kellee Savage (d.), Joanne first met him fourteen years prior during the Tom Kelsoe case.

VALENTINE "VAL" MASLUK: thirty-five, writer, and neighbour to the McCallums. Formerly Val Massey, Joanne's journalism student fourteen years ago. Author of *Steven Brooks: A Biography* and *Two Journalists*, a novel based on the Tom Kelsoe investigation.

RAINEY ARCUS: Val's researcher for his books and another former journalism student of Joanne's.

STEVEN BROOKS: father of Leah Drache and the reclusive bestselling and award-winning author of *Medusa's Fate* and *The Iron Bed of Procrustes*.

GEORGIE KOVACS (née SHEPHERD): mid-forties, Jo's former writing partner on *Sisters and Strangers*, wife of Nick Kovacs, and former girlfriend of Steven Brooks.

LAUREL WOODROW (d.): an author whom Steven Brooks potentially plagiarized. She took her own life fourteen years ago, two years prior to the publication of *Medusa's Fate*.

REBECCA WOODROW: Laurel Woodrow's granddaughter who is bringing a plagiarism suit against Steven Brooks.

PATRICK O'KEEFE: lawyer representing Rebecca Woodrow in her suit.

TOM KELSOE: killer, sociopath, and Joanne's former co-lecturer at the School of Journalism. Currently in prison for the murders of journalism student Kellee Savage and professor Reid Gallagher fourteen years ago. Jo's friend Jill Oziowy had formerly been in an abusive relationship with him.

ANNIE AND WARREN WEBER: friends of Jo and Zack; parents to older son Simon and baby daughter Maeve.

SIMON WEBER: wedding photographer and son of Annie and Warren; former associate at Falconer Shreve who had to stop practicing law after suffering a psychiatric break.

ED MARIANI: sixty, the head of the School of Journalism; work associate of Joanne's and close friend. She was his best man at his wedding to his partner Barry.

DEBBIE HACZKEWICZ: head of Major Crimes who knows Joanne and Zack well.

KAM CHAU: mid-thirties, executive producer for Charlie D at MediaNation.

NORINE MacDONALD: Zack's executive assistant at his firm.

SAWYER MacLEISH: twenty-nine, a long-time friend of Joanne's son Angus and like family to Joanne.

CHAPTER ONE

MORNING, AUGUST 27, 2022

In spring, summer and early autumn, when we're at our cottage at Lawyers Bay, my husband, Zack, and I usually sleep with our windows open. Except for the occasional tang of skunk, the air we breathe in is a gift, and on the Saturday morning of August 27, our bedroom was fragrant with the scent of stargazer lilies and summer's last roses.

Zack and I were lying side by side, our hands touching. I stretched lazily. "We seem to be in for another day of glorious weather," I said. "It looks as if our seemingly endless summer knows it's time to pull out all the stops to remind us that nothing lasts forever." My husband chuckled softly, but he didn't respond.

I would be turning sixty-four in a month, and Zack was fifty-seven. From the day we stood in front of the altar at St. Paul's Cathedral and promised to love and to cherish until death did us part, "seize the day" had been our byword. But as benevolent as the weather promised to be, a large question mark loomed over the hours ahead.

Our grandsons Charlie and Colin were going to choose their first puppy, and, still at the sweet age of nearly six, they wanted their grandparents to be part of the adventure. Zack and I were both dog-lovers. From the time I'd left boarding school, I had owned a dog — but our most recent, Pantera, had been Zack's first dog. Pantera had been abandoned at our son Peter's animal clinic. His young owners brought the bullmastiff in to be neutered, but, despite repeated calls from the clinic, they never picked him up. Finally, they severed their connection to Pantera with a brief and pithy text: "He was real cute when we got him, but he just kept getting bigger. Stop guilting us."

I'd asked Peter to bring Pantera to my house to discuss his future and to see how he got along with my old dog. They were doing well, then Zack wheeled into the backyard; Pantera loped over to him, and it was love at first sight for both man and mastiff. Pantera turned out to be "a Velcro dog." He had chosen Zack, and he was determined to stay by his side, come hell, high water or whatever perils awaited the man we both loved. Over the next eight years and eight months, Pantera was an intrinsic part of our family, and then, in early July, his big heart simply stopped beating. He had nine happy, healthy, loving years of life and a sudden and painless death.

The average lifespan of a bullmastiff is eight to ten years. That was a fact, and as a trial lawyer Zack was accustomed to dealing with unpalatable facts, but Pantera was the first dog Zack had ever owned, and he grieved. I was grateful that Pete and Maisie were with us the day Pantera died. Pete made the arrangements, and the next week we buried our much-loved mastiff in the spot under the Amur maple that he favoured for sunning.

In the almost two months since Pantera left us, Zack was always on the mark professionally and personally, but I knew he was suffering.

Saturday was the day we'd promised to meet the twins and their parents at breeder Neil McCallum's acreage, sixty-seven kilometres east of Regina. The boys wanted to get an early start, so we'd arranged to meet them at nine thirty. When Zack came into the kitchen for breakfast, I knew he was miserable, but I also knew he was determined not to let the boys down. I'd made blueberry waffles, one of Zack's favourites. When he saw them, he smiled appreciatively. "Thanks," he said. "Your blueberry waffles could get me through just about anything."

I watched as he poured on melted butter and maple syrup and then just stared at the plate.

"Zack, we don't have to go," I said. "I can call Pete and Maisie."

"And tell them what? Jo, you remember how insistent Charlie and Colin were that I was the one who could help them pick exactly the right pup."

"I do. And I remember that when you pointed out that their father is a veterinarian who could tell them everything they needed to know, Colin said, 'But Daddy can't read a story the way you do, Granddad. When you read a story I can *feel* it in my stomach.'"

Zack shook his head at the memory. "That sealed the deal," he said. "Let's eat our waffles and hit the road."

"Would you like me to drive?" I said.

"You read my mind," he said. "It's an hour's drive to the breeder's, and I can use that hour to man up."

* * *

For the first ten minutes of our drive, Zack was silent. Seemingly, manning up took time.

Finally, he said, "Okay. I think I'm ready to join the human race again. Tell me about Neil McCallum."

"Well, for starters, I know you'll like him. I haven't seen Neil in fourteen years, but we talk on the phone a couple of times a month. And, of course, he always sends us a holiday letter with news and photos of his dogs."

"I'm not big on holiday letters," Zack said. "But I enjoy Neil's. They seem to capture the spirit of the season."

"That's because Neil is always filled with the spirit of the season," I said. "He's made a very good life for himself. When I met him, he had his first Bouvier, and he was planning to breed her."

"Judging by the photos, Neil's built quite an empire with his Bouviers."

"He has," I said. "Neil has Down syndrome, and he and his mother work hard to maintain that empire. They have the town's only concession stand, and they move it to wherever the action is. Neil says when you own a concession stand, there's always something to look forward to. In the spring, there's tee ball, baseball and horseshoes, so Neil and his mum set up in the park. In fall, there's football, and the big fowl supper and then comes Christmas, so Neil and his mother set up in the hall that the town uses for the holiday market. After Christmas, there's curling at the curling rink. According to Neil, 'It's all just so good.'"

Zack was pensive. "Seems like Neil's figured life out," he said. "A lot of us buy into the argument that our reach should always exceed our grasp — that life is about making it to the next rung."

"Neil doesn't see it that way," I said. "He's content with what he can reach, and he's a happy man. And it's not because he's settling for less than the best. He recognizes that what he has *is* the best."

Zack reached over and stroked my leg. "What you just told me about Neil may be exactly what I needed to make it through the morning. Bring on the pups!"

I covered Zack's hand with mine. "Welcome back," I said.

* * *

When we arrived at Neil McCallum's, Maisie and Peter's Volvo was already parked in the driveway, and Neil was waiting for us. He was holding a squirming puppy, and he seemed remarkably unchanged from the young man I remembered. Neil was a little below medium height and had a stocky build. He was wearing blue jeans, a green and white Saskatchewan Roughriders long-sleeved shirt and a Riders ball cap. The hair not covered by his cap was brown, and he had the almond-shaped eyes, small nose and distinctive mouth of a person with Down syndrome.

He moved close to us as I got out of the car. "I'm so happy to see you, Joanne. I'm happy to see you too, Mr. Shreve." Zack had reached into the back seat and was snapping the pieces of his wheelchair into place. When the chair was secure, he transferred his body from the passenger seat to his wheelchair. Neil was fascinated by the sequence. "You do that so fast, Mr. Shreve."

My husband smiled. "Practice makes perfect."

Neil spoke slowly, and he stuttered a little when he was excited. "That's right. It took me a while to find the right puppy for you, Mr. Shreve. But I found him, and here he is. He's a boy, and you get to choose his name." Neil handed the squirming puppy to Zack, and the pup immediately settled in. Zack was clearly gobsmacked. Neil was beaming. "See how happy he is! I'll take a picture."

Bouvier puppies look like little black bears. They're hard to photograph, but in Neil's photo, Zack's new pup did indeed appear to be content, and Zack did indeed appear to be gobsmacked. But Neil had already moved on to the next item on his agenda. "Maisie, Peter and the kids are waiting, but there are two things I have to tell you. Mr. Shreve, we have a bathroom on the main floor that your wheelchair can fit in."

The enthusiasm with which the puppy in Zack's arms was licking his new master's face had apparently short-circuited my husband's thousand-megahertz brain, and he was slow on the uptake. "That's good to know," he said finally. "And Neil, please, call me Zack."

"I will," Neil said. "Here's the second thing I have to tell you. Joanne, my neighbour Valentine Masluk wants you and Zack to come to his house for lunch today."

"Valentine Masluk, the writer?"

Neil nodded. "His house is only ten minutes from our house. Joanne, when I told him last night that you were coming today, Valentine asked me to tell him asap if your answer to lunch is 'yes' or 'no.'"

I glanced at Zack to see how he felt. But Zack and his new puppy had bigger fish to fry than consider an invitation from a stranger. "Please tell Valentine yes," I said. "But Neil, I'm curious, did Valentine Masluk say why he wanted to have us over?"

Neil's head shake was vehement. "No. Do you want me to ask him, or do you want to be surprised?"

"This seems to be a day for surprises," I said. "Please just tell Mr. Masluk we'd be pleased to join him for lunch."

* * *

The next hour was a happy blur. Zack's wheelchair was manual, so he handed his new pup to me and wheeled over to the boys. At the first whiff of puppy breath, I knew this little Bouvier belonged with us, but there was another puppy to choose, so our pup stayed with me while Charlie, Colin, their father and grandfather made their deliberations.

As soon as she saw that I was alone, our daughter-in-law was by my side. When Pete brought Maisie home to meet us for the first time, she'd just come from a lacrosse game, and her upper lip was split. Her smile was crooked but winning. Zack said when he shook hands with Maisie that night, she crushed three of his fingers.

Maisie was now a senior partner in Zack's law firm. That morning she was wearing white cotton shorts and a black T-shirt with an image of the scales of justice and the words "born to argue" printed on it in white block letters. Like my husband, Maisie was a trial lawyer, and like him, she loved her work.

"Jo, I want to tell you how grateful Pete and I are that you suggested giving our sons this chance to spend time with Neil McCallum. Before we came, we explained to the boys that Neil is a person with Down syndrome, and that the way he looks and speaks is a little different from the way most of the people they know look and speak. But Neil didn't need our intervention. He's so patient and kind with Charlie and Colin, and, of course, he has puppies. The twins think he's amazing. Pete and I do too."

"I'm glad we were able to bring Neil and your family together."

"So you're not angry about the way Zack got ambushed and you ended up with a potential new dog?"

When I glanced down at the pup and saw his dark eyes peering up at me with frank curiosity, I felt a sudden rush of something very close to love. "No," I said. "We're not angry."

"That's a relief," Maisie said. "It was just a misunderstanding. When the boys were looking over the puppies, they told Neil that their granddad has been sad since his dog died, and he needed a puppy too. Neil didn't miss a beat. He said, 'If your granddad needs a dog, we'll find the right dog for him.' And then he told them that people always make easy things hard and he just didn't get it. Pete was going to straighten out the situation, but we realized that Neil and the boys were right. Zack did need a dog."

"And there was no point in making an easy thing hard," I said. "So our new dog comes with a life lesson."

"It's a lesson worth holding on to," Maisie said. "And now that we've discovered that the key to life is clearing our path of the blocks we throw in our own way, let's join our crew."

* * *

Colin and Charlie had chosen their dog's name before they set eyes on any of the puppies. The name was secret, but according to the twins it was a good name for either a boy or a girl. That sunny morning when Zack pointed to the pup that was the liveliest in the litter and said, "I kind of like that one for you," the boys turned to each other: "That's the one," Charlie said. And Colin said, "That's Goldie," and his tone made it clear the matter was settled.

* * *

Margaret McCallum came over with her phone and took photos of the twins with Goldie and then some of the whole Crawford-Kilbourn family with Goldie.

"Neil tells me he already has some photos of Zack and you with your new pup, Joanne."

"He does," I said. "And we'd appreciate copies of those photos."

"Now, Margaret, I'd like to take some photos of you and Neil with our as-yet-unnamed pup," Zack said.

"You might want to make a photo album for your pup," Margaret said. "We keep photos of each of our puppies with their new owners in albums. Sometimes when Neil is feeling blue, we take out the albums, and he's back to being himself in no time flat."

"As soon as we get back to the city, we'll buy an album," Zack said. "Jo and I sometimes feel blue ourselves, and it would be good to have a pick-me-upper handy."

* * *

Decisions had been made. Zack and I both took advantage of the main-floor wheelchair-friendly bathroom, paid our puppy deposit and thanked Neil for giving us and the twins a sticky note that said "Pickup day — Saturday, September 10." In two weeks, Goldie and our still-to-be-named dog would become part of our lives. Neil walked us to our car, and after we were settled and he'd given us directions to Valentine Masluk's place, he said, "This was nice, wasn't it?"

"It was," I said.

When we were back on the highway, Zack turned to me. "So what just happened?"

"You needed something, and Neil was able to give you what you needed," I said. "Easy-peasy. Now, in all the hullabaloo, did you pick up on the fact that we are now on our way to Valentine Masluk's place?"

"I did," Zack said. "I also picked up on the fact that you're the one he's interested in seeing. Do you have any idea why?"

"None. He's writing Steven Brooks's biography, and Steven's daughter is marrying our son in a little over a week," I said. "Angus and Leah have been together on and off for fifteen years, but when Steven arrives in Regina for the wedding rehearsal, it will be the first time we've set eyes on him."

Zack raised an eyebrow. "He certainly takes his role as the reclusive author seriously."

"Leah told us he bought that cabin on Anglin Lake because he was suffering from a severe case of writer's block, and he was hoping the move back to Saskatchewan would kickstart some new ideas," I said.

"And it worked," Zack said. "The year after he moved to the cabin, he finished the manuscript for *Medusa's Fate*, a bestseller and an award winner."

"And six years later there was *The Iron Bed of Procrustes* — also a megahit. But last February when we thought Leah's father would be coming to her engagement party, I reread Steven's first three novels. They're not very good, Zack."

"Maybe he was just a late bloomer," Zack said.

"Still, he must be feeling the pressure." I shrugged. "Or maybe he's just satisfied with what he has already accomplished."

"Well, the biography should answer that question. It could be a real tell-all. Angus showed me the contract Brooks signed. It gives Valentine Masluk unrestricted access to his papers, his work, his interviews, his friends, his enemies, his lovers — free access to everything and everybody."

I was incredulous. "He doesn't get to vet the manuscript?"

"No. He does not," Zack said. "The only revisions Steven can make are to correct factual errors. Essentially, the agreement gives Valentine Masluk permission to gather together everything he's learned about Steven, decide what the evidence reveals about the man and write five hundred pages proving his point."

"Land mines everywhere," I said.

"Yep, and the contract is ironclad. Why Steven Brooks signed it is beyond me. He's a smart guy. But that contract leaves him wide open." Zack glanced at me briefly. "Jo, has Leah said anything to you about her father giving Masluk unrestricted access?"

"No. She did tell me that when she and her aunts tried to talk Steven out of signing the contract, he quoted William Blake. 'If the doors of perception were cleansed every thing would appear to man as it is, infinite.'"

Zack snorted. "So Steven Brooks wants to cleanse the 'doors of perception' about himself so the world can see that he's 'infinite'? Sounds like we're approaching batshit crazy territory, Jo."

"Mila and Reva are both psychiatrists, and Leah's an MD. They're knowledgeable about people whose view of the world has become skewed. But Steven did sign the contract. I imagine at this point Leah and her aunts are just hoping for the best. They've all met Mr. Masluk. According to our soon-to-be daughter-in-law, they all like him. Apparently, he answered all their questions and addressed all their concerns. He was upfront about his commitment to telling the truth. He said he wouldn't whitewash Steven Brooks, but he would make every effort to understand why Steven has made the decisions he's made."

"That's pretty much the way I approach my clients," Zack said. "But my clients are in my office because they're facing charges and a team of Crown prosecutors eager to see that justice is done. I'm their last hope. Steven isn't facing charges, he's just a guy who, for some reason, has decided to open up his life and let Valentine Masluk give the public a guided tour."

"Mr. Masluk has been working on the biography for close to five years. The official publication date is September 7, but *Steven Brooks: A Biography* is already being shipped to book suppliers. There's been so much going on, I don't think I told you that we received an advance reading copy last week. I figured you and I could wait till all the excitement settles before we sit down to read it."

"A 480-page book demands a serious commitment," Zack said.

"It does," I said. "And the week ahead might be a good week to start on that commitment. Leah's aunts are coming to Lawyers Bay tomorrow for a visit, and after we get the cottages ready for Leah, Angus and their friends to stay in over the Labour Day weekend, we can go back to the city and take care of everything that needs to be taken care of before the first week in September, which is going to be jam-packed. Monday is Desmond Zackary Dowhanuik's second birthday party. Monday night is the rehearsal dinner and the rehearsal itself. The first day of school is Tuesday: Colin and Charlie are starting grade one. Lena will be headed for grade nine at LeBoldus and Madeleine will be in grade ten. Angus and Leah's wedding is on Tuesday, and after that, we have quite a few more family birthdays to celebrate and a pup that will need to be named and housebroken."

Just then, a disembodied bass voice announced, "You have now reached your destination."

"Why does that guy always make arriving at the address we punched into the GPS sound like the Day of Judgment?" Zack said. His tone was easy, but when I didn't comment, he was quick to pick up on my mood. "You're apprehensive about this meeting with Valentine Masluk, aren't you?"

"I am," I said. "And there's no reason why I should be. I just wish I knew why he wants to see us."

As I turned off the motor, Zack leaned closer to the windshield. "You'll know soon enough," he said. "Mr. Masluk just came out of his house to greet us, and he looks harmless. Check him out for yourself."

When I followed through on Zack's suggestion, it was my turn to be gobsmacked. Valentine Masluk turned out to be another man whom I hadn't seen for fourteen years, and, like Neil McCallum, he had played a central role in a dark episode of my life.

Those many years earlier, Valentine Masluk or Val Massey, as he was then known, was a student in a cross-disciplinary seminar on politics and the media that Tom Kelsoe, a lecturer and rising star in the School of Journalism, and I co-taught. Val was twenty-one, but he had been a very young and vulnerable twenty-one, and, like all the students in the seminar, he idolized Tom Kelsoe.

The slender man in blue jeans approaching our car had a confident stride and an open smile. Seemingly, Valentine Masluk had left behind the naïveté that had once made him the willing acolyte of a sociopath.

Zack had already snapped his chair together and was transferring his body to the seat of his wheelchair before I had the presence of mind to unsnap my seat belt and slide out of the Volvo. Val Massey met me with an outstretched hand. "Dr. Kilbourn, I can't tell you how pleased I was when Neil told me you were coming to his place this morning. It's been too long since we've seen each other."

"It has," I agreed. Zack had wheeled over to join us. "And you're not the only person whose name has changed. I'm Joanne Shreve now, and this is my husband, Zack."

After they shook hands, Zack said, "So what do I call you — Val or Valentine?"

My former student shrugged. "When I'm with friends, Val is fine, but Masluk is my family name. The day I dropped Massey and began using Masluk was the day I started to grow up. But let's go inside. I'm sure the three of us can find topics more riveting than how I finally came of age."

Val lived in an old farmhouse, and surprisingly, there was a ramp to the front porch. Zack grinned and wheeled over when he saw it. "My lucky day," he said.

"And there's an accessible bathroom on the main floor," Val said. "Time to buy a lottery ticket, Zack."

The front door opened into the kitchen. The house had been sensitively renovated. The kitchen was at least twice as large as many old farm kitchens, and Val had combined the best of what was available in the second decade of the twenty-first century to some memory-evoking pieces from the past. The old wood stove and the chrome kitchen table and chairs were a graceful nod to the past, but the stainless steel appliances were top of the line. The table was set for three with an earthenware pitcher filled with sunflowers as a centrepiece. A pot simmered on the stove. It was difficult to imagine a more welcoming room.

"Please make yourselves comfortable," Val said. "As you can see from that very large quantity of borscht, since I talked to Neil last night, I have been busy. I'm really glad you can stay for lunch."

My husband and I exchanged a glance. "Wild horses could not drag Jo and me away from this meal," Zack said.

"Good," Val said. "Now, I like a lager with borscht, but if you'd prefer something else . . . ?"

"Lager's fine for me," I said.

"And with me," Zack said. "Val, thank you for removing one of the kitchen chairs to make room for my wheelchair. You're a considerate host."

"My dad was in a wheelchair, so I picked up on a few things."

Val opened three bottles of Stella Artois and placed them on the table next to three beer glasses. After we'd filled them, Zack raised his glass. "To friendship," he said.

I sipped my beer. "Seeing you and Neil on the same day is wonderful, but I'll have to admit, it's a little overwhelming."

"Overwhelming but serendipitous," Val said. "Joanne, over the years, I've started to call you a dozen times, but I never knew what to say or where to start. But thanks to your grandsons' search for the perfect puppy, here we are together as I had hoped we would be. But first things first. Did the boys find the pup of their dreams?"

"They did. Our son is a veterinarian, but his twins were insistent that Zack make the choice because when their granddad reads a story, they can *feel* it in their stomachs."

"High praise," Val said. "As you may have heard, I have a book coming out this month — if your grandsons are up for a chapter book, I could use a blurb!"

"Charlie and Colin are fine with chapter books as long as the chapters aren't more than three and half pages long," I said.

Val groaned theatrically. "Mine are on the long side, so I guess I don't qualify. But right now, I'd just like to hear about you two. Joanne, when you stepped out of the car today, I noticed something different about you."

"Fourteen years will do that to a person," I said.

Val shook his head. "No, it's not that. You don't look older. You just look happier."

"I am happier," I said.

Zack took my hand. "We both are. We caught the brass ring."

"So once again, you're lucky," Val said.

"We are indeed," my husband said. "Because Colin and Charlie weren't the only ones who got a new dog from Neil today."

"I didn't realize a puppy for you and Joanne was part of the plan," Val said.

Zack shrugged. "Neither did we, but not long after the pups were born, Charlie, Colin and their parents came out to see the new litter. The twins told Neil that since Pantera, our mastiff, died, I'd been sad and I needed a dog. By the time Jo and I arrived, Neil was ready for us. He had a handsome little pup in his arms; he handed it to me and said, 'I found the right puppy for you. He's a boy, and you get to choose his name.'"

I picked up the narrative. "And before Zack could protest, Neil whipped out his phone, snapped photos of Zack with his new dog, handed the phone to me and said that if the pictures weren't good enough, he could take more."

Val's laugh was warm. "That is a classic Neil story. For every problem, there is a solution. Don't make something that's easy hard."

"Words to live by," Zack said. "Val, how did you come to know Neil?"

Val had beautiful blue eyes, large, clear and long-lashed. He turned them to Zack. "It's a long story, so let's save it till after we've had lunch. My dad and I didn't agree on much, but we did agree that meals were for serious eating, not serious talk. If you'd like to wash up, now's your chance. I'll get everything on the table."

"Everything" turned out to be quite a spread: Borscht with dishes of sour cream and fresh dill; a selection of sausages — kovbasa, bratwurst, bratwurst with cheddar, bratwurst with apple and gouda; and a platter of Ukrainian cheeses, including bryndza, which, Val explained, was made from sheep's milk and was tangy and smelly. A loaf of black bread, butter, an assortment of mustards and a bowl of dill pickles that Val had made himself were arranged on a small lazy Susan.

The borscht was sublime, and Zack had opted to butter a slice of bread and sample everything on his plate so he could mix and match. After he tried the bryndza, he winced. "My palate was not ready for that experience." He took a large sip of lager. "But sheep's milk cheese is worthy of a second try." He popped another chunk of bryndza in his mouth and nodded approvingly. "Excellent," he said.

I turned to Val. "The last time I saw you, you were walking across the stage at Conexus to receive your Bachelor of Journalism degree. You've made quite a mark since then. How did that come about?"

Val's smile was apologetic. "It's the old story," he said. "I knew somebody who knew somebody, and I was in the right place at the right time."

"No need to apologize," Zack said. "That's the story for most of us. What happened?"

"Ed Mariani, the head of the School of Journalism, had a friend at CBLT in Toronto who hosted a weekly show about books: interviews with writers and segments on different genres — kids' books, YA, mysteries, speculative fiction, romance — the spectrum. My first degree was in English, so Ed suggested I make a video talking about what I could bring to the show and send it to his friend Mehwishan Joohi. She liked my ideas, and I was hired to write scripts about what was new and hot in the genres. It was a great entry-level job, and when Mehwishan received an offer she couldn't refuse, she went to Current Affairs and I began hosting *The Uncommon Reader.*

"Here's where the right place at the right time comes in, and it's not a happy story," Val continued. "I'd done a twenty-minute in-depth interview with Blythe Paley, a twenty-four-year-old Toronto woman who'd written a debut novel that was already on the New York Times Best Seller list. *Tap Dancing the Tightrope* was the story of a bride who falls in love with her brother-in-law after a single dance at her wedding reception. The writing was gorgeous, and the novel was hilarious, heartbreaking and absolutely compelling.

"The day after the interview aired, Blythe was riding her bike downtown and a car swerved into the bike lane and killed her. The first printing of *Tap Dancing the Tightrope* was sold out that week. My interview with Blythe was the only in-depth interview she'd done, so it was played and replayed. Publicists for major writers started approaching our show about interviews, and the rest, as they say, is history."

I'd made a serious inroad on my borscht, so I was up for conversation. "Is that how you came to meet Steven Brooks?" I said.

"It is, but that's another story." Val drew a long breath. "Right now, I want to hear about you two — starting with you, Joanne. I've watched *Sisters and Strangers* four times. It's brilliant, but it's disturbing. Is that really the way it was for you?"

"It's six episodes of a made-for-TV miniseries, so there's a lot left out," I said, "but what's in the production is accurate."

Val leaned towards me. "You and Georgie Shepherd did a terrific job with the writing. Incidentally, Steven knows Georgie Shepherd — in fact, he mentioned that, for a while, they were a couple."

"Since Georgie is now married to one of Zack's closest friends, perhaps we'd better let that sleeping dog lie."

Val grinned. "Got it. So is there a sequel to *Sisters and Strangers* in the works?"

"No. Once was enough."

"Do you regret doing it?"

"Not at all. It was painful, but facing the truth about that period in my life helped me put many things in perspective." I looked at the smorgasbord of Ukrainian delights in front of us. "Now that I've cleared the hurdle of my past, I think I'm ready for the bryndza."

Zack slid my beer glass, still half full, towards me. "Lager at the ready," he said.

CHAPTER TWO

AFTERNOON, AUGUST 27, 2022

With my first bite of bryndza, I knew this was a taste I would have to acquire, and I swallowed the lager gratefully. When I saw that Val and Zack were watching me carefully for a response, I raised my hand, palm up. "I'm still assessing."

The men laughed, and Val turned to Zack with a question about his work on the defence team in a high-profile murder trial that ended in mid-June. The trial had taken its toll on my husband, and it had been difficult for me, as well, because I was very fond of the defendant's parents. The outcome of the trial was the best the defence could have hoped for, but my husband's succinct review of how the case had played out over the difficult weeks of the trial made it clear that he was not keen to revisit that time in our lives, so we moved on to a second helping of borscht and some pleasantly innocuous talk.

Finally, Zack took up his napkin, patted his lips with it, placed it on his plate with a gentle groan of contentment and said, "That meal was nothing short of sensational."

"I'm glad you enjoyed it," Val said. "But there are leftovers. Would you accept a doggy bag?"

"Gratefully, but our dog, Esme, will never see it," I said. "If she ever tasted kovbasa, her desiccated liver treats would forever lose their charm."

Zack leaned forward in his chair. "Hey, slow down. You two are sending out signals that it's time to pack up and say goodbye, but Val, you said that after we'd finished eating, you'd tell us about how you and Neil met. Joanne and I are now sated and content, and I know we would both like to hear that story."

Val took a moment, seemingly considering his options. "I'll start with the condensed version," he said finally. "Zack, fourteen years ago, I attempted suicide. Joanne knows this story because she's a part of it. When I was released from the hospital, I drove out here to the graveyard behind the United church. I'd brought flowers for the grave of Kellee Savage, a young woman who had died in mid-March.

"It was near the end of April when I finally left the psychiatric ward and was able to come out of the city to her grave. By then the air smelled of warming earth and new life. I'd always loved that time of year, but that year the awareness that there would be no spring awakening for Kellee overwhelmed me. I couldn't find words, so I'd placed the flowers on Kellee Savage's grave and started to leave, and then Neil McCallum appeared.

"He asked me if I had been a friend of Kellee's. The question was a body blow, but I told him the truth. I said, 'No, but I wish I *had* been her friend.' Neil considered what I said, and then, being Neil, he came up with a solution. 'I *was* Kellee's friend, and I miss her. You wish you'd been Kellee's friend. Now you can't be her friend because she's gone. You and I could be friends. We could think about Kellee together.'"

"Why make something hard, when the answer is easy," Zack said. "Val, that is a beautiful story."

"It is, and it opened a path for me." He got up and returned with two manuscripts, which he passed to Zack and me. "I knew I could never make amends to Kellee for my part in the cruel hoax that caused her such pain and ultimately led to her death. But I could write about her strength, her commitment to the truth and her courage in exposing Tom Kelsoe for what he was.

"Nine years later, I started to write *Two Journalists,* the novel that I just gave you. I'd tried to write a true account of what happened that March a dozen times, but dealing with the truth ripped me apart. Finally, the therapist I was seeing suggested that I use the tragedy of Kellee Savage's death as material for a novel. She said that my guilt was blocking my ability to take the one step that could save me, and that knowing I was writing fiction would give me the freedom and perspective I needed to explore the roles all of us who knew Kellee had played in the tragedy of her death."

Val's emotions had always run close to the surface, and Zack picked up on his anxiety about how we would react to *Two Journalists.*

My husband's smile was reassuring. "So writing this novel gave you the freedom to take a hard look at the truth."

"It did. It was a long, strange trip, but it helped me understand where my descent from pretty decent guy to monster began."

"Was it a trip worth taking?" Zack said, and his tone was intimate and earnest.

Val didn't answer immediately. He seemed to be turning the question over in his mind. Finally, he said, "Yes, it was a trip worth taking." He paused. "Many times I was certain I'd lost my way, but I kept at it, and one day I began to see through the eyes of my characters. The closest I can come to describing that feeling is that it was as if a tuning fork in my body resonated.

"Suddenly, I knew how it felt to be Kellee Savage, and I was able to see the world as Tom Kelsoe saw it."

"That must have been unsettling," I said.

"It was terrifying," Val said. "But it also revealed how Tom Kelsoe was able to manipulate people. And that was transformative because it made me begin to understand the truth about myself."

"And that truth is something you can live with?" Zack said.

When he answered, the curve of Val's lips was boyishly hopeful. "The last time Joanne visited me, in the hospital, I told her I didn't see how I could pick up the pieces of my life. Joanne said that I could do it because there was no alternative. She said that after her husband Ian Kilbourn died, she'd been where I was and that every morning she would remind herself that when Pandora's box was emptied of all the horrors, only one thing remained, and that was hope. That's pretty much where I am now, Zack. I'm doing my best and living in the hope that that will be enough."

My husband was seldom physically demonstrative with anyone outside the family, but when he held out his arms to my former student, Val leaned in. "Finding a self you can live with is not easy," Zack said. "It took me years. But it sounds as if you're well on your way." He paused. "Stay in touch, Val."

Val stood and grinned. "Our first chance to stay in touch is coming very soon. I've been invited to Angus and Leah's wedding. I suspect Steven Brooks engineered my invitation, but I jumped at the chance to connect with you again, Joanne, and, of course, I was eager to meet Zack."

"Sometimes the cosmos just gets everything right," I said. "This is great news. Will you be bringing a plus-one?"

"I will, and my plus-one is someone you know: Rainey Arcus."

I turned to my husband. "Rainey was in the Politics and the Media seminar," I said.

"She was," Val said. "Rainey also did most of the research for Steven Brooks's biography. That book would not exist without her. And that's all I'm going to say except when you read *Two Journalists*, I guarantee that you'll be surprised at the role Rainey Arcus plays in bringing our story full circle."

* * *

Ten minutes later, Zack and I were in our car, headed back to Lawyers Bay. The day had been intense, and we were both grateful for the time to be alone together to take a stab at processing everything that had happened. Neither of us spoke until we turned from the highway onto the grid road.

This time it was my turn to ask the question: "What just happened?"

Zack took in a long breath and exhaled. "We just spent a very pleasant two hours with a man who's been through hell, survived and is now on his way to making peace with himself."

"'On his way,'" I repeated. "Those *are* the operative words aren't they?"

"They are," my husband said. "Because, despite his undeniable success, Valentine Masluk still seems to be on shaky ground."

"I felt that too," I said. "From what he told us about his novel, Kellee Savage's death still haunts him."

"Should it?" Zack's tone made it clear that the question was not casual, but it was one I was reluctant to answer.

"Yes, for the same reason it still haunts me."

"Joanne, we've talked about this. You didn't do anything wrong."

"I didn't do anything," I said. "And *that* was wrong."

Zack reached over and squeezed my hand, but he knew me well enough to stay silent.

* * *

As she always was, Esme was at the front window waiting for us. And as always, we made a fuss of her.

"We're going to have to break the news to Esme about the new addition to our family," Zack said.

"Esme's slowing down a little these days," I said. "A puppy may be just what she needs to get her groove back, but let's give her a few more days as an only dog before we tell her that life is going to change around here."

"Fair enough," Zack said. "So, how would you like to spend the rest of our day?"

"First, a nap — my panacea for all the complexities of the world."

"Want me to tuck you in?"

"I'd like it better if you slid in beside me," I said. "Zack, more than anyone, I know how much you're missing Pantera. I miss him too. But it's time to get back to doing the things that comfort us both. You remember what Ron Lancaster said."

Zack nodded. "The Little General said you never lose a game, you just run out of time. And he knew whereof he spoke. He was the Roughriders starting quarterback for sixteen seasons, and in four of those seasons the Riders played for the Grey Cup — even won it once."

"They did indeed. You and I are not kids, Zack. We know our time together is not limitless. The science behind your former client's claim that 'a heavy-duty love sesh cleanses the body of toxins' might be sketchy, but a heavy-duty love sesh has other benefits."

I was watching Zack's face closely. Our love-making was a sensitive subject. We both knew that since Pantera's death, our sex life had changed, and not for the better. My husband's smile started slowly, but it was worth waiting for. "Are you up for a heavy-duty love sesh?" he said softly.

"I am," I said.

An hour later, toxin free and goofily happy, we lay side by side watching the shadows from the forsythia bush outside our window dance on the ceiling.

"That was stellar," I said. "You're always great, but that was a four-star performance."

Zack drew me closer. "It was probably just the bryndza," he said.

"No, it was just you being you — the sexiest guy I will ever know," I said. "But just to be on the safe side, tomorrow I'll call the Ukrainian Co-op and place a standing order for a weekly delivery of bryndza."

"But today," I went on, "I think we should sit outside on the little patio and read and enjoy the late afternoon warmth." The copies of *Two Journalists* Val gave us were on my bedside table. I handed Zack one. "Are you ready to read?"

"I am," Zack said. "Are you?"

"I honestly don't know, but Val deserves to know that you and I value him enough to make his novel our first priority."

Those were brave words, but when I settled on the chaise longue and opened the book, the opening paragraph hit me with the force of a slap.

> First year students in a print journalism class are often given the assignment of writing their own obituary. It's a useful exercise because it teaches students how to make words count and helps them focus on their goals. The obituary Kylie Sauvage wrote for herself concludes with a line that poignantly reveals the person she could have been. "Kylie Sauvage was a great journalist because although no one ever noticed her, she was always there."

The names of the characters had been changed and some of the details had been altered, but I had lived this story, so as I read I found myself unconsciously translating Val's words into my own subtext of truth.

On the last day of a life blighted by her limitations, Kellee Savage had clipped bright shamrock barrettes in her hair, confident that her twenty-first birthday would bring her the recognition she yearned for and had earned. Later, we would all learn that, as a journalist, Kellee was as indefatigable and meticulous as she had been as a student. She was never without her small pink tape recorder. With the permission of all concerned, Kellee had used it to record classes and seminar discussions. And as she built her case that Tom Kelsoe's *Getting Even* was a betrayal not only of Kelsoe's subjects, but of the principles underpinning responsible journalism, Kellee had recorded her sources and the dates and times of their meetings.

On the morning of March 17, Kellee was prepared to make public everything that would reveal the truth about Tom Kelsoe. All the dominos were lined up, and when I read Val's text I suddenly realized that I was the first domino. If I believed Kellee's assertion that the note inside *Sleeping Beauty* had been written by Val Massey and confronted him, Val would not have denied the truth. Kellee had been certain of that, and so had I. Kellee believed Val would attempt to justify what he had done and that would mean disclosing the fact that he lied to protect Tom Kelsoe. The second domino would have toppled, then it would be just a matter of time before all the dominos would fall, and Tom Kelsoe would be revealed as a liar and a manipulator.

Kellee had counted on me to give her a fair hearing, but I had made it clear that I not only didn't believe her, but that her concern was not my concern. I had washed my hands of the matter and directed her to Student Affairs.

Several times on the evening she died, Kellee had attempted to get in touch with me. When finally she did, she had been at the student pub and was very drunk, and my offer to help had been perfunctory. I volunteered to call a cab and said that I would see her the next morning.

As the week went by, and Kellee's absences from her classes reached a worrying number, I had reported her missing. When the ravaged, barely identifiable as human body of a female was found in a farmer's field thirty-two kilometres east of the university, the police had asked me to identify the remains. It was one of the worst moments of my life. Kellee's bright St. Patrick's Day barrettes were the only reminder of the Kellee who had believed her twenty-first birthday would mark her coming of age as a journalist.

I wanted to close the book and never open it again, but I knew I had to stay the course, and so I read on. When the air grew chilly, Zack and I went inside, made ourselves sandwiches, cracked open two bottles of Stella Artois and sat down at the partners' table in the dining room to read until we'd both finished the book.

* * *

Two Journalists was stunning. The writing was powerful, and Val's pain was evident in every word. There were details I'd forgotten or never known and, although Val had changed the names and blurred the identities of the characters, to me, we were all recognizable. We were not monsters. We were flawed but decent people who knew right from wrong and who, most of the time, made an effort to do what was right — yet we had all failed Kellee Savage.

Kellee had taken the first step on the path leading to her death when she presented Reid Gallagher with irrefutable evidence that Tom Kelsoe was a fraud, but that step had not sealed her fate. The path to her death was cluttered with instances of "if only." If only just one of us had listened and acted, the tragedy could have been averted. *Two Journalists* was a cautionary tale for our time with a lesson as old as time itself: When good people fail to acknowledge the desperate needs of another human being, the other human being can be lost.

* * *

As Val Massey had predicted, Rainey Arcus's role in *Two Journalists* surprised me.

Unlike the rest of us, Rainey had no reason to plague herself with the unanswerable question of "what if." Rainey's focus had been on another question: "What made Tom Kelsoe do what he had done?" And she had the skill set and the financial wherewithal to find the answer.

Rainey had paid her way through J school by working as a freelance researcher. She had a gift for finding sources in areas that were not immediately obvious to most people. She was a whiz at online searches and at gathering information from offline sources — print documents, audio recordings and videos — and she knew how to present information, whether in writing or in person.

Not long after Tom had been incarcerated, Rainey wrote to him, saying that she was interested in hearing his side of the story. She offered Tom a friendly ear, and he pounced. He and Rainey began a correspondence that proved mutually beneficial. Their exchange of letters gave Tom a lifeline to the world outside the Prince Albert penitentiary, and it gave Rainey a rare insight into the mind of a brilliant man who was a sociopath.

Tom Kelsoe's letters were frank and seemingly without illusion. He knew he was up the proverbial shit creek, but he was prepared to create his own paddle. Between his words, Kelsoe's message pulsed with confidence. He knew his chances of being paroled were slim, but he was certain that because the collective brain power of the members of the parole board was no match for the power of his own brain, they were adversaries he could outwit.

Tom Kelsoe decided to make life in the penitentiary work for him. Determined to gain parole as soon as possible, he created a pattern of behaviour that would offer the parole board concrete proof that he was a model prisoner, remorseful and eager to contribute something to his new community. Funding for programs educating prisoners had been slashed, and when Tom volunteered to teach other prisoners how to write their stories, the prison authorities accepted the offer with alacrity. The stories were collected in a series of chapbooks titled *The Pen*. Not surprisingly, Tom Kelsoe's fellow prisoners protected and adored him. Seemingly, once again, Tom Kelsoe had landed on his feet. Life in prison was bearable and Tom had big plans for the future.

Fourteen years after Kellee Savage's horrific death, the lives of Linda van Sickle, Jumbo Hryniuk and Neil McCallum, who were all innocent of wrongdoing, were still marred by Kellee's tragedy. Only Tom Kelsoe had walked away emotionally unscathed, prepared to build himself a new life with no regrets and no self-doubt. He was, to use that much overused cliché, a survivor — more than that, he was the person who walked away from the horror and, without missing a beat, created a new world for himself.

* * *

As we readied ourselves for bed, my husband and I were silent, absorbed in our own thoughts. After he had transferred himself from his chair and settled himself in our bed, Zack said, "That really is one helluva book."

"Val had one helluva story to tell," I said. "And he told it so powerfully. Zack, do you remember that trial?"

"Are you kidding? I even managed to get into the courtroom a few times thanks to my wheelchair. There aren't a huge number of advantages to being paraplegic, but access to hot ticket events is one of them. Everything about that trial was unforgettable. Kelsoe had planned and executed the murders of two innocent people, but there were groupies outside the courthouse carrying signs with hearts drawn on them and the message 'Free Tom' written in pink. The Tom Kelsoes of this world always manage to land on their feet. Kelsoe was sentenced to two life sentences to be served concurrently, but most often those sentences are commuted to eleven years."

"So Tom Kelsoe could be living among us . . ."

"Jo, don't think about that. A lot can happen inside a penitentiary in eleven years."

I shuddered. "I don't want to think about that either," I said.

"In that case, don't. Let's call Val tomorrow and tell him how deeply affected we both were by his novel. You may not agree with me on this, but that book deserves more than a private printing of one hundred copies. I think we should encourage Val to submit *Two Journalists* to the company that's publishing his biography of Steven Brooks."

"I agree with you," I said. "Reading that book was painful for me, but what I felt is not even one-hundredth of the pain Kellee Savage lived through in the last days of her life. She deserves to be remembered and honoured."

SUNDAY, AUGUST 28, 2022

That night we both slept well, and Sunday morning we awoke to sunshine and birdsong. "Another lollapalooza day," I said. "The Drache sisters will see Lawyers Bay at its late summer best."

Zack stretched lazily. "And in ten days, we'll be attending Angus and Leah's wedding. Let's hope the great weather sticks around."

"Outdoor weddings are always chancy," I said. "But Leah and Angus have made plans for any contingency, and since the renovations, the Scarth Club really is a great choice. The club is over a hundred years old, and the renovations left all that beautiful cherry wood untouched and brought the old kitchen into the second decade of the twenty-first century."

"Thank God for that," Zack said. "Because the food prepared in the old kitchen all tasted the same — awful. Anyway, now the chef in charge of the kitchen knows what he's doing, and the club still offers its signature old-fashioneds, which are irresistible but lethal."

"And for that reason," I said, "old-fashioneds will not be served at the reception. Our son says he and Leah want everyone to have a great time, and that means no drunks, no drama. Hence the split-second schedule."

Zack ticked off the sequence of events on his fingers. "Four o'clock, the wedding ceremony starts in the back garden; five o'clock, cocktails and photographs, also in the back garden; six o'clock, sit-down dinner, speeches, cake-cutting and dancing; ten o'clock, sharp, the evening ends. That plan definitely sounds as if it was drafted by our daughter-in-law-to-be."

"Apparently, it was mutually agreed upon," I said. "As was the decision to pass on the bachelor and bachelorette parties in favour of a weekend with friends at Lawyers Bay."

"Angus gave me the rundown on that agenda too," Zack said. "Saturday is for water skiing, swimming and boating, lunch across the lake at Magoo's and a bonfire on the beach. Sunday is for hiking, throwing around a football, watching the Labour Day Classic between the Roughriders and Blue Bombers and finishing the day with a barbecue."

"And Monday, after lunch, everybody drives back to the city, rested and ready for the wedding rehearsal," I said. "It's perfect."

Zack placed some pillows against the headboard and propped himself up. "Certainly a helluva lot better than a bachelor party," he said. "Those things really are rank: too much booze, too much porn, too much sex on offer and too many boyish hijinks that get out of control." He shook his head in disgust. "At the first bachelor party I attended after law school, the groom got so drunk he passed out and someone shaved off his pubic hair."

I grimaced. "Ugh!"

"It gets worse," Zack said. "The guy doing the shaving was hammered too, and he used a straight razor."

I raised my hand in a halt gesture. "Enough. Did the groom-to-be come out of the experience —"

"Intact?" Zack said. "Yep, not even a nick. Of course, seeing his nether parts the next morning was unsettling, but the groom soldiered on, and the wedding went off without a hitch."

"There were no straight razors at the bridal showers I attended, but there were many times when I would have welcomed one," I said. "Those showers were so earnestly sweet they made my teeth ache. I was maid of honour five times for girls I went to school with — that meant I had to attend all the showers held in their honour."

Zack cocked his head. "So what did you do at the showers?"

"We drank weak tea from fancy cups and ate sandwiches made from tinted bread the hostess had rolled out so she could create pinwheels from ham salad or egg salad. For dessert there were pastel-coloured meringues. After we'd had our fill of pinwheels and meringues, we all sat in a circle so we could watch the bride-to-be open her gifts.

"Showers were most often connected with either the kitchen or the bedroom: the two rooms where a newly married woman was expected to excel. The kitchen gifts were predictable, but the bedroom gifts for the bride — crotchless lacy black panties, masks and sex toys that no one, including me, could ever figure out — were just weird."

Zack's face creased with sympathy. "And you endured all this?"

"I did, and as maid of honour, it was my job to write down the bride's exact words as she opened each gift, and when all the gifts were opened, I had to read aloud what I'd written and explain that this is what the bride would say when she saw her new husband's penis for the first time on their wedding night."

Zack was pensive.

"The perennial favourites were 'This one is so big I'm going to need some help with it,' and 'This one's soft and squishy — it has to be a joke.' While the merriment was going on, the bride's mother would be taping the bows from gifts on a paper plate, and when the last gift had been unwrapped, the mother would tie the paper plate on her daughter's head and the shower was officially over."

Zack held up his arms in a gesture of surrender. "You win," he said. "The ham salad pinwheels and the paper plate hat beat the groom's shaved groin, hands down . . ."

"So to speak," I said.

Zack slid down the pillows and pushed himself into a half-turn so he was facing me. "Right, so to speak," he said, and his laugh, deep and hearty, was the laugh I hadn't heard for a while. He drew me close. "To the victor go the spoils. Choose your prize."

"I choose you," I said. "But I'll have to wait to receive my prize because the Drache sisters and their brother-in-law, Steven, will be here at ten."

* * *

The first time I met Mila Drache was when she and her sister, Reva, hosted a Valentine's Day party at the Scarth Club to announce Angus and Leah's engagement. That evening I was struck by how alike the sisters were. Both were in their early seventies, fine-featured, with deeply set, knowing hazel eyes, enviable complexions and delicately sculpted, expressive mouths. They were petite, but their contralto voices rang with confidence, and both could effortlessly command a room.

The sisters' similarities went beyond the physical. Both women were recently retired psychiatrists — Reva practised in Toronto; Mila, in Regina. Neither had married, both were protective of Steven and doted on Leah, the niece they had raised after her mother died in childbirth. Planning the wedding had been a source of delight for them, and they had been conscientious about checking with Zack and me about every decision.

The Drache sisters — intelligent, genial and witty — were good company, and Zack and I were looking forward to introducing them and Leah's father to life at Lawyers Bay. When my phone rang fifteen minutes before the Draches were due, my first thought was that they'd overshot the turnoff that led to our place. The turnoff was in a treed area, and it was easy to miss. But my caller was our son-in-law, Charlie Dowhanuik.

Charlie was the host of *Charlie D in the Morning,* a wildly successful national radio show. I had been in the delivery room when Charlie was born. I had heard his first lusty cry, and thirty-five years later, I still welcomed the sound of his voice.

"All's well at your house?" I said.

"Everybody's blooming," he said. "I'm just waiting outside the library for your granddaughters. They were in need of books."

"A need I understand," I said.

"Actually, Jo, I'm calling you about a book. You have an advance copy of the Steven Brooks biography, don't you?"

"I do. It's in the stack I'm going to read when life gets back to normal after the wedding."

"Good, then you can help me. I just received a weird message. Pub date for the book is September 7, but Valentine Masluk will be on the book tour by then, so I'm taping an interview with him tomorrow afternoon. Anyway, the email said, 'When you're interviewing Mr. Masluk tomorrow, ask him if pages 329ff of the Brooks biography tell the whole story.'"

"And no information about the sender, of course," I said.

"It's 'signed' 329ff with a Hotmail address that's probably a burner."

"Hang on. I'll get the book," I said. I went to our bedroom, picked up the biography and began leafing through until I found page 329. "Okay, got it," I said. "Do you want me to read it to you?"

"No, just give it a quick look and tell me what it covers."

I started reading, but when it became apparent that the passage was going to continue for a while, I said, "The section focuses on the period when Steven Brooks had that incapacitating attack of writer's block after his third novel was not well received." I skipped a couple of pages ahead. "It seems to end when Steven happens upon the story of Medusa and writes *Medusa's Fate*, which was published in 2010, nine years after his failed novel, and then the biography moves right into the writing of *The Iron Bed of Procrustes*, which was published in 2016.

"I've been leafing through the research Randi, our assistant producer, gave me. One of the pieces referred to *Medusa* and *Procrustes* as 'two blips of genius after three competent but unremarkable novels.'"

"That's harsh," I said after a pause.

"Harsh but true," Charlie said. "All the critical pieces I've read say they anticipate with great interest Steven Brooks's next novel."

"So the pressure is on," I said.

"Yes, and apparently there's nothing at the publishers yet. I've been pondering the wisdom of asking Valentine Masluk if he found anything in his interviews with Brooks or with his agent and publisher to suggest when novel number six will appear. The agent and the publisher aren't saying anything, and Brooks refuses to discuss what he's working on. He suffered a debilitating writers' block for the nine years before he produced *Medusa's Fate*, so rumours are cropping up."

"And there's speculation that he's suffered a relapse?"

"There's that, and then there's an uglier rumour. The disparity between Brooks's first three novels and the two that won all the awards and kudos is marked. Randi is diligent about research, and she says there's speculation that Brooks was not the sole writer of *Medusa's Fate* and *The Iron Bed of Procrustes*."

I felt a knot in my stomach. "And you're thinking of asking Valentine Masluk about this?"

"The rumours are out there, Jo. Randi tells me the reviews that will be online this weekend are already making oblique references to the possibility that if Steven Brooks does not produce a new novel as exceptional as *Medusa's Fate* or *The Iron Bed of Procrustes*, there will always be question marks surrounding his legacy. My interview with Valentine Masluk will be aired on the day the biography is published. By the end of the week, the unsettling question 329ff is raising will be the one people want answered, and I'm paid to ask the questions our audience wants answered."

"I know that," I said. "But when you have your pre-interview chat with Val, it might be courteous to ask him if that's a question he's able to answer."

Charlie D was quick off the mark. "'Val?'" he said. "Are you and Mr. Masluk on 'Val' and 'Jo' terms?"

"We are," I said. "It's a long story, but Valentine Masluk was a student of mine. He was Val Massey then, so I didn't make the connection, until yesterday when he invited Zack and me for lunch."

Charlie's tone was teasing. "And your son-in-law, the intrepid journalist, was told none of this? Joanne, you and I are going to have a talk about sharing." He sighed theatrically. "But — thanks to your granddaughters — for the time being, you're off the hook. Madeleine and Lena just came out of the library with loaded bags. I suspect half the books are for Desmond. The girls love reading to him, and he loves being read to."

"Madeleine and Lena are reveling in being big sisters," I said. "Des is a lucky boy." I paused. "Charlie, how many people would know that you're interviewing Valentine Masluk tomorrow?"

Charlie whistled. "Good point," he said. "Only a handful on my end. Of course, it's possible Masluk mentioned it to somebody."

"I doubt that. Val didn't mention it to Zack and me, although we would have been a logical choice. Anyway, I guess you'll find out soon enough."

"I'll send you an MP3 of the interview tomorrow night," Charlie said.

"Leah's father and her aunts are coming to Lawyers Bay this morning," I said. "They'll be here any minute. If I hear anything that might clarify that email, I'll text you."

CHAPTER THREE

Zack and I were both outside to greet our guests. Mila and Reva were quick to get out of Reva's Lexus and approach us, but their brother-in-law was nowhere to be seen. We exchanged greetings, and Zack said, "No Steven?"

"No, he's a little under the weather," Mila said.

"I'm sorry," Zack said. "I was looking forward to sitting down with him, lighting up our Primo del Reys and having the father of the groom, father of the bride talk."

Mila smiled. "I'm afraid you're going to have that talk with the bride's doting aunts."

"So no cigars?" Zack said.

When we all laughed, I felt my nerves unknot. My chat with Charlie D had been disquieting, and I wasn't ready to face Steven Brooks.

The fashion choices of the Drache sisters were very different, but each had chosen exactly the look that worked for her. Reva, the Toronto psychiatrist, wore her thick, lustrous iron-grey hair long, held back from her face by one of the extraordinary copper hair clips I'd noticed on her visit in February. She wore no jewelry, and her clothing was beautifully cut but simple. That morning she wore black slacks, white Skechers and a grey blazer in a cropped, unstructured silhouette that looked both fashionable and comfortable.

Mila's silver pixie bob with side bangs was elegant and playful, as was her clothing choice: a creamy Irish Aran sweater, silver and turquoise drop earrings, close-fitting tan wool slacks and intricately tooled turquoise western boots.

I'd set out a tray with tea and scones on the partners' table in the sunroom. When she spotted the table, Reva clapped her hands in delight. "That oak table is absolutely glorious."

"The designer who made the decisions about the interior of our cottage bought it at a country auction," Zack said. "It came from a long-defunct law firm. I've tried to track down the firm, but no luck."

Reva was looking closely at one of the twenty-four chairs that came with the table. "And those chairs are in perfect condition," she said. "Your decorator found a real gem."

"Agreed," Zack said. "Joanne will tell you that I'm never happier than I am when every seat at the table is filled and there are a couple of high chairs pulled close." He turned his wheelchair towards the hall. "Now, if you'll excuse me, I have a Zoom meeting that will probably last longer than it should, but I'll be back in plenty of time for us to take the boat across the lake to Magoo's for lunch."

"Good," Mila said, "because we are both looking forward to the famous Magoo's onion rings."

"Mmm," Reva said, but she was gazing out the window, her attention elsewhere. "The view of the lake from here is so calming."

"It is," I agreed. "Even when there are just the two of us, Zack and I eat dinner here. We have busy lives, and in every season, the view gives us a reason to draw a deep breath and take stock."

"Rabbi Shoichet often talks about the importance of stillness in our lives," Reva said. "Incidentally, he asked us to apologize for not meeting with you again before the wedding. He'd planned to, but his wife had a baby on Wednesday. Another boy, so the Shoichets now have three boys under the age of five."

"Wow. Three boys under five. Please tell them mazel tov from Zack and me."

"I will. Joanne, Dan also asked me to tell you that coming to know Angus and Leah has been a gift. He says he's never counseled a couple more deeply in love and more realistic about what a successful marriage involves than they are."

"Angus and Leah have been dating one another on and off for fifteen years, so they've had plenty of time to work a lot of things out," I said. "Angus brought Leah home for dinner with us the week he started high school. She was wearing shorts and a black Doctors Without Borders T-shirt, and Angus was wearing shorts and a white T-shirt with a picture of Homer and Bart Simpson yelling 'Wait. There is Intelligent Life here' at a spaceship that's vanishing into the stratosphere."

Mila's laugh was low and warm. "There *are* studies that support the old wives' tale that opposites attract."

"The attraction was definitely there from the beginning," I said. "And as they grew older, Leah and Angus seemed to grow more alike, but coming together and drifting apart had become a pattern for them until the summer Angus, Leah, Taylor and I spent here at Lawyers Bay."

"Leah says that was the most formative summer of her life."

"It was formative for us all. I'd rented my friend Kevin Hynd's cottage. He was one of the founding partners of Falconer Shreve Altieri Wainberg and Hynd, and the four remaining cottages were owned by the other partners. They'd been friends since law school, and they took care of one another. Because Kevin and I were close, that summer his partners were taking care of my family and me. Before we arrived, they had arranged for Angus and Leah to have summer jobs running The Point Store."

"We've heard a great deal about those summer jobs," Reva said.

"Your niece was a godsend, and not just to The Point Store. I'm sure Leah told you that the week after we arrived, Christopher Altieri drove his MG off the dock into the lake. Angus and I dove in and tried to open the car doors, but Chris had locked himself in. It was a terrible, terrible loss, and the four remaining partners were ripped apart. Zack was the only partner I'd ever really talked to, and I told him that I thought my family and I should go back to the city so they could mourn privately, but Zack said his partners and their families needed us, and so we stayed.

"The grief of Chris's partners was a tsunami — overwhelming and unpredictable," I said. "Zack and the others did their best, but there were times when the pain of their loss overwhelmed them, and it was difficult for us, as outsiders, to know how we could help.

Leah, with her uncommon common sense, offered our family the anchor we needed to moor us, so we were there, steady and predictable when we were needed."

Mila was thoughtful. "I'm glad she was there for you. The suicide of a loved one is a crushing blow."

"It is," I said. "But having Leah with us lightened the burden. And she definitely lightened the burden of the owner of The Point Store." I checked my watch. "If we're going to visit the scene of Leah's triumph, we'd better make tracks. Is there anything I can get either of you before we go?"

"Thank you, no," Reva said. "Those scones were delicious, but Leah tells us that lunch at Magoo's demands a healthy appetite."

"It does indeed," I said. "So I guess it's time for what our grand-daughters call a bio break. There's a bathroom on the right as you turn down the hall, and if you keep on going, there's another just inside the guest room."

* * *

When our seat belts were snapped and we were on our way, Reva turned to me. "Angus says that running Stan Gardiner's Point Store was, and I quote, 'a sweet gig.'"

"It was," I said. "But it came with a price. Times were changing at the lake, and a battle was brewing between the old-timers who'd grown up here and the slick young matrons who lived in the huge summer homes that had sprung up along the lakeshore.

"Stan Gardiner not only owned The Point Store, he lived above it, and whenever he heard the bell tinkle to announce a customer,

Stan shuffled downstairs to see what was up. If it was one of the old-timers who'd been meeting in front of the pop cooler since they were pups, Stan would join them to chew the fat."

"A clash between squatters' rights and the rights of the entitled," Mila said.

"Exactly," I said. "The old-timers believed they'd earned the spot in front of the coolers; the young matrons resented having to detour around the old gents in a space where stock was already teetering on overcrowded shelves and spilling off display racks."

"A quandary," Reva said.

"It was. But since we are now at The Point Store. You can see Leah's solution to the problem for yourselves." I parked, and we walked over to the shady area next to the store. Picnic tables had been set up beneath the branches of the old green ash tree. The tables were covered with cheerful blue-and-white checked vinyl cloths.

"Welcome to Coffee Row," I said. "Leah found rolls of vinyl in an old shed behind the store, and she made those tablecloths. She and Angus plugged in a party-size coffee pot and declared that Coffee Row was ready for guests. On opening day, egg salad sandwiches were served. Leah had added a touch of cumin to the old recipe, and the matrons and the old-timers agreed it was the best egg salad they'd ever tasted. After the gala opening, the refreshments were scaled back to plates of no-name cookies, but no one seemed to mind, and dogs were welcome, so Coffee Row was a hit with us all.

"When Angus and Leah are at the lake, they always drop by Coffee Row." I gestured towards the gents settled at the picnic tables. "As you can imagine, Leah has many fans here. I'll introduce you to a couple of them."

Stan Gardiner was sitting at one of the tables with his friend of seventy years, Morris, a dedicated smoker of Player's plains. They were not alone; Morris's old yellow dog, Endzone, was curled up on the piece of rug his owner always put down to keep Endzone from getting rheumatism. When I introduced Reva and Mila, Stan and Morris rose to shake their hands.

"That Leah of yours is a very pretty girl," Morris said. When he heard his master's rasp, Endzone raised his head to listen, but the conversations did not involve Endzone or a piece of bologna, so he flattened out on his piece of rug and fell asleep.

"And that Leah's not just pretty," Stan said. He tapped his temple. "She's smart too. Nothing gets by that little lady."

Morris turned to me. "Your Angus is a lucky young man," he said. "He got the cream of the crop."

"He did indeed," I said.

Stan and Morris both removed their John Deere caps. "To the happy couple," Stan said.

It was a graceful toast, and when the Drache sisters and I said our goodbyes we were all glad we'd stopped by to visit.

It was a great day for a walk along the beach. The sun was warm, the air was still and the lake was placid. The Drache sisters were dog lovers, and they had found a stick for Esme to chase. Esme's stick-chasing days were behind her, but she was game and so were the sisters.

We continued walking in companionable silence until we came near the gazebo at the tip of the bay's west arm. "This is where Maisie and Peter's wedding took place," I said. The gazebo, an octagonal structure of wood and glass, offered a breathtaking view of the lake and of the bay.

"What a perfect spot to get married," Reva said.

"It was," I said. "Maisie and Peter took their vows standing in front of the gazebo. The entrance was draped in pink magnolias."

"It must have been beautiful," Mila said.

"It was, and I know Leah and Angus's wedding will be just as lovely."

"I hope so," Reva said, and the anxiety in her voice was palpable.

Mila put her arm around her sister's shoulder. "It will be," she said, and her tone indicated the issue was off the table. She gave Reva's shoulder a quick squeeze. "Time for us to get back to the house. It's lunch time."

When we returned, Zack was sitting on the patio reading *Sports Illustrated*. I bent to kiss him. "Been waiting long?" I said.

"Nope, just long enough to read about Notre Dame's chances this year."

"Are they good?"

"Very good."

"Excellent, I'm going to put Esme inside and grab a sweater. I'll meet you down at the dock."

Sweater in hand, I was just about to walk out the door when our daughter Taylor called from Saskatoon.

"Nothing on my mind," she said. "I just thought I'd check in."

"We're always glad to hear from you."

"Is Dad there?"

"No, he's down at the dock. We're taking Leah's aunts to Magoo's for lunch."

Taylor groaned. "Now I'll be thinking about onion rings all afternoon."

"You and Gracie will be at Lawyers Bay for Labour Day weekend," I said. "And I have it on good authority that includes a trip to Magoo's."

"In that case, as Madeleine would say, 'I'm mollified.' Now people are waiting for you on the dock, so I'd better let you go. Say hi to Leah's aunts for Gracie and me, and give Dad a hug from us both."

When I arrived at the dock, Reva and Mila were already putting on life jackets and Zack was gripping the device that allows him to lower himself into the Chris-Craft. The mechanism was sophisticated structurally, but simple. It depended not on electronics, but on dexterity and strength, and I was struck again by the power my husband's arms had to hoist his body from land to boat.

I waited until the transfer was complete and then took my place beside him and gave him a hug. "We just had a call from our younger daughter. That hug was from Gracie and her. And Reva and Mila, Taylor and her girlfriend say hi." I slipped on my life jacket. "Ready when you are," I said.

It was a pretty day for a boat ride, and when we'd crossed the lake, Zack took the scenic route along the shoreline so the sisters could see the cottages. As always, we could hear the music from Magoo's while we were still on the water. That afternoon, the authentic Wurlitzer jukebox that was the first thing you saw when you came into Magoo's was booming. This time it was booming out Slim Whitman's "I Remember You." All the selections on the jukebox were vintage, evoking the uncomplicated innocence of mid–twentieth century American pop.

The menu at Magoo's called up memories too: burgers on kaiser rolls, coleslaw, greasy hand-cut shoestring fries, onion rings, and milkshakes so thick they were a challenge to slurp through a straw. Everything was homemade from ingredients produced locally, and everything was delicious.

From the moment we walked through the door, the Drache sisters were enchanted. Zack had reserved a table for us on the deck, but the walls of the restaurant were covered with cheerfully faked photographs of flesh-and-blood female movie stars of the '50s and early '60s posing with Mr. Magoo, the crotchety, myopic W.C. Fields–like cartoon character. Reva and Mila checked out every photograph and then turned their attention to the selections the jukebox offered.

When we finally sat at our table, Mila looked around, shook her head and said, "I wish Steven could have seen this place. The fun might have helped." Her voice was wistful.

"There's always next time," Zack said.

"There is," I said. "And now that you're both retired, you and Steven could come here for a weekend or for as long as you like. Magoo's closes after Thanksgiving, but that still gives you plenty of time to introduce your brother-in-law to the pleasures of the Wurlitzer."

"That's a generous offer," Mila said. "But I've always believed in that old adage: house guests, like fish, begin to smell after three days."

Zack chuckled. "Luckily, for us all, that will not be a problem. The cottage closest to ours on the west side belongs to Joanne and me. We wanted a place for our family and friends to stay when they visit. You, Reva and Steven are family *and* friends, so you qualify for the cottage on both counts."

"And, to set your minds at ease, Zack and I believe that the fish-guest axiom applies to hovering hosts too," I said. "Our arrangement with our adult children works for us all. They're responsible for their family's breakfast and lunch, and we all have dinner together at the partners' table."

"So we're *always* there without always *being there*," Zack said.

"A very lawyerly solution," Reva said, and her smile was open. "That works for us. We may take you up on your offer, sooner rather than later. With the wedding, the biography coming out next week and the new novel Steven's writing, there's a great deal of stress in his life, and it's taking its toll."

"Lawyers Bay is a great place to rest and recharge," Zack said. "But there's a server a couple of metres from us who's looking expectant. Magoo's never rushes a customer. It's family owned, and they understand that a meal is often a place where problems can be addressed; but they are a restaurant, and they do like to get food on the table."

"In that case, let's not keep that handsome young man waiting," Reva said.

The sisters were both slender, but seemingly, they were trencherwomen, and they each ordered the loaded Magoo burger with sides of onion rings, shoestring fries and coleslaw, and a vanilla milkshake to fill in the cracks.

The excellence of Magoo's food makes conversation a fool's option, and the Drache sisters were not fools. Once the food arrived, the four of us were content to savour our meals and listen to Paul Anka's plangent plea to Diana to stay with him, Fats Domino's memories of finding his thrill on Blueberry Hill and Chuck Berry's celebration of Johnny B. Goode, the little country boy who could surely play a guitar.

When Roy Orbison began singing "Only the Lonely," Reva's eyes widened. "I took voice lessons when I was young, and my teacher told me that Roy Orbison and Enrico Caruso were the only twentieth-century tenors who could hit E over high C," she said.

Mila looked fondly at her sister. "Every day, I learn something from you," she said.

"Maybe that E over high C is the secret of that song's enduring power," I said. "A client of Zack's told him that 'Only the Lonely' is so sad it could make a dog cry."

"Sensitive client," Reva said.

"No, like most of us, that client was a mixed bag," Zack said. "He was charged with dropping a barbell on the windpipe of his sleeping grandmother."

Reva grimaced. "Was he guilty?"

"Absolutely, but he did have a good ear for a ballad of doom."

"We all have our gifts," Reva said. "Zack, I'm interested in your comment that your client was 'a mixed bag, like most of us.' That's a remarkably non-judgmental assessment."

Zack shrugged. "I'm a trial lawyer. I have to approach every client as being a 'fucked-up, fallible human being just like everyone else.'"

"The Albert Ellis approach," Reva said.

"I was sure you'd recognize that. Joanne and I read one of his books this summer. The idea of understanding and accepting all parts of yourself resonated with us."

"Ellis is a contentious figure," Reva said. "But he's right about the need to remember our shared humanity in our dealings with others. For my sister and me, that means helping clients chip away at the narrative they've created that keeps them from recognizing that we are all 'a mixed bag.' Acknowledging that is the first step towards freeing the self to live a purposeful life."

Val Masluk's inability to accept the fact that, like every human being, he had made terrible mistakes in the past, was still very much on my mind, and I knew it was on Zack's mind too. He was clearly pleased with the turn our conversation was taking. "Reva, I know that, like me, Joanne looks forward to hearing more about the narratives we create to keep ourselves from understanding and accepting all parts of the self."

"I do," I said. "And it's exciting to know that today was just the first of the many times we'll all have to talk about that, and about all the other perplexing problems that come with being a human being."

Mila's laugh was low and warm. "We all have so much to learn," she said. "It's comforting to know that we have thoughtful friends to talk to along the way."

We all recognized an exit line when we heard it. Zack motioned to our server for the check, and we headed for the boat. Once we were in our life jackets, Zack started the motor and Reva turned in the direction of the restaurant, waved and said, "Farewell, Magoo's. We shall return." Her comment was lighthearted, and I smiled. Seemingly lunch at Magoo's had worked its magic, and the shadow that had crossed Reva's face when we talked about Leah's wedding had been banished.

When we were safely home, Zack said, "Recess is over for me. I have to get back to the Zoom meeting. Reva and Mila, this has been a pleasure. I hope you know that whether Jo and I are in town or here at Lawyers Bay, you are always welcome to join us to talk about the mysteries of human life."

I walked the Drache sisters to their car. Mila took my hand. "Thank you for everything." She looked over at the Amur maples. "Those trees will be spectacular in a few weeks." She sighed. "Lawyers Bay is a hard place to leave."

"But it is an easy place to come back to," I said. "And I hope you both will."

Reva cocked her head. "Joanne, how did Lawyers Bay get its name?"

"The original owners of the land on which all our cottages are built were Kevin Hynd's parents. The cottage Leah, Angus, Taylor and I stayed in that first summer was the one Harriet and Russell built. Harriet kept guest books — one for every summer — and Leah, Taylor and I spent many happy rainy evenings leafing through them. Every guest commented on Harriet and Russell's hospitality, so Zack and I are trying to continue their open door, open arms example. Now, about the name — Russell Hynd was a lawyer, and everyone in this community liked and respected him and his wife. I don't know who coined the phrase 'Lawyers Bay,' but I do know the reference was affectionate, so Zack and his law partners hung on to it."

"And very wise they were to do so," Mila said. "Now, we really must be on our way."

I put my hand on Mila's arm. "One last thing," I said. "Mila, for nine and a half years I've been wanting to thank you for something. The first night Zack and I spent together, I asked Leah if she'd stay with Taylor while I was gone. She said yes, and then she asked where I was going. When I told her I was going to Zack's place, she asked the question everyone would be asking me until the day Zack and I were married. She said, 'Are you sure about this?' When I said I wasn't sure, but I was going anyway, Leah said, 'Well, good for you. My aunt Mila always says that summer is for bad boys.'"

Mila's laugh was low and warm. "Of all my attempts at offering wise counsel, that's what my niece remembers. Well, I'm glad it did the job."

* * *

Zack wheeled out to meet me when I came back to the house after watching the sisters' Lexus disappear down the road. "This is a pleasant surprise," I said. "I thought you'd be tied up in your meeting for another hour or so."

"No, we actually dealt with everything we had to deal with. And I think we were all getting sick of each other."

"So we're both free. My plans for our immediate future are modest and within easy reach," I said. "I want us to stretch out on the chaise longues on the little patio outside our bedroom and talk about *Two Journalists*."

"Fine with me," Zack said. "But it's too nice a day to plumb the depths of Tom Kelsoe's twisted psyche. Besides, we could plumb forever and never find a satisfactory answer to the question 'What makes Tom tick?' He's a sociopath, and they are a species unto themselves."

"George Bernard Shaw says that just as some unfortunate people are born without a thumb, some people are born without a moral compass."

Zack was thoughtful. "I guess that's as good an answer as any. Let's start with an easy question . . . Val said that you'd be surprised by the role Rainey Arcus played in gathering the research for the book. Were you?"

"I was," I said. "The Rainey Arcus I remember was painfully shy. The J school is small, and the members of our seminar group had taken many classes together. They knew and trusted each other, and class discussion was always lively. The students made my job easy, but Rainey was a concern. She spoke only if someone asked her directly about her thoughts on the topic we were discussing. Her responses were always insightful, but she never said more than the bare minimum. The other students and I made every attempt to encourage Rainey to expand on her ideas, but it was obvious that she found speaking to a group agonizing, so we stopped pressing her."

"That does not sound like the gutsy journalist who went after Tom Kelsoe's story."

"No, it doesn't, but somehow it doesn't surprise me. Students at the School of Journalism have disparate goals, so it's useful for the instructors teaching the class to know what those goals are. Rainey Arcus wrote that her goal was to become a journalist committed to providing Canadians with 'dimensional journalism,' which she defined as 'telling the story behind the story, fully, fairly and accurately.'"

"And that's exactly what she did with Tom Kelsoe," Zack said. "She knew he was a sociopath who had murdered two people, but she obviously felt she was a match for him. To me, that suggests a very healthy ego."

"It does, and that surprises me," I said. "Do you remember Cowichan sweaters?"

The smile Zack gave me was wry. "And just like that, the conversation takes a turn. But I adapt quickly; and, to answer your question, I do remember Cowichan sweaters. In the seventies they were everywhere — at least, in our province. I remember hearing them referred to witheringly as 'the Saskatchewan dinner jacket.'"

"I heard that too," I said. "They *were* everywhere, and most of them were knock-offs, manufactured by workers far from the Coast Salish people in BC who'd made the original sweaters. I never saw Rainey without her Cowichan, and hers was the real McCoy. It was also so large that it seemed to swallow her. She was an attractive young woman: waist-length white-blond hair and extraordinarily luminous grey eyes — they were the colour of a stone that washed up close to shore.

"One afternoon when the other members of the seminar left for their Friday bitch and brag session at the student pub, Rainey stayed behind. I saw a chance to break through the wall she'd built around herself, and I took it. I told her how much I admired the pattern and the craftsmanship of her genuine Cowichan. She thanked me and said, 'It's my silver bullet. When I wear it, I disappear.' I smiled but Rainey's brow furrowed. 'I wasn't joking,' she said. 'Whenever people look my way, they don't see me. They just see the sweater.' She paused. 'I like that.' Then, without another word, she picked up her laptop and disappeared.

"It will be fun to see her at the wedding. I'll bet you a box of Timbits that Rainey won't be wearing her Cowichan."

"Nope, I never bet against a sure thing," Zack said. "But back to the topic at hand. Did you notice that there was no mention of Tom Kelsoe's abusive relationship with Jill Oziowy?"

"I did, and I was glad for Jill's sake that Val decided not to deal with it. Zack, you wouldn't have recognized the person Jill became when she entered into her relationship with Tom. She'd always been her own woman: bright, independent and focused . . . but she was slavishly devoted to that man. Her one concern was pleasing him, and when he beat her, which he repeatedly did, she always went back for more."

Zack shook his head. "That's hard to believe."

"It was the classic abusive relationship," I said. "Tom cut Jill off from all the people who mattered to her."

"Like you."

"Yes, like me, and that stung. Kelsoe convinced Jill that he was the only person in her life whom she could trust. If Jill began reaching out to someone, Tom beat her for belittling the love and devotion he was heaping upon her. The day after the beating, he would rub lotions on the fresh bruises and cuts, sobbing with contrition as he touched the still open wounds."

CHAPTER FOUR

MONDAY, AUGUST 29, 2022

On Monday morning, Zack and I awoke to the sounds of Esme whining; the wind whistling; the staccato beat of a hard rain on the roof and the soft patter of it into the water that had come in through the open window to pool on the bedroom floor. Zack took his phone from his nightstand, tapped, looked at the screen and said, "Well, hell. A storm front has moved in, and it's not going anywhere until late Tuesday at the earliest."

I slid out of bed. "I'm going to let Esme out long enough to take care of her immediate needs." After I closed the window and sent Esme on her way, I went into my bathroom for a towel for me to skate around the puddle on the floor. When it was soaked through, I pitched it in the laundry hamper, brought out another bath towel and made a second pass. The third bath towel did the job, and after I threw it in the hamper and let Esme in, I sat down on Zack's side of the bed.

"I vote we have breakfast and drive back to the city," I said. "That road between Lawyers Bay and the highway is 'improved,' but it's not improved enough for a three-day rain."

"I vote with you," Zack said. "I'll make breakfast, and you can pack up any food we should take back."

* * *

We were at our house on the creek by noon. We have an attached garage, so Zack and I have mastered the art of unpacking. After I take Esme inside, Zack reassembles his chair and transfers his body to it from the car. I hand whatever needs to be moved to him, and he puts it where it needs to be.

That day, when I handed him the box of leftovers Val had packed for us, Zack leaned close to one of the containers, opened the lid and breathed deeply. "The scent of bryndza," he said. "And we haven't had lunch. Yay or nay to include bryndza on our menu?"

I leaned over the container and took a deep breath. "Definitely a yay," I said.

* * *

After lunch and a deeply satisfying interlude, we had a nap and then went for a swim in the indoor pool that had been the deciding factor when we made the offer on our house. When I was towelling off, Charlie D called.

"I know you're at the lake, but there's something you need to hear that won't be on the edited MP3 of my interview with Valentine Masluk. I was planning to drive to Lawyers Bay so we could talk about it face to face, but Mieka vetoed the idea of me driving on the highway on a day where there's zero visibility. If you have a minute, I'll play the excerpt now."

"We have a minute, but after a white-knuckle drive from the lake, we're back in the city — so we can talk face to face after all."

"I'll be there in ten minutes, and Desmond Zackary will be with me. He has a surprise for you."

* * *

Zack and I were at the door when Charlie and Des arrived. Father and son were both wearing yellow slickers. After Charlie removed Des's slicker and boots and handed him to his grandfather, he turned to me. "Check out the message on Des's sweatshirt, Jo."

I read the words aloud. "'I can read!'"

I was my husband's resident expert in the field of child development, and he looked up at me questioningly. "Is that the right age?"

"Des is almost two years old, and we all read to him all the time."

"And we read the same books over and over and over again," Zack said.

"Right, so it's not surprising that he can look at some words if we point them out," I said. I turned to Charlie. "Time for show and tell. Did you bring a book for Des?"

"Right here." He handed Zack the book, and Des scrambled onto Zack's lap.

"Okay, Desmond Zackary, time to do your stuff." Zack pointed to the first word on the book's cover, but Des leapt ahead of him. "*The Snowy Day* by Ezra Jack Keats," he said triumphantly, and he turned to the first page. Zack began by reading three words. "One winter morning," he said. When Zack pointed to the next word, Des was off to the races. "Peter woke up," he said, his finger on the page.

It was a virtuoso duet, and when *The Snowy Day* ended, Des slid off Zack's lap and I handed Des his favourite toy — a ten-piece vividly coloured set of wooden arcs that, when fitted together perfectly, formed a rainbow. The great-grandfather for whom Des was named had been a significant figure in the world of visual art. Our daughter Taylor was also an artist, and the wooden rainbow had been a gift from her. She had been delighted when she saw how carefully Des arranged the pieces. "He'll be an artist," she said. At the time, Des was eleven months old, but when I pointed that out, Taylor's response was enigmatic. "Doesn't matter. He already has what he'll need."

Des was soon engrossed in the coloured arcs, so I sat down on the floor next to him and turned my attention to Charlie. "Let's get started," I said.

"The good news first," Charlie said. "The interview with Valentine Masluk is one of the best I've ever done. On his show *The Uncommon Reader*, he dealt with a wide spectrum of writers, illustrators, critics and academics, so Valentine knows exactly what to do when he's the one answering the questions.

"He politely turned down my offer to do a pre-interview. He said, correctly, that if the interviewer does not anticipate the answer to a question, the listener can hear the ring of truth in both the answer and in the interviewer's response to that answer."

Zack chuckled. "So you walked the high wire without a safety net."

"We did," Charlie said, "We did not risk life or limb, but when you hear the MP3, you'll understand how doing the interview without the safety net of a pre-interview makes for great radio. Anyway, that's the good part. I finished the interview, did my usual wind-up, and then I told Valentine I had one more question. He didn't have to answer it, but if he answered and believed his answer would strengthen the interview, I could add it. If he answered and decided that he didn't want the answer to be part of the interview, I would delete it. That's when the bad part came. I told Valentine about the email I'd received and asked if he understood the reference to pages 329ff."

Zack moved his chair closer. His voice was deep and intimate. "And Val did answer your question, but you both decided not to air it. Charlie, it seems to me that the issue is resolved. Why do you want Joanne and me to listen to something that will never be made public?"

Charlie raked his fingers through his hair. "Because in a little over a week, Angus is marrying Leah Drache, a woman we all truly love, and my spidey sense tells me there's something out there that could blow up Steven Brooks's world."

I felt a coldness in the pit of my stomach. "Let's listen to the tape," I said.

"Okay," Charlie said. "What you're about to hear happened immediately after I set out the terms for asking *The Question*. Valentine Masluk took control immediately."

Charlie started the MP3, and Val's voice, measured but with an underlying note of tension, filled the room.

"Charlie, I respect your work, and I owe my life to your wife's mother, so I'm going to tell you the truth. I know what your question will be before you ask it, because it's the question that seems to be inevitable in all the interviews I'm doing for the biography. The approach is always slightly different, but the inference is always the same: that someone other than Steven Brooks wrote *Medusa's Fate* and *The Iron Bed of Procrustes*."

Charlie D paused the MP3. "Did Val go into any details?" I said.

"No, Valentine is a very contained guy, but at that moment, he looked stricken. What the note suggests is as obvious as it is devastating."

"Plagiarism," I said. "But Charlie, Medusa and Procrustes are both characters in Greek myths. Their stories are powerful, and there must be many adaptations."

"And there are — at least for Medusa," Charlie said. "As soon as my interview with Valentine Masluk was scheduled, I dug into the mythical Medusa's origin story. It's fascinating and definitely R-rated. Medusa was a triplet. Her sisters were Gorgons with fangs and claws and scales, but Medusa was drop-dead gorgeous, and she sang like an angel. Poseidon fell in love with her. Some versions of the story say she seduced him; others say he raped her. The classic 'he said, she said' situation, but however it happened, it happened in Athena's temple, and Athena was so enraged that her temple had been defiled that she turned Medusa's hair into snakes and put a curse on her: after that day, every man who looked upon Medusa would turn to stone."

"The underpinnings for *Medusa's Fate* certainly come from the mythology," I said. "But it's a contemporary novel, and Steven Brooks's Medusa has a complicated history that destroys her relationships with every man who loves her. Charlie, Greek myths are adapted all the time. George Bernard Shaw used the myth of the sculptor who falls in love with the statue of a woman he created for his play *Pygmalion*. And Shaw's *Pygmalion* was adapted as the musical *My Fair Lady*. Offhand, I can't think of any adaptations of the myth of Procrustes."

"The story of a man who invites passersby to spend the night on a bed that he promises will fit anyone and then cuts off their heads or limbs to make their bodies fit the bed does not strike me as promising musical comedy material," Charlie said.

I laughed. "True enough, but there are hundreds of examples of writers taking source material and reshaping it into an original piece of work that is their own."

Zack had been listening with interest. Now he moved his chair so he was facing both Charlie and me. "And that's exactly what Steven Brooks claims he did. But if the source material was not the myth but an adaptation by another writer, we're left with only one possibility, and it's an ugly one: Steven used source material without adapting it, and plagiarism is not only unethical, it's illegal. The publishing contracts Steven Brooks signed for his books would require that the work he submitted be original. Plagiarism is a breach of that contract and, in all likelihood, would result in a lawsuit."

"A couple of years ago, there was a case where that nearly happened," Charlie said. "The author submitted a manuscript that had been turned in to them by a student in their writing class. They avoided a breach of contract lawsuit from their publisher by giving back their advance."

"I remember that case," Zack said. "The consensus among lawyers is that the writer in that particular instance was lucky. The legal ramifications could have been far more serious, and in Steven Brooks's case, they would be more serious, more complicated and far more costly. Not only did Brooks receive advances for those novels, but after he earned back those advances there would have been many years of royalties. Both novels have been adapted for stage and film. Brooks's reputation is not the only thing at stake here. My guess is that if this is, indeed, a case of plagiarism, there will be lawsuits from the publisher, from the producers of the plays and from the production companies that financed the films. There's a whack of money involved, and the law is always serious about anything involving a whack of money."

Charlie's expression was grave. "I had to make a quick call, but I still believe it was the right one. I advised Valentine Masluk to ask Steven to tell him the truth about his source material for both novels."

"And he refused?" I said.

"He fell apart. Listen to his voice." Charlie D played the MP3 again:

"As I predicted, Charlie, this is déjà vu all over again. And I really cannot talk about this. Just know that I am aware of the situation, and I am not going to exacerbate it. I was responsible for two people losing their lives. I'm not going to let that happen again with Steven Brooks. Unless someone moves a piece on the board, the situation is in hand."

"And if someone does move a piece?" Charlie D's recorded voice asked.

The question was followed by an uncomfortably long silence. When he finally spoke, Val's pain was palpable. "Then I don't know what comes next. And really, that's all I can say. Charlie, this part of the interview must not be made public."

Charlie turned off the recording. "So, our best hope is that our anonymous seeker of truth will just fade away."

Zack's tone was gentle. "Do you really think the person who sent that email will just fade away?"

Charlie's laugh was short and angry. "Not a chance," he said. "But like it or not, that's where we are, and there's nothing we can do to keep that piece on the board from moving inexorably towards checkmate."

As the enormity of the inevitable hit us, Charlie, Zack and I were silent, but Valentine Masluk had an eight-week-long book tour ahead, and he sounded as if he was already at the brink.

"There's nothing we can do to change the path of the inevitable question to Val Massey, but we can't leave him without a recourse," I said. "And I have one — a story that went viral and would be familiar to many of your listeners. Roy Brodnitz, the well-known theatre writer, had fallen into a deep depression after his partner died. He was on the brink of taking his own life when he came upon a painting of the northern lights that was so brilliant it gave him a new life filled with hope and creativity. Referencing it in an interview might give Val the escape route he needs. I'll call him tonight, and he and I can talk it through."

"Finally, a small glimmer of light on the horizon," Charlie said. "This doesn't solve the big problem, but at least it might take the pressure off Val. I've been concerned about him too."

The three of us had been keeping our voices low, and Des, wholly absorbed in his wooden rainbow pieces, had been oblivious to us. But Charlie had raised his voice when he reacted to the glimmer of light, and he'd caught Des's attention. Our grandson looked up, took in the situation and ran into my arms.

"Des is ready for a nap. Come to think of it, so am I," Charlie said. "But I'm glad we talked, and I'm glad you're calling Val tonight, Jo. Valentine said that you once saved his life. He didn't elaborate, and I didn't ask, but I think if anyone can get to him, it's you."

I stood. "The wedding is in a week. Someone has to do something."

"At this moment, Valentine has either boarded the plane for Toronto or his flight is already underway," Charlie said. "If you need it, I have his cell number."

"I have it too," I said. "Charlie, this is such a mess."

"Truer words were never spoken," our son-in-law said. When he and Des were both dressed for the weather, Charlie kissed Zack on the top of his head and me on the cheek. "God, I'm glad you two are around."

"That goes both ways," Zack said.

* * *

The rain and wind had worsened by the time Charlie and Des left, and I was grateful Charlie had been able to park close to the house. When I closed the door, Zack said, "Val doesn't deserve this, Jo. Relating the Roy Brodnitz story will give him breathing space, but it won't change anything."

"The only person who can change what happens next is Steven Brooks, and he's not going to open up," I said. "Really, what difference would it make if he did? His reputation would still be shot, and all the legal repercussions you mentioned would still be set in motion. It's six of one, half dozen of another. The only thing Steven can control is the timing."

The lines that bracketed Zack's mouth like parentheses deepened. "And Leah and her aunts will be collateral damage. Jo, do you think they know?"

"Steven's sisters know something's wrong. Mila and Reva's time with us yesterday was idyllic, but there was a moment of darkness. I didn't tell you about it because at the time it seemed inconsequential, but in retrospect, I wonder. We had a good walk along the beach with Esme then I took them out on that finger of land at Lawyers Bay where the gazebo is."

Zack's face softened. "Where Peter and Maisie were married."

"Exactly. I knew the sisters would be interested in hearing about the wedding, and they were. When we arrived at the place in front of the gazebo where Peter and Maisie exchanged vows, they wanted to hear all the details."

"And you obliged," Zack said.

"I did, and after I'd finished describing the dresses and bouquets of Maisie's attendants, and how Madeleine and Lena tossed rose petals on the grass, I told them about that heart-stopping moment when the ceremony was over and Maisie and Peter turned to face us all with their arms raised in victory.

"Mila was clearly moved. When she said that Peter and Maisie's wedding sounded absolutely perfect there was such sadness in her voice, and I realized that somehow my words had touched a nerve. I tried to be reassuring. I said that I knew Leah and Angus's wedding would be just as perfect as Peter and Maisie's had been. For a long while, both sisters were silent, then Reva whispered, 'We're hoping it will be but . . .'

"Mila didn't let Reva finish the sentence. She drew Reva close to her and said, 'It will be the wedding Leah and Angus have earned: solemn, joyous and flawless.' When Reva's eyes filled with tears, Mila tightened her grip on her sister's shoulders and said that it was time for us to get back to the house."

"So Steven's sisters definitely do know that something's wrong."

I nodded. "But I'm sure Leah doesn't," I said. "When she and Angus were here for dinner last week, they were as happy and excited as two people in love should be in the days before their wedding."

"And they deserve to stay that way," Zack said. "Joanne, rolling over and playing dead is not your style, and it's not mine. We need to let Reva and Mila know that we're aware of the fact that something is wrong, and that we don't need an explanation, but we do want to help."

"The direct approach. I'll call Mila and Reva while you make the martinis. Let's keep dinner simple. We have lentil soup in the freezer and some very nice wild rice bread. Does that tickle your fancy?"

"It does. For the record, you can tickle my fancy any time you like."

"The night is young," I said. "And martinis always get things off to a promising start."

* * *

I had no luck with the Drache sisters. Reva wasn't answering her phone, and Mila thanked us profusely for the offer of help and said that there are always problems but that, for the time being, everything was going smoothly. When I told Zack that Mila's answer was "thanks, but no thanks," he said her response sounded definitive and that the ball was now in the Drache sisters' court.

That evening, following Rabbi Dan Shoichet's suggestion that all of us involved in Leah and Angus's wedding should watch *Father of the Bride,* Zack and I took our after-dinner coffee to the family room and settled in. The movie was thirty years old, but Steve Martin as the bride's befuddled father and Martin Short as the wedding planner were still hilarious, and Steve Martin's explanation of the difference between a marriage and a wedding was still right on the mark. By the time we turned in for the night, the darkness in Steven Brooks's past no longer dominated my thoughts, and when I heard Zack snore, I knew it no longer dominated his.

* * *

In the week before the wedding, Zack and I tried to stay focused on the daily business of living, but like the dull pain of an aching tooth, the threat posed by 329ff was always there. We both knew that it was only a matter of time before the truth about Steven Brooks's plagiarism was revealed and that the effect on Leah, Angus and all who loved them would be devastating.

Every time my phone buzzed, my pulse quickened, but, mercifully, the calls were simply the familiar calls of my everyday life: Madeleine and Lena asking if they could each bring a friend over for a swim; Mieka putting Des on the phone because he wanted to invite us to his birthday party; Peter letting me know that the twins' visit to the schoolroom where, in a few days, they would start grade one had been a success. And many friends called just to tell Zack and me that they were thinking of us in the hectic days before the wedding.

In fact, our days were far from hectic. We had both pared down our commitments for the week before the wedding so that we'd be ready if needed, but apparently, we were not needed. The morning after I told Mila that Zack and I were aware there was a problem and we were ready to help, the Drache sisters sent us a basket with a generous assortment of red wines to pair with the heavier dishes of autumn, but when I called to thank them, they were both warm but brisk. I was certain the sisters feared that if our call continued, I would ask a question they didn't want to answer, so I didn't call again. As Zack said, the ball was in their court.

* * *

FRIDAY, SEPTEMBER 2, 2022

I'd talked to Val twice after he arrived in Toronto. He had embraced the idea of using the Roy Brodnitz story to deflect interviewers, and it seemed to be working. By Friday afternoon, I allowed myself to consider the possibility that somehow we had managed to dodge the bullet. Taylor and Gracie's flight from Saskatoon was arriving at 5 p.m., and Ed Mariani had invited the four of us to enjoy the late summer view of the university campus from their balcony while we savoured the paella made by Ed's husband, Barry Levitt. A tension-free evening with people we loved was exactly what Zack and I needed, and we were both looking forward to it.

Zack had just left for the airport when my phone rang, and, as seemed to be my default reaction these days, my pulse quickened.

When I saw Georgie Kovacs's name on caller ID, I exhaled. Georgie was a friend, and I always welcomed the prospect of a conversation with her.

Roy Brodnitz had written the first two episodes of *Sisters and Strangers*, and when he died, the responsibility for writing scripts for the remaining episodes fell to Georgie and me. As someone accustomed to writing either academic papers or political speeches, I found the learning curve steep, but *Sisters and Strangers* was the story of two formative periods of my life. Getting the narrative right mattered to me, and I was a willing student.

By the first day of principal photography, Georgie and I had created a script we believed honoured the vision of the writer who died, and we had become so close that I held her bouquet as she and Zack's long-time friend, Nick Kovacs, exchanged wedding vows.

Georgie and Nick had now been married for over two years, and both were quick to say their life together was a gift. They were now a family of four, with a two-and-half-year-old son and Nick's eighteen-year-old daughter, whom Georgie had adopted. After we exchanged quick sketches of the latest news about our families, Georgie got down to business. "I've found a novel that I think would make a great limited series for us. You know my criterion for a proposal worth developing: if my loins twitch when I read it, I'm in."

"And your loins are twitching," I said.

Georgie's laugh was deep and throaty. "I am aware that the loin-twitch criterion is a tad bizarre, but yes, my figurative loins are twitching for this one. Are you interested?"

"Of course," I said. "But I don't have a lot of time. Zack should be at the airport by now, waiting for Taylor and Gracie's flight from

Saskatoon to arrive. The four of us are going to have dinner with Ed Mariani and his husband."

"Lucky you," Georgie said. "But I think you and I may also be lucky with the novel that I just finished reading. The plot is riveting, and it has characters that an audience will want to explore because of the choices they make."

"That does sound tempting," I said. "Do you want to give me an overview or would you rather wait for me to read the novel myself?"

"I'll go with the overview," Georgie said. "You have a busy week ahead, and you won't be able to get to the novel for a while. I think we should move on this quickly before someone else goes after it. Do you have enough time to hear an ill-thought-out-but-fervent pitch?"

"You have never in your life done anything that was 'ill-thought-out,' but I am curious." I glanced at my watch. "And I do have some time. Go for it."

"Okay, the story is contemporary, and the setting is academic. It's a world you know, Jo, and you don't have to be a Rhodes Scholar to smell the whiff of reality in the plot. The names may be changed, but those characters are real and so are the decisions they make. When a basically decent female professor dismisses a female student's accusation that a member of the class is harassing her sexually, the consequences are tragic.

"The novel's focus is on a small group of students who've been together for three years. They know one another well, and they trust one another, so when the young woman tells them that a member of their group is making sexual advances to her, they turn their backs on her. The young woman is not physically attractive, but she is dogged and through her diligence she pieces together a scandal that will reveal the truth about a sociopathic faculty member of the School of Journalism. No one, including the decent but flawed professor the young woman turns to, will hear what the young woman has to say, so the path is clear for the sociopath to kill her.

"The rest of the book happens now, fifteen years later, and we revisit the students and see how their lives were shaped by their failure to reach out to someone in desperate need. Jo, you and I could really do something with this. What are your thoughts?"

I was dumbfounded. I couldn't seem to pull my thoughts together. When I failed to respond, Georgie said, "I'm hoping your silence means that you're as bowled over by this possibility as I am."

Finally, I said, "Where did you get the book?"

"I can bring you the copy I have," Georgie said. "But I take it your question is about something more complex than the name of a bookstore."

"It is. I don't know where to begin, but here's what I know about *Two Journalists.*"

I was certain 329ff was somehow involved in getting the book to Georgie, so I included what we knew about their ultimate goal. It was a long story, and Georgie listened without comment.

When I finished, she whistled. "Wow, talk about a tangled web. I'll start by giving you a simple answer to your question about where the book came from: It was in our family's mailbox. The envelope it came in had my name on it, but no stamps."

"So *Two Journalists* was hand delivered," I said. "No signature, of course."

"No, and I had zero concerns about that. It's not easy to get a potential property to a person in our business who might help push

85

your book along to production. I was so wowed by *Two Journalists* that I was just grateful that I'd opened the envelope. But I did look up Valentine Massey online. There was nothing, so my assumption was that Massey was a novelist who either lived in Regina or who lived close enough to us to look us up on Canada 411 and drop the book in our mailbox." Georgie paused. "Jo, do you have any idea at all about what's going on here?"

"None, and you know me well enough to know how uneasy I am about loose ends."

"I do know that. That's why I'm so glad that we talked about this. Remember the mantra we had when we were writing the scripts for *Sisters and Strangers*?"

"A burden shared is a burden halved," I said. "And I actually do feel less weighted down by all this now that I've talked to you. You're a good friend, Georgie."

"Jo, I have no idea what's going on here, but I'll do whatever I can to help, and if that includes simply listening, count me in."

"Thank you. It's good to know you're there. Now, I guess the next time I see you will be at the wedding. You'll recognize me because I'll be wearing the suit I wore when Zack was the best man and I was the best friend at your wedding."

"And look how well that turned out," Georgie said, and her voice was filled with contentment. "Just to make certain that everything comes up roses for Leah and Angus, I'll wear the suit I wore at my wedding. Nick loved that outfit, but silk shantung does not have much of a role in our family life. I'll be happy to get some mileage out of that outfit — even if it is pink."

"It's a very pale shade of pink. You're a natural blond, and you really rocked that outfit."

"Winner, winner, chicken dinner," Georgie said. "I get to wear that suit again, and I don't have to shop. And Jo, I'll see you before the wedding. Mieka and Charlie have invited us to Desmond's birthday party. A birthday party and a wedding in two days — Chloe is beyond excited to be part of everything."

"Good. And Georgie, you're right about *Two Journalists*. There really is a lot we could work with there. Who knows? Maybe we still can."

CHAPTER FIVE

I was still pondering the adaptation possibilities of *Two Journalists* when Zack arrived home with Taylor and Gracie. Their plane had been on time, and they were ready for a weekend that started with paella, continued with the long weekend at Lawyers Bay with the members of the wedding party and their significant others and culminated in the marriage of two people who were exactly where they hoped they'd be when they heard the Oracle in *The Matrix* tell Neo that being the One is like being in love: "No one can tell you you're in love, you just know it. Through and through. Balls to bones."

Zack and I had agreed not to tell Taylor and Gracie about the threat 329ff posed not only to the wedding, but also to Leah and Angus's future happiness. Taylor was close to both Angus and Leah, and the knowledge would weigh heavily on her. Our younger daughter's emotions were always close to the surface, and those who knew Taylor knew immediately when something was troubling her.

* * *

When we arrived at our hosts' door Friday evening, Taylor and Gracie were in high spirits. Ed Mariani had a face made for smiling, and as he greeted us, his smile was on, full-wattage. Ed self-identified as a "portly" man, and his closet was filled with variations of a shirt he, himself, had designed that was both comfortable and flattering. Tonight's shirt was apricot cotton, and after the usual round of hugs, he led us into the kitchen where Barry's justifiably famous paella was a work in progress.

Since Taylor and Gracie had become first housemates and then partners, Gracie had enjoyed the hospitality of our hosts often, but this was her first paella, and she was keen to watch it come together.

Taylor's drink of choice the first time she had dinner with Ed and Barry had been a Shirley Temple. After Ed gave Zack and me our martinis, he handed the young women the Shirley Temples with paper umbrellas they had requested because Taylor wanted to share everything about our first dinner with Gracie.

That long-ago night when Taylor and I attended that first dinner, Barry had pulled out a stool for Taylor to sit on so she could learn how he made the paella. Tonight he pulled out two stools. "One for you, Taylor, and one for Gracie," he said. Barry was a small, compact man with looks that would be described as "boyish" until his eightieth birthday. He had a twenty-four-inch waist that he measured daily and retained by a rigorous daily exercise program.

Taylor and Gracie took their places, and Taylor began. "As everybody knows, I love seafood, and that night, Barry let me watch him dump a steaming pot of seafood into a mixing bowl of rice. He asked me if I knew the names of any of the different 'critters' he had poured into the rice. I recognized the mussels, shrimp and scallops, and I asked Barry if he could help me with the names of the others."

Barry turned to Gracie. "I told our friend here that I thought I remembered throwing a squid into the pot. I described it and asked Taylor if she could point out the squid. She did, and we followed through on our game: me describing, Taylor pointing out."

"I was able to identify the clams, some chicken and a lobster," Taylor said, looking fondly at our two hosts. "Barry congratulated me and said that the next time Jo and I came for dinner, I was in charge of the paella. That was the night I knew I loved Ed and Barry."

"And we loved her too," Ed said. "And after we met you, Gracie, we knew Taylor found the right person to love."

After dinner, Barry led Taylor and Gracie inside to show them some new art he and his husband had acquired. Ed stayed behind, and as soon as Barry and the young women were out of earshot, Ed took Zack and me aside.

"I received a troubling message in my university email today," he said. "I wouldn't classify it as threatening, but it sets out a path the writer says I would be wise to follow."

"And the path is?" Zack said.

"To remember that as head of the School of Journalism, I have an obligation to remind Valentine Masluk, who holds a degree from our school, that an ethical journalist must tell the complete story."

"And the sender identified themselves as 329ff," I said.

Ed's jaw dropped. "I'm not the only one to receive a message from 329ff?"

"No — 329ff challenged our son-in-law, Charlie Dowhanuik, to ask Val Massey on air to tell the complete truth about Steven Brooks's activities in the nine years between the failure of this third novel and the amazing success of *Medusa's Fate*."

Ed sighed and smoothed his apricot shirt over his chest and stomach. "I love these shirts," he said. "No matter how much I eat, my clothing no longer punishes me. Did Charlie D accept the challenge?"

My eyes were still focused on the quiet beauty of a manicured university campus in the days between the summer and fall semesters, and I didn't turn to face Ed when I answered his question. "Yes and no," I said. "The interview was taped. Charlie ended the interview, but he didn't stop the tape. He told Val that he had another question, but if Val chose not to answer it, he wouldn't press him. Then he asked Val a series of questions that were leading inexorably to the question 329ff wanted answered. Val saw what was happening and hit the brakes. He said that particular series of questions was familiar to him, that Charlie's wording might be different but the inference would be the same as it always was: that someone other than Steven Brooks wrote *Medusa's Fate* and *The Iron Bed of Procrustes*."

Ed had also been drinking in the peace of the campus, but my words shook him. "Plagiarism," he said. "My God, that's devastating. That would end Brooks's career."

Zack turned to Ed. "It would, and the legal ramifications would bankrupt him. Brooks would have to pay back all the money that had been advanced to him in good faith by his publishers, all the royalties he'd earned and all his earnings from adaptations of both books."

"And this is happening days before Angus and Leah's wedding," Ed said, and his dismay was palpable. "Why would 329ff want to hurt them?"

"I don't know." I paused. "Ed, we haven't told Taylor any of this. As you have no doubt noticed, our daughter's emotions run deep."

Ed nodded. "And her face always reveals what she cannot find the words to say. She never visits this house without going to our bedroom to see Sally's painting *Two Old Gardeners*. She always stays a few minutes, and when she comes out she doesn't hide the fact that she's been crying. Once, I asked her if there was anything I could do to help. Taylor said it was too late. She said she wished she'd been able to tell Sally how much joy that painting brought to Barry and me and to everyone who saw it." Ed had been watching me closely. "Now I've made you tear up," he said.

"Happy tears. It took Taylor a long time to get past her anger and see that her birth mother did the best she could with the life she'd been given."

For a few moments, we were silent, then Ed said, "Jo, do you remember that poem Barry and I read together at our wedding?"

"I do. Sir Philip Sidney's 'The Bargain.' I'll remember that moment forever."

Ed's voice was fervent. "We have to do everything we can to make certain that the moment when Angus and Leah exchange their vows is as meaningful for them as our moment was for Barry and me." Ed managed a small smile. "For my part, I can assure you that the floral arrangements Leah, her aunts and I have decided upon will be perfect. The late summer flowers we've chosen are still in my garden, and they will be at their peak on the wedding day."

* * *

Overall, the evening had been a joy, and we were all sorry to see it end. Taylor and Gracie were driving to Lawyers Bay the next morning, and they wanted to get an early start. That meant an early bedtime. After we hugged them goodnight, Zack yawned and stretched. "I wouldn't mind turning in early myself."

"Neither would I," I said. Esme was looking at me expectantly. "It looks like my pal here wants a little backyard time," I said. "I won't be long."

When I came into the bedroom, Zack was in his robe, sitting by the window. I sat in the chair across from him, and he moved his wheelchair close. "When Taylor, Gracie and I got back from the airport, I knew something was bothering you. Are you ready to talk about it now?"

"Was it that obvious?" I said.

"Just to me."

"I do need to talk about this," I said. "Georgie called not long before the three of you came in." As I told him about our conversation, Zack listened closely. When I finished, he uttered his second favourite curse word and covered my hand with his own. "So the book that Val believed would be seen only by those who were part of the tragedy has found a larger audience. What did Georgie think of *Two Journalists*?"

"She thought she and I could make a dynamite limited series from it."

"I'm assuming that proposal is now off the table."

"I don't know," I said. "Zack, I'm not sure of anything anymore. I have no idea what's going to happen next, or when it will happen. All I know for certain is that whatever happens next is going to be a blow to people we love, and we don't know how to ward it off."

Zack looked at me closely and frowned. "I believe this is a double massage night," he said.

"Even hearing the words 'double massage' makes my muscles unknot," I said. "You always know what I need."

"You always know what I need too," Zack said. "And there's something I need now."

"I'm always up for that," I said.

Zack grinned. "Second best thing about being married: the roller coaster of joy is always within reach. But this is something else. We're picking up our puppy in a week, and we haven't settled on a name."

"True," I said. "But we *have* narrowed our list down to five names we both like." I counted the names off on my fingers: "Cooper, Woody, Duke, Lucky and Bailey."

"Those are all fine names," Zack said. "But last night after you fell asleep, I thought of another. You remember Ned Osler."

"I do. He was a lovely man — an old-school gentleman." I tried to read Zack's face. "So, you want to call the new puppy Ned?"

"That's not a bad thought," Zack said, "but I was thinking of the name Ned Osler gave his big gentle dog. The dog was a lot like Pantera, but of an uncertain lineage."

"A 'Heinz 57' dog," I said.

Zack chuckled. "I'd forgotten that. A Heinz 57 dog, like the brand with fifty-seven varieties! Anyway, the secret sauces that came together to make Ned's dog produced a winner. He was the best, and his name was Scout. What do you think about Scout as a name for our new pup?"

"I like it. In fact, I like it a lot. So it's decided. Next Saturday, we'll drive out to Neil McCallum's and pick up our dog Scout."

Zack rubbed his hands together gleefully. "I can hardly wait."

"Well we do have a few things that should help you cope. Sunday is the Labour Day Classic between Saskatchewan and Winnipeg. The Riders are having a good year, and the Grey Cup will be held in Regina, so fingers crossed, we'll win; Monday, we're celebrating Desmond Zackary's second birthday. The party theme is *The Very Hungry Caterpillar* because it's one of Des's favourite books, and we'll all be at Charlie and Mieka's place with Maddy and Lena, the twins and their parents, and Georgie, Nick and their kids. Mieka tells me there will be caterpillar cake. And if that's not enough to fill your dance card, Monday night there's the dinner and wedding rehearsal at the Scarth Club, and Tuesday there's the wedding, but it's also back-to-school day, and we're invited to Pete and Maisie's to take photos of the boys going off to grade one. After that, you only have to endure Wednesday, Thursday and Friday before we can pick up Scout."

Zack's brow furrowed. "Did I sound childish when I said, 'I can hardly wait'?"

"Just a tad, but it's your first puppy. You're entitled."

* * *

The weather on Saturday and Sunday was picture perfect, and Zack and I received a steady stream of photos of the handsome young people in the bridal party swimming, waterskiing, chowing down at Magoo's, watching the Labour Day classic, tossing around a football or just plain goofing off.

Idyllic, but I noticed that Angus's closest friend and best man, Sawyer MacLeish, who had always been front and centre in every aspect of his life, remained on the sidelines during all the fun and games. The previous January, Sawyer had suffered an injury perilously close to his spinal cord, and he had spent the months dedicated to his physical and emotional rehabilitation living with us.

Sawyer could not have asked for a better guide than Zack during the bleak months when he was struggling to regain the life he had known. Zack rarely spoke of the spinal injury that he sustained when he was ten. He was coming home from baseball practice, dreaming of a career in the major leagues, when a drunk driver blew through a red light and Zack's dream of a career in the major leagues ended.

When Dylan Haczkewicz, the son of Regina's head of Major Crimes, was in a motorcycle accident that left him with paraplegia, he refused to accept a life with a disability. He wanted to die, and his mother, Debbie, asked Zack for help. Every day for a month, Zack went to the hospital to talk to Dylan, and every day, Dylan pushed him away, often physically. When Zack brought Dylan a T-shirt with a cartoon of a guy in a wheelchair saying, "I'm only in this for the parking," Dylan gave in and listened. He enrolled in courses focused on teaching English as a second language, became a teacher, went to Japan and married a colleague at the school where he taught. They now have two sons and a full life.

In the years after Dylan, Zack became the go-to guy for staff at the rehabilitation centre confronted with young male patients who refused to face the prospect of life in a wheelchair. Zack understood what they were going through, and he knew, intimately, the question they were afraid to ask: "Will I still (a) be a real man and (b) have a normal sex life?" He also knew the answer to (a) was "yes," and the answer to (b) was "yes, but you may need to redefine 'normal.'"

Zack had been able to reassure Sawyer that, for him too, the answer to the two-part question was affirmative. And recently, Sawyer and a therapist in the rehab centre had found a relationship that, while still new, was definitely checking both "yes" boxes. As Zack and I watched the videos Angus, Leah, Taylor and Sawyer sent, we both noticed that while Sawyer stayed on the sidelines, Lorelei, the therapist, was increasingly in the thick of the action with Sawyer cheering her on. It was a bright flag celebrating a landmark for both Sawyer and Lorelei, and Zack and I cherished it.

The plan had been for the members of the wedding to extend the pleasures of the long weekend into Monday, staying at the lake until mid-afternoon and arriving at the Scarth Club in time for dinner at six and the wedding rehearsal afterwards. By Sunday night, I crossed my fingers, hoping against hope that the buoyant ebullience of the weekend would continue, and that, in the words of the old Irving Berlin song, there would be "nothin' but blue skies from now on."

* * *

MONDAY, SEPTEMBER 5, 2022

When we awoke Monday to heavy rain and a leaden sky, reality hit. For a few sun-splashed days, 329ff had drifted off the radar. I had welcomed the respite and willed myself to ignore the increasingly strident voice inside me, reminding me that 329ff's silence was not a white flag accepting defeat but simply the silence of someone biding their time. Their intent all along had been to expose Steven Brooks as a plagiarist and a fake. A large event where Steven Brooks's family and friends gathered to celebrate his daughter's marriage would be a magnet for the person determined to shame him.

As I listened to the rain pounding on our roof, I remembered the sorrowful Irish lilt in the voice of my grade nine English teacher, Miss Boucher, as she explained that in literature, the term "pathetic fallacy" describes the imparting of human emotion to something not human. "For example, girls," she said, "if the day when you bury a loved one is stormy, you might see in the turbulent weather a reflection of what you, yourself, are feeling — if the skies seem sad, that is pathetic fallacy."

That morning, the Drache sisters and I began texting weather forecasts to one another. The forecasts were as gloomy as the weather, and the outdoor wedding we'd all hoped for was seeming increasingly unlikely. The three of us continued to reassure one another that we weren't worried. Nonetheless, we kept checking forecasts and texting.

* * *

The party celebrating Desmond Zackary Dowhanuik's second birthday was in the early afternoon. The weather could not have been gloomier, but the moment we stepped inside the Dowhanuik house, my spirits lifted, and when I looked at Zack, he grinned and shrugged. "If you hang in long enough, something good always comes around the corner."

I squeezed my husband's shoulder. "Albert Camus shares your optimism. He said that no matter how hard the world pushes against him, he has, within him, 'something stronger — something better, pushing right back.'"

Zack drew a deep breath. "I think we may need to hang on to that for a while."

"Here's a nice start," I said. "Our youngest grandson has spotted us, and he's on his way over."

There were many reasons that children were drawn to my husband. He had an actor's voice: sonorous and musical. As Colin said, when Zack read a story, you could feel it in your stomach. Zack never talked down to children. He addressed them with the same directness and humour he used with adults. And there was another reason for his popularity with the young: sitting in a wheelchair, Zack was closer to a child's level than most adults were, and his lap was one a child could easily climb onto. And when Desmond reached his grandfather, that is exactly what he did.

The theme of the party was inspired by *The Very Hungry Caterpillar* by Eric Carle, and the family room was bright with the lively and vibrant images that Taylor told me Carle created by dabbing tissue paper with acrylic paint and then cutting the paper into the shapes he needed. The book had been a favourite of my children and our grandchildren when they were very young.

Eric Carle had died the year before. He was ninety-one years old, and he left a rich legacy for children and for all those who loved and read to them. The story he tells is as simple as it is universal. The hero moves from innocence through experience to a new beginning, which can, and often does in many stories, lead to the beginning of a new life. Carle's hero, a caterpillar with a voracious appetite, eats almost everything in sight for almost a week. Not surprisingly, his binge ends in a stomach ache. After the caterpillar eats a single green leaf, it is ready for the job at hand, spinning a cocoon. Two weeks later, the caterpillar emerges from the cocoon. In an ending as satisfying as it is surprising for the very young, the drab caterpillar has become a gloriously coloured butterfly.

That afternoon, Des was wearing Very Hungry Caterpillar overalls, and after Des settled in my husband's lap, he pointed to the vibrant images on his overalls and said, "Granddad, look! Same as our book!" My camera phone was already focused.

Mieka was never far behind her son. "Hey, Mum, you just took the first photo of Des in his new outfit."

"Those overalls are perfect," I said. "Where did you get them?"

"They were a gift from Maeve Weber."

"For an eight-month-old, Maeve is a savvy shopper."

Mieka laughed. "And a generous one. She also brought a pair for Erik Kovacs. She didn't want anybody to be left out."

"Maeve takes after her parents," I said. "Warren and Annie are among the most generous and inclusive people I know."

"They're certainly among the happiest," Mieka said. The Webers had been married five years before Maeve came along. Warren was eighty-one and Annie was thirty-one. My older daughter's smile was wide. "Maeve's parents believe she's a miracle," she said. "And I believe that too. Wait till you see her in the little girl version of these overalls. Maeve Weber will be the star of Desmond Zackary's second birthday party."

Mieka had hosted hundreds of birthday parties in the years since she'd purchased the café and play centres, UpSlideDown and April's Place, and she had always used my rule of thumb for the number of guests that the parents should invite to the party: the birthday child's age plus two. Mieka was now thirty-six, and I had long since forgotten where the party formula came from. It had always worked for us, and it worked that day. Desmond Zackary Dowhanuik, Erik Kovacs and Maeve Weber were happy little people in their matching Hungry Caterpillar gear. No tears and no tantrums, and that meant jubilant parents, siblings and grandparents. It was a good party.

* * *

The presents had been opened, Des had blown out the candles on his caterpillar cake and we'd all eaten our slice, but when I went over to Georgie to say goodbye, she took me aside. "Just before we left for the party, I received an email," she said. "Very short and to the point: 'You and Dr. Shreve could make something great out of *Two Journalists*.' So, the connection between what we've done in the past and the possibilities of us doing it again with *Two Journalists* is definitely there."

"And the note referred to me as Dr. Shreve," I said, "and that suggests another connection. Georgie, unlike Tom Kelsoe, I never encouraged students to call me by my given name. And the only place I've ever used 'Dr. Shreve' is at the university."

"So you think 329ff might be a former student?"

"That, or a faculty colleague." I shrugged. "I don't know. But I do know that I've had enough of this game of cat and mouse."

By the time the birthday party ended, the rain had stopped and the sky was clearing. The sun had come out — pale and watery, but it was making an effort. Another pathetic fallacy, and definitely one to emulate.

The wedding rehearsal would be held in the recently revamped private dining room in the Scarth Club. It was now called the Heritage Room, and it was one of my favourite venues. When the Club had opened over 125 years ago, the guests were male only, and the room was reserved for meetings and meals where the men who were our city's decision-makers were free to drink the club's signature old-fashioned and speak privately of matters beyond the ken of women.

Warren said that in his father's day the private room was charming, but age had taken its toll. The room had become shabby, and people simply stopped using it. When Warren told Annie that he wished the space could once again become a place for good talk and celebration, Annie, as attentive to her husband's wants as he was to hers, granted his wish.

The room had two features worth retaining: high ceilings and large windows. Everything else had to be replaced, repaired or restored. And the Webers saw to that. Annie and Warren hit all the farm estate sales and they scored some handsome pieces: dark oak hutches and sideboards, mismatched dining tables and chairs. All were old beauties, and the hands that restored them to former glory had been knowledgeable and loving. The floors were now gleaming pine planks. Annie had chosen to paint the walls in the colour of clotted cream, and the inviting warmth was the perfect complement to the stark black-and-white photographs of Saskatchewan farmhouses that families had simply walked away from during the Dirty Thirties.

Warren's son, Simon, had restored many of the photographs and taken others himself. The Heritage Room was an eloquent tribute to Ansel Adams's observation that "not everybody trusts paintings, but people believe photographs." It was impossible not to be moved by the photographs of homes that farm families, beaten by dust and despair, had simply walked away from, leaving behind bibles, children's schoolbooks, tables set for dinner and dreams.

Zack and I had invited Warren, Annie and Simon to join us at the rehearsal dinner. Annie and Warren's knowledge of the process of the restoration and the history of the furnishings was encyclopedic, and we knew the other guests would enjoy talking with them.

At first glance, Simon Weber seemed to have it all: dark-haired, tall, slender and fine-featured, he was a handsome man. His millionaire father and stepmother loved him deeply, and he had graduated from law school near the top of class. But throughout his life, Simon had been plagued by psychiatric problems. He was a lawyer at Zack's firm when he suffered a breakdown so severe that he had been hospitalized. Practising trial law is high pressure, and Simon and his analyst agreed that Simon needed to find another path to recovery.

Photography gave him that path. The Webers' gift to Leah and Angus would be Simon's photographs of their wedding starting that night with the rehearsal and the next day, through the ceremony, the dinner and the dance afterwards. The last picture would be one of the newlyweds as they drove off to begin their honeymoon, Mila and Zack and I had already ordered full sets of photos. Simon was a gifted photographer, so it was a meaningful gift for us all.

* * *

We were dining in the Heritage Room. The Webers were at our table with Steven Brooks and his sisters and Rabbi Dan Shoichet and his wife, Tamar. Everyone had sent in their menu choices two weeks earlier, so after appetizers, the food arrived promptly. Leah and Angus sat with the members of the wedding party and their significant others. All were tanned, relaxed and full of stories about their weekend; Angus and Leah were quiet, seemingly content just to absorb the laughter and love that surrounded them. The mood was exuberant at all the tables but ours.

A golden evening, but the shadow Steven Brooks cast was as undeniable as it was impenetrable. In interviews after the publications of his two blockbuster novels, Steven Brooks was the picture of someone who is the person he always imagined he would become. He was good-looking, with an elegant mane of silver hair, strong features, penetrating black eyes and a confident smile. As famous people often are, he was smaller than I'd imagined him to be, but in the interviews he had a star quality that made you forget what he was not and focus on what he was: a distinguished writer of fiction with a career studded with accolades, a still-profitable backlist and the promise of more novels to come.

That was how Steven Brooks appeared in the interviews and photographs I remembered, anyway. But all that had changed by September 6. He was diminished, both physically and emotionally. Physically, he was thinner and weaker emotionally, the vitality seemed to have been drained from him. The Steven Brooks who was sitting across the table from us had the air of someone who had suffered through a long illness and is unsure if they will ever return to robust good health.

Like his sisters and me, Steven had ordered the La Ronge pickerel, with wild rice and a simple salad of the mixed greens that were grown in raised beds just off the patio behind the club. It was the perfect meal for early September, and Reva, Mila and I savoured every bite. But Steven picked at his food, and when the server came to collect our dishes, Steven had left so much on his plate that the server asked if there had been a problem with anything in the meal. Steven muttered something conciliatory and waved him off.

After dessert, we moved to another of the private rooms for coffee, and by the time we returned, the Heritage Room was rehearsal-ready. The chuppah was in place, and Angus, his best man Sawyer MacLeish and the groomsmen were standing in front of the wedding canopy wearing their kippahs. Chairs had been arranged for those of us who were observers only, and the female members of the wedding party were at the back of the room ready to proceed up the aisle to join the groom and groomsmen.

As they had done at Maisie and Peter's wedding, a string quartet would be playing old standards as we took our seats. At four o'clock, the ceremony would begin.

Dan Shoichet had explained to us that the modern Jewish wedding has three parts: the betrothal, in which rings are exchanged; the reading of the ketubah, the marriage contract; and the reading of the seven traditional blessings by the rabbi.

That evening, when Leah joined Angus in front of the chuppah for the betrothal and held out her hand, as she would to receive her ring during the actual ceremony, Angus said, "You are sanctified to me with this ring, according to the law of Moses and Israel." He then offered his hand to Leah, so he could receive his ring, and

Leah made the same declaration. It was a powerful moment, and I swallowed hard.

Rabbi Shoichet read the first paragraph of the ketubah in Hebrew and then read all of it in English. He explained that at this point in the ceremony, Leah and Angus would read the vows they had written to each other, but they wanted to keep what they would say private until the wedding.

Finally, the rabbi began chanting the seven traditional blessings in Hebrew, translating each blessing into English after. The traditional breaking of the glass would immediately follow the final blessing. Rabbi Shoichet explained that the breaking of the glass is a reminder that there are such moments in every human life, which the couple, united by love, will each help the other to get through.

By the time the rabbi had explained the significance of the breaking of the glass, the tears came, and when Zack offered me his handkerchief, I made good use of it. Angus and Leah came over as soon as the rabbi had finished. Angus bent for a closer look at my face. "Are you okay, Mum?"

I gave my eyes a final mopping, blew my nose and dropped Zack's handkerchief in my bag. "Yes," I said. "Just happy. I'll work on a quieter way of being happy by tomorrow afternoon. But right now, I would welcome a hug from both of you."

After Angus and Leah hugged us, Zack said, "It's going to be a sensational wedding, and as a former Boy Scout, I am always mindful of our motto: 'be prepared.' I'll bring a man-sized box of tissues with me."

Leah shook her head in disbelief. "I cannot imagine you as a Boy Scout, Zack."

"Then I will recite the Scout Promise," my husband said. He raised his hand in a salute and stated:

> *On my honour;*
> *I promise that I will do my best;*
> *To do my duty to God and the Queen;*
> *To help other people at all times;*
> *And to carry out the spirit of the Scout Law.*

"Are you convinced?"

Leah and Angus were laughing. "Not yet," Angus said. "Here's the final test. I was a Boy Scout, and I need to hear you recite the Scout Law."

Zack nodded. "Then perhaps we can recite it together." My husband and son raised their hands in a solemn salute. "The Scout Law," Zack said, and then in unison, they began:

> *A Scout is helpful and trustworthy,*
> *Kind and cheerful,*
> *Considerate and clean,*
> *and wise in the use of all resources.*

As we headed for the double doors that opened onto the main dining room, we were all laughing. Dan and Tamar Shoichet were the only ones left in the dining room, and when we said goodnight, Dan asked if Zack and I could stay behind for a few moments. Tamar said goodnight to us and told her husband that she'd wait for him in the club foyer.

When we were alone, Dan Shoichet said, "Joanne, why don't you and I sit down? This may take a while." His hazel eyes were troubled. "At dinner, Steven Brooks's distress was palpable," he said. "As a spiritual advisor and close friend of Leah and her aunts, I would like to help, but I wouldn't know where to start. I met Steven Brooks for the first time two hours ago. He has never been present at any service I was a part of, and according to his sisters, he has not been inside a synagogue since he was a boy. Steven says he is Jewish by culture, but not by religion. If you can suggest a way I might help, I'll do it, but I don't believe Steven would welcome any attempt on my part to reach out."

"You're right," I said. After my husband and I exchanged a quick glance, I carried on. "Zack and I believe we know what the problem is, but we have no proof. Confronting the man we saw at dinner with our suspicions would shatter him. Neither of us has any idea what our next move could or should be."

Dan's face was grave. "Angus tells me your family are regular congregants at St. Paul's Cathedral. At this point, I think all we can do is pray for guidance and hope for the best."

CHAPTER SIX

TUESDAY, SEPTEMBER 6, 2022

It was six thirty when Esme and I returned from our run Tuesday morning. The sun was rising — a ball of gold in an aureole of orange and peach; a glorious omen for the day — and when I opened the kitchen door, I was prepared to ask Zack to join me so we could watch the sun rise together. But Zack wasn't alone in the kitchen. Leah was sitting opposite him at the butcher-block table.

I dropped Esme's leash and went to Leah. My words came in a torrent. "What are you doing here? Are you all right? Is Angus all right?"

Leah was always the still point in the middle of the storm, and that morning her voice was calm and her tone, reassuring. "I'm fine, Jo. Angus is fine. The wedding will be fine. To answer your question, I'm here because I wanted you and Zack to know that all is well and that all will be well.

"Steven Brooks will not be at the wedding. Angus and I had decided to be mindful of that old saw that it's bad luck for a bride and groom to see each other on their wedding day, so I spent last night with my aunts. When we came down for breakfast, there was a note on the table from Steven saying he needed to get away 'from prying eyes.' He noted that he did not want us to make any attempt to find him. That he would come back when he was ready." Leah's smile was small and sad. "And that's all he wrote."

"But you're all right with this?"

Leah nodded. "I am. Given that Steven made no attempt to hide his self-pity last night, I think his decision not to be part of the wedding is a gift to us all. Maybe his indifference to me from the day I was born was a gift."

"I am so sorry your father chose not to be part of your life," I said.

"That's nothing to be sorry about, Joanne. You know that. You and I have talked about the difference between a life observed and a life experienced. Your mother didn't want you, so you spent thirteen years in residence at a private school for girls. My mother died, and my father didn't want me, so my aunts took me in. To an observer, the fact that you and I were both abandoned when we were very young would appear tragic."

"The truth is, that, given the circumstances, we were both lucky," I said. "Bishop Lambeth was the best choice for me. It was a great school; I received a first-class education; I had structure in my life; I made good friends and, most importantly, I didn't have to live with my mother's constant rejection."

"And it was the same for me," Leah said. "My aunts gave me a loving home and raised me in a religion that gives me comfort, purpose and a connection with those who came before me. Mila and Reva offered me an identity, and the support and love they gave me was unconditional.

"I'm under no illusions about my father. When I asked my aunts why Steven Brooks didn't want to be part of my life, they didn't lie to me. They made me see my father for what he was: a man torn apart by insecurity and self-doubt. When I was growing up, Steven was obsessed with his belief that his work was not getting the attention and respect it merited. He saw writers whom he believed were lesser creatures than him picking up the big prizes, and it infuriated him. He believed fame would come to him eventually, but until then he could take pride in the fact that although his number of readers was limited, the readers he had were the crème de la crème. He wrote 'for the few and for the future.'

"Anyway, Steven is who he is, and his absence will simplify everything," Leah said. "That's brutal, but it's also true."

"Sometimes the truth is brutal," Zack said. "Leah, I'm sure you noticed that Rabbi Shoichet stayed behind last night to talk to Jo and me. It was obvious to him and Tamar, his wife, that Steven is deeply troubled. Dan wanted to help with whatever problem Steven is facing, but since he'd only met Steven hours earlier, he thought Steven would not be receptive to any attempt Dan made to reach out."

"And he was right," I said. "Leah, Dan's final words to us were 'at this point all we can do is pray for guidance and hope for the best.' That's wise counsel, and I think we should heed it."

"Dan is a realist," Leah said. "Whatever is troubling Steven will be connected to his writing. That's all he's ever really cared about." There was no bitterness in her voice. Like Rabbi Shoichet, Leah was a realist too. She started towards the door and then pivoted to face Zack. "One last thing," she said. "Zack, I'd like you to give the father of the bride's speech at the dinner. Are you up for that?"

"I'd be honoured," Zack said.

"Thank you," Leah said. "Now that that's settled, I'll see you at four."

I'd better get a move on too," I said. "The boys' school bus comes at eight fifteen, and it's already past seven. Zack, can you start breakfast while I get showered and dressed?"

"Of course. What's your pleasure?"

"That Boursin au poivre is getting close to its best before date, and I love the scrambled eggs you make with it. You can surprise me about the rest."

When I returned to the kitchen, the eggs and Boursin were in a bowl, waiting for the butter to bubble in the pan; the juice was poured, and slices of sourdough bread were in the toaster. "Anything for me to do?" I said.

"Nope. You always say scrambled eggs is a job for one. But while I finish off here, could you check online and see what the father of the bride's speech should cover."

By the time Zack was doling out the eggs and buttering the toast, I had found what he needed.

"Got it," I said. "The father of the bride's speech should include a welcome to guests, thanking them for coming; a heartfelt anecdote of the bride; a mention of your new in-laws; and words of wisdom to the new couple. And remember to be genuine and acknowledge your emotions."

Family life always means tumult for someone, so our rule is to exclude serious talk from the table. That morning, Zack and

I both had concerns that merited serious conversation, but the eggs Boursin were excellent, and my friend Terry Toews's rhubarb marmalade raised our sourdough toast to new heights. It was a meal that deserved a light heart, and so we talked about the next item on our agenda: Charlie and Colin's first day of grade one.

The boys would be in different classes, and their mother, who was herself an identical twin, was not wholly sold on the idea. The arguments against having the twins in the same classroom were solid. If one twin was dominant, the less assertive twin would never have the chance to grow in confidence. If the twins were in the same room, both would lose the ability to develop their identity as individuals. In the minds of their teachers and school-mates, if the boys were in the same class, they would never be Colin and Charlie — they would always be "the twins."

Maisie and her twin sister, Lee, had lived on a farm and attended a rural school. Through grade school and high school, Lee and Maisie had always been in the same classrooms, and they had flourished: Maisie, graduating from the College of Law near the top of her class, and Lee earning a PhD in agricultural science. The sisters were very different people with very different interests. They had developed as individuals without sacrificing their closeness.

When Lee died suddenly, not long before Charlie and Colin were born, Maisie was devastated. But she was strong, and she survived as much as anyone can survive that deep a loss. She and Pete had a good marriage, and they loved their sons, but Maisie told me once that every landmark in her sons' lives reminded her of a joy Lee would never know.

Maisie had agreed, albeit reluctantly, to the school's decision to separate Charlie and Colin in kindergarten. The arrangement had worked well, and I was confident that when her sons climbed onto the school bus, their mother's smile would be wide.

* * *

After Zack and I had cleared the breakfast table, I said, "Do you want me to run through the points the speech made by the father of the bride should cover again?"

"No, I've got it: Welcome the guests and thank them for coming. Share a heartfelt anecdote of the bride. Be genuine and acknowledge my emotions. Mention the new in-laws. Offer some words of wisdom to the newlyweds."

"I always forget what a quick study you are," I said. "That was excellent."

"Thanks," Zack said. "Now that we've finished breakfast, I can rant."

I was surprised, but from the set of his jaw, I knew he was genuinely angry. "Go for it," I said.

"Okay. Well, I'll start with something we already know. Steven Brooks is a selfish prick and a snivelling coward who ran away on his daughter's wedding day because he couldn't face 'prying eyes.' Goddammit, Jo, he's the one who should be giving the speech. He's the one who should be sharing the heartfelt anecdote and talking about his new son-in-law.

"As soon as I saw Leah's face this morning, I knew that she realized that her father ran away because years ago, he did something that, if discovered, would ruin his reputation, and now he's been caught. It's only a matter of time before everyone knows the truth about him — that he's a liar, a thief and a hack. Isn't that just the greatest fucking gift a father could give his daughter on what should be one of the happiest days of her life?"

I put my arms around him. "I agree with every word you just said. Do you feel better now that you've got all that off your chest?"

Zack sighed. "Actually, I do. Now, it's time for us to move along. And we'd better take two cars, because Peter, Angus, Charlie D, Sawyer and I are going to my barber's for an old-fashioned shave and a great haircut."

"Turn your phone off," I said. "You deserve a break. If anyone needs a lawyer, they're going to have to talk to me."

* * *

When the school bus pulled away, Colin and Charlie's faces were pressed against the bus window, and both boys were grinning. Maisie and I were fighting tears, and Peter and Zack were both swallowing hard.

"And so, ready or not, another chapter begins," I said.

"The boys were certainly ready," Maisie said. "They came into our room at 5 a.m. I laid out school clothes last night, and Colin and Charlie were fully dressed."

"Good for them," Zack said.

"Hold that 'good,'" Maisie said. "Colin was wearing the outfit I laid out for Charlie, and Charlie was wearing the outfit I laid out for Colin." Her smile was wry. "Oldest twin trick in the book, but I am wise to the ways of twins."

It was the first time I could remember Maisie alluding to her life with Lee without pain. Another new chapter had begun.

Angus arrived just then. "Damn," he said. "I missed the big moment. Sorry — something came up."

I felt a flutter of unease. "Anything that needs to be dealt with immediately?"

Angus shook his head. "Not immediately, but maybe later in the day. My best man was out for his daily walk around the lake this morning, mentally rewriting his speech for the dinner reception tonight, and he tripped over something and hit the sidewalk." Angus saw the concern in my eyes. Since Angus was in the second grade, Sawyer MacLeish had been like a member of our family. I had always looked upon him as a third son. In the year after my first husband died, I had three children at home, and Sawyer MacLeish had always been there with a box of Hamburger Helper to get the kids and me through the worst time of our lives.

The year before, Sawyer had faced the worst time in his own life, and Zack and I had brought him into our home for months while he had to piece together a life after a serious spinal injury. In the past year, Zack and I had cared for him and brought him back to the point where he was able to live independently and function as a lawyer. Angus knew that any injury to Sawyer would be a concern to me, and he was quick to be reassuring. "It wasn't his back, Mum. He sprained his thumb, and he was trying to figure out how to tie a Windsor knot and lost track of time. Anyway, he'll meet us at the barber shop."

"Charlie D is meeting us there too," Zack said, "so let's boogie."

* * *

The men had just left when my phone rang. My caller was Zack's executive assistant, Norine MacDonald. She had been with Zack since the day Falconer Shreve was pulling in enough money to hire an EA for each of the partners. Norine was the only EA to stay the course, and after three decades together, she was indispensable to Zack.

When I met him, Zack's life was trial law, and he resented any demand that interfered with his work. Norine ordered every item of Zack's clothing. She was his sounding board for trying out his opening and closing statements. He respected her opinion; he seldom ignored her advice and regretted it when he did. She placated difficult clients, made certain every space Zack would be entering was accessible and, from the day Zack and I were married, she was among my closest friends.

"Hi," I said. "Norine, I hope you're not calling to tell us you can't be at the wedding."

Despite her myriad responsibilities, Norine never seemed hurried, and she always waited a few moments before she answered. Norine had been raised up north, on Poundmaker Cree Nation near Cut Knife. She told me once that the Elders believed answering a question quickly was an insult to the questioner because it suggested their question was not worthy of thought. Norine's words resonated with me. My first husband, Ian Kilbourn, had been elected to the legislature when I was pregnant with Mieka. Much of my adult life had been involved with the politics of our province, and I remembered how often I had regretted an off-the-cuff response.

As always, Norine's tone was gentle but firm, but this time the message she delivered was not one I welcomed.

"I'm aware of the situation with Steven Brooks," she said. "Zack just had a phone call from Patrick O'Keefe. He's representing Rebecca Woodrow. Ms. Woodrow has presented Mr. O'Keefe with what he believes is substantive evidence that her late grandmother, Laurel, is the person who wrote the first drafts of both *Medusa's Fate* and *The Iron Bed of Procrustes*."

My hands were shaking, but I managed to keep my voice steady. "I knew this would happen at some point, but learning that there's proof that Steven plagiarized those novels is a blow."

"I know," Norine said. "And it gets worse. Apparently, Laurel Woodrow worked with Steven Brooks on the *Medusa* manuscript until they both believed it was ready to send to a publisher."

"But Laurel Woodrow's name doesn't appear in the books. After Zack and I became convinced that *Medusa* and *Procrustes* were plagiarized, I went over the dedications and the acknowledgements in both, and in the interviews that Steven gave when the novels were published. There was never a mention of Laurel Woodrow."

Norine's voice was even. "Given the circumstances, I guess that's not surprising."

"No, I guess it's not." I drew in a deep breath. "Peter, Charlie D, Angus and his best man, Sawyer MacLeish, are with Zack at his barber's getting the full treatment: shaves with a straight razor and haircuts. I'm not going to call Zack now. He's really been looking forward to this morning of male bonding. I'll tell him when he gets home."

"Understood," Norine said. "Jo, I am so sorry this is happening."

"Welcome to the club," I said, and there was no mistaking the note of defeat in my voice.

After Norine and I ended our call, I checked my texts. Zack had sent Maisie, Leah, Mieka and me photos of the men in our lives at the barber shop. Norine's news had been bleak, but the sight of my husband, our son-in-law, our sons and Angus's best man sitting side by side in old-fashioned barber chairs all lathered up buoyed my spirits. I forwarded the photos to Norine, and texted Zack, saying I wished Simon Weber had been there to take official photos of the four men. Zack's reply was speedy. "Way ahead of you. Simon is snapping away as I speak."

* * *

Zack came home ebullient, looking and smelling, in Dolly Parton's pithy phrase, "better than a body has a right to."

He held his arms out. "How would you like to go to a wedding with me this afternoon?"

I leaned in. "I'd love to. Zack, you can always wrap my heart around your little finger, and I don't want to spoil this moment, but something else has cropped up."

After I gave him a précis of what I'd learned from Norine about Rebecca Woodrow and Patrick O'Keefe, Zack said, "Well, shit," and picked up his phone. "I'm calling Pat." When I started to leave, my husband motioned for me to stay, and I did.

Patrick and Zack exchanged pleasantries, and then Zack asked if he was okay with putting the call on speaker, telling him Norine had made me aware of the situation with Steven Brooks and I might have questions.

After Patrick consented, Zack got straight to business. "So what's going on?" He listened without comment to Patrick's account and then nodded. "Okay, I'm up to speed. Joanne has information about Steven Brooks that you and your client should have."

"I'm sure Norine told you that Steven Brooks's daughter, Leah, and our son Angus are getting married this afternoon," I said.

"She did, and I feel like hell dumping this on you on your son's wedding day. But you needed to know that at nine thirty tomorrow morning Rebecca and I will be in a Zoom meeting with Steven's publishers and their lawyers. The publishers are aware of the fact that Rebecca Woodrow has concrete proof that her grandmother Laurel Woodrow wrote both *Medusa's Fate* and *The Iron Bed of Procrustes*. Tomorrow will be focused on how best to handle the situation."

"So the wheels are in motion," Zack said. "One more question: Has your client been emailing people urging them to press Valentine Masluk to look into the source material for *Medusa's Fate*?"

Patrick didn't hesitate. "No," he said. "She has not. Rebecca Woodrow has been not only circumspect, but ethical. If she'd wanted to sandbag Valentine Masluk, she would have involved the media. Instead, as I told you, Rebecca is meeting privately with Steven's publishers, who coincidentally are also publishing Valentine Masluk's biography of Steven. Tell me about the emails."

"They're individualized, and they're targeted," Zack said. "Whoever is sending them has enough information about the recipients to know the approach that will work with them. I'll let you know if I learn anything more. Pat, I really appreciate the heads up. Thanks."

"And thank you, Zack. I've always liked you . . . even in the days before you realized that criminal law doesn't have to be a contact sport."

Zack chuckled. "I've always liked you too, Pat. You know, I don't remember ever seeing you outside the courthouse. Why don't you and Melanie come over for drinks and dinner? It would be good to see you again and to finally introduce Joanne to you both."

Esme was at the front door barking. Now that she was older, Esme was losing interest in activities beyond her immediate sphere. When I went to check out the problem, Zack, wise in the ways of our Bouvier, smiled and waved me off. By the time I returned, Zack and Patrick's call had ended.

"So when can we expect Patrick and Melanie for dinner?"

Zack raised an eyebrow. "Never," he said. "Apparently, Melanie is long gone. There have been two Mrs. O'Keefes since her departure, and Pat and Wife Number Three are in the process of clearing the path for Wife Number Four."

"So, we should hold dinner until Wife Number Four has settled in."

"No, Pat still wants to meet you, but we agreed that if he and I are on opposite sides of the Brooks-Woodrow case, we should wait till that's played out."

"So, the die is cast," I said. "We have three hours before we need to start getting ready for the wedding. Let's use them wisely."

* * *

Zack and I had separate bathrooms and dressing rooms. Getting dressed was not a simple process for Zack, and before we were married, he had a spacious dressing room for me added to the second bathroom that would be mine.

The decision had been pragmatic, but it came with a surprising delight. For a special event, like the wedding, the first time we saw each other dressed and groomed was when we stepped out of our respective dressing rooms. That afternoon, we both liked what we saw. Zack looked great in a tuxedo and his new Italian leather dress shoes. The shoes were in a deep, almost iridescent shade of red, and they were exquisite, but the fact that, like all my husband's shoes, their soles would never touch the earth was a reminder that pierced my heart.

"You look good enough to eat," I said.

"So do you." Zack gave me a satyr's smile. "But you always do."

"A couple of splashes of bay rum, and you turn into a smooth talker," I said. "How do you see our roles in the rest of this? I know that, as a lawyer, you're an officer of the court, and you have to report a crime. Perjury is a crime. And we have to tell Val Massey about this land mine he'll be stepping into the day *Steven Brooks: A Biography* is launched."

"What time does his flight leave for Toronto tomorrow?"

"Early — 7:30 a.m. Zack, we can't let him get on that plane without knowing the truth about what Steven Brooks did with Laurel Woodrow's manuscript. He should also know about Rebecca's and Patrick O'Keefe's meeting tomorrow morning with the publishers of Steven's books and of Val's biography."

"And that means we have to tell him before he leaves the reception tonight."

"There's no other option," I said. "No matter what we do, we will wound a man who's still reeling from past wounds. At least this way, Val will have a chance to process the bombshell and come up with a strategy for dealing with it."

Leah called at one thirty to ask how Zack and I felt about taking our chances on having the wedding outdoors. The day was sunny and windless but crisp. A perfect late summer day for a wedding, and as Zack and I pulled up in the club's back lane, it appeared everything was in order: the chuppah was set up, as were the two rows of chairs where guests would witness the wedding; Ed Mariani had delivered the flowers, and they were perfection.

There was a place for everything, and everything was in its place, but one puzzle piece had yet to be slid into its spot: the wedding favours. A small hard-polished black delivery van was parked in the lane, and three delivery women, identified by the logo on their nicely cut serge uniforms as employees of Sandy's Reliable Deliveries, were purposefully carrying delivery boxes inside.

"Hold on!" Zack wheeled up to the mover whose monogram identified her as Sandy Latimer. As he introduced us to Ms. Latimer, my husband's smile was wide and guileless. "We're Joanne and Zack Shreve," he said. "We're the parents of the groom, and in his absence, Steven Brooks has asked us to act in loco parentis."

Sandy Latimer nodded. "So, if the need arises, you're able to act in Mr. Brooks's place," she said. "And in that capacity, you're now making a decision."

Zack's smile dimmed. "We are," he said. "It's a snap decision, but Joanne and I believe it's the right one." We were just in time to vet Steven Brooks's selection, something his erratic behaviour of late had us feeling was an absolute necessity.

Zack opened a carton and removed a meticulously wrapped gift. Already, I was almost positive that beneath the wrapping paper would be something wildly self-serving, but "almost positive" is not "dead certain," and my heart was pounding as Zack peeled back the shining paper enclosing Steven's gift for each of the guests at his daughter's wedding — an autographed copy of *Steven Brooks: A Biography*.

Zack slid out an enclosed note. Steven's soaring, egotist's handwriting was distinctive, and so was his message to the 263 guests who had come to wish his daughter and her new husband a lifetime of love and fulfillment.

> *We work in the dark*
> *We do what we can*
> *We give what we have.*
> *— Henry James*

Words to live by — perhaps for Henry James, but not for a young couple beginning their life together. But Steven had included the full names and addresses of each of the guests at the wedding, and a copy of his own address care of his sisters.

Once we had seen what was inside the packages, Zack didn't hesitate. "These gifts aren't needed. Please return to sender."

Sandy Latimer's reliable delivery crew were invaluable. The boxes were sealed and back on the truck in a flash.

Zack turned his chair towards me. "The guests will be arriving soon," he said. "I know Angus's groomsmen will show them to their seats, but it might be nice if we are there to greet everyone."

And it *was* nice. It was fun introducing ourselves to Leah's friends, and it was fun to have a quick chat with some of our favourites: Ed and Barry; Warren and Annie Weber; Elder Ernest Beauvais and Peggy Kreviazuk; Howard Dowhanuik; Vince Treadgold and Dr. Jay-Louise Yates; and, of course, the members of our own family, Mieka, Charlie D, Madeleine, Lena, Maisie and Peter.

There had been last-minute cancellations. Jill Oziowy — who described her position at MediaNation as "Vice President in Charge of Making the Decisions Everyone Else Is Too Chickenshit to Make" — had to fire MediaNation's director of digital programming for verbally harassing staff. After Jill had handled that ugliness, she had to restructure the department.

Decisions about personnel — shifting some employees to positions that would place them in the fast track for promotions while leaving others behind, knowing that they had been passed over — called for a thoughtful and sensitive handling of the situation, but it was the first week in the new season, and Jill did not have the luxury of time. She was frustrated — already second-guessing her decisions — and she did not disguise her disappointment about missing Angus and Leah's wedding day. I tried to reassure her by saying that we all understood the situation was not of her making and that I'd send photos. It wasn't enough, but it was the best I could do.

Brock Poitras and Margot Hunter were last-minute cancellations too. Their six-year-old daughter, Lexi, fell off the monkey bars at school and broke her arm — a nasty fracture that required surgery. Lexi was on the mend, but Brock and Margot wanted to be close by to care for her and her five-year-old brother, Kai. The Poitras-Hunter family had been living in Toronto since the middle of July, and Zack and I had been looking forward to seeing them, but they would be coming to Saskatchewan for Thanksgiving, so all was not lost.

When the river of arriving guests had slowed to a trickle, Zack said, "Looks like it's time for us to take our places." We'd just settled in in the front row when Zack said, "Hey, Val Masluk just came in with his plus-one."

I turned to look. Val and Rainey were standing at the back of the garden, waiting for a groomsman to show them to their seats. Zack and I were both dreading telling Val about Steven Brooks, and Rainey was a welcome diversion. She and Val were a striking couple. In his well-cut pinstripe two-piece suit, Val was definitely worthy of a second look, but Rainey's pale apricot one-shoulder silk dress with a leg slit was riveting.

Zack turned to me and raised an eyebrow. "It seems Ms. Arcus has retired her Cowichan sweater."

The guests were still chatting quietly as they waited for the ceremony to begin, and I kept my voice low. "Indeed, she has," I said, "and good for her. Rainey was always attractive, but she seemed determined not to let anyone get past the sweater that swallowed her and the waist-length hair."

Zack shrugged. "My guess is that somewhere along the line Rainey realized what she was capable of doing with her life and she didn't need to hide anymore."

"Very insightful." I squeezed my husband's hand. "Zack, I know there's a sword hanging over our heads, but it's not going to drop until Rebecca's meeting with the publishers at nine thirty tomorrow morning. Our son is about to marry a young woman we all love. Let's just be grateful for this moment and for all the good moments ahead for Leah and Angus and for us."

Zack raised my hand to his lips and kissed it. "Fair enough," he said.

* * *

Reva and Mila Drache had been with Leah until the members of the wedding party lined up for the procession. They greeted Gracie, Mieka, Charlie D, Maisie, Zack and me warmly. Reva was in silvery-grey silk, and Mila, in burgundy. Both looked lovely; more significantly, both seemed free of care.

"Leah was right about Steven's absence from the wedding being a gift for us all," Reva said. "After all our fretting, the weather couldn't be better."

"An omen," Mila said. "This day may turn out to be all we hoped it would be."

* * *

The air was still and, freshened by the rain, the vegetable and herb gardens glistened in the dappled late-afternoon sun. On the stroke of four, the quartet hit the first notes of "Dodi Li," and my eyes stung, but it seemed I'd shed all my tears at the rehearsal. So, dry-eyed but deeply moved, I watched the solemn and beautiful ceremony that joined together our son and the woman we all loved.

Angus and Leah had chosen "A Tuscan Garden" as the theme for their wedding. As Leah's attendants processed up the aisle wearing full-length, cap-sleeved chiffon gowns in the vibrant colours of the late summer palette — silver sage, dusky green, deep lavender, burgundy and goldenrod — carrying bouquets Ed Mariani had arranged from the newly cut flowers of his own garden, the effect was breathtaking.

A full-length, cap-sleeved chiffon gown in dusky green would not have been Taylor's first choice, but Leah had been careful to choose a gown that would flatter each of her attendants, and her choice of colour for Taylor, a brown-eyed brunette, had been right on the mark. When Taylor's eyes met Gracie's as she passed by, Gracie mouthed the words "I love you," and lines from Puck's final speech at the end of *A Midsummer Night's Dream* flashed through my mind. "Think but this, and all is mended."

Leah had told her aunts she wanted to look like herself on her wedding day, and that meant no new hairstyle and, except for a touch of gloss on her lips, no makeup. In her simple, sleeveless, form-fitting silk gown, Leah was as fresh-faced and as filled with joie de vivre as the girl Angus brought home almost fifteen years ago. The hands that held her bouquet of white orchids were steady, and her intelligent hazel eyes were focused on the man with whom she was about to make a lifelong commitment. Leah was a woman at peace with herself and with the vows she was about to take.

* * *

As the betrothal portion of the service began, I was struck by Rabbi Shoichet's ability to make us all feel we were part of the ceremony without compromising the intimacy of the words Leah and Angus spoke as they exchanged rings. True to his promise, Zack had a stash of tissues in his tux pocket, and I knew he was watching my face as Dan read the ketubah that Angus and Leah had chosen first in Hebrew and then in English. When he handed me a tissue, I whispered. "Thanks, but no need. Everything just seems so right."

And as we moved towards the completion of the ceremony, everything continued to seem so right. Leah and Angus had asked

Elder Ernest Beauvais to say a prayer before Rabbi Shoichet chanted the seven traditional blessings.

I had never seen Ernest wearing anything other than blue jeans, a fresh cotton shirt and his leather jacket with the crest of the Iron Workers Union of Canada. Ernest was a big man: tall and powerfully built. His two-button navy pinstripe suit was the work of an expert tailor, and Ernest did it justice.

Ernest's voice was powerful and deep; he was a person who cherished language, spoke slowly and made every word count. He began by thanking Rabbi Shoichet for the talks about faith they had shared over the summer and for allowing all of us at the wedding to hear the beauty of the Hebrew and then to have it translated into English.

"The prayer I'm about to say is only a fragment of a much longer poem I heard at a wedding many years ago," he said. "The Elder who gave the prayer was Apache. Most of the people at the wedding were Apache. I am Cree, and I didn't understand the language. But like my friend, Dan Shoichet, the Apache Elder believed that some things — like faith and love — are universal, so we must make what we say accessible to all. That Elder taught me the prayer in English. As I said, it was many years ago, so this is all I remember.

> *Now you will feel no rain,*
> *for each of you will be shelter for the other.*
>
> *Now you will feel no cold,*
> *For each of you will be warmth to the other.*
>
> *Now there will be no loneliness,*
> *for each of you will be companion to the other.*

Now you are two persons,
but there is only one life before you.

May beauty surround you both in the
journey ahead and through all the years.

It was a beautiful prayer, and it hit home with Zack. I handed him the tissue he'd brought for me. The smile he gave me was shamefaced, but he made use of the tissue.

When Ernest started to leave, Dan Shoichet motioned him to stay. Seeing these two fine men stand together as Rabbi Shoichet chanted the seven traditional blessings, translating each from Hebrew into English, was a memory to cherish.

And there was another piercingly beautiful moment. After Angus crushed the glass, he and Leah turned to take their first steps together as a married couple. At that moment, seemingly out of nowhere, a blue jay appeared and perched on the chuppah.

Blue jays were rare at this time of the year, but Ernest was sanguine. He joined Angus and Leah. "Brother Blue Jay dropped by to let you know you are heading in a good direction."

Rabbi Shoichet moved to the opening of the chuppah and faced the guests. "This is where we all shout 'mazel tov' to Leah and Angus," he said.

Zack and I added our voices to the chorus of congratulations, and my husband took my hand. "Could that have been any more perfect?"

"No, it couldn't, and I am so relieved."

CHAPTER SEVEN

As soon as the wedding party and Rabbi Shoichet walked back down the aisle, those of us in the first row followed, and soon all the guests' chairs were emptied and the servers in their black-on-black Scarth Club uniforms were moving quickly to arrange the chairs in conversational groupings with small tables for appetizers. The air was still and the sky, cloudless. We would be able to have the antipasto course outdoors.

Zack and I were watching the servers work their magic when Reva and Mila came over. Mila was ebullient. "It was exactly the wedding Angus and Leah wanted," she said.

"And no matter what happens in the future," Reva said, "no one can take that away from them." Her voice was steely and her words silenced us, so I was relieved when Simon Weber joined our small group.

"I knew the four of you would like to see these," he said, and he handed me his Leica rangefinder. The closeups of Angus crushing the glass; a wide shot of the blue jay arriving and perching on the chuppah just as Angus and Leah took their first steps together as a married couple; and another closeup of Ernest Beauvais welcoming Brother Blue Jay and explaining the meaning of his arrival — all stunning.

Mila couldn't take her eyes off the photographs. "These make everything we've done, and may have to do, worthwhile," she said finally, and the undercurrent of resolve in her pleasant contralto suggested that she knew the battle was far from over.

It was another unsettling moment and, once again, I was grateful for Simon's presence. I returned the camera to him. "Leah and Angus will love seeing these, but they'll be surrounded all evening by people who want to wish them well."

Simon was sensitive to nuance, and he'd picked up on the tension in Mila's voice. His glance towards me was quick but a sign that he'd received the message. "So now's my time to congratulate the newlyweds."

"No time like the present," Zack said.

Simon's lips twitched towards a smile. "I'm on my way, but first I'd like to take a photo of you and Joanne in front of the chuppah and also one of Leah's aunts."

"We would treasure that," Zack said.

"My sister doesn't like having her picture taken," Reva said. "But I'm certain she'll make an exception today."

"I will indeed," Mila said. "Today is a day that has been exceptional in every way."

*　*　*

Zack and I made the rounds of the guests separately. The pleasures of sitting in the late summer sun, sipping Chianti or Pinot Grigio and enjoying Tuscan antipasto were considerable, and our guests were in a mellow mood. It was fun to meet new people and catch up with old friends and expand our knowledge base of cultures who see blue jays as spiritual animals. By the time we joined Annie and Warren Weber, we had learned that various cultures regard blue jays as representing everything from courage and faithfulness to mischief and mimicry. The information we acquired was intriguing, but we were both ready for a change of topic, and the Webers were always good company.

They were also a striking couple. Annie was a natural blond with a peaches-and-cream complexion and aquamarine eyes that could melt a heart, or turn to ice when she sensed that a situation might cause her husband distress. Before she and Warren were married, Annie managed Wheelz, a biker bar. She was coolheaded, and she could effortlessly bring a troublemaker to their knees or remove them from the scene before tension erupted into violence — useful skills in an uncertain world — and I had seen Annie in action more than once.

Tongues had wagged when Annie married a multimillionaire fifty years her senior, but the Webers were truly in love. Maeve's birth had been a blessing neither of them anticipated, and to see them with their daughter was to understand the meaning of the word "joy."

The Webers had an idiosyncrasy that puzzled Zack but that I found charming. Warren and Annie coordinated their clothing choices. Warren loved colour: primary, pastel and everything in between. That September afternoon, Annie was wearing a sleeveless silk floral print midi that was a swirl of muted pastels, and Warren's dove grey tuxedo, lavender dress shirt and pastel floral-patterned tie were the perfect complement for the ethereal muted tones of her dress.

When we asked if we could join them, Warren's smile was as wide and open as the prairie that had taught him everything he needed to know about how to bring the farm equipment company his father, Alastair, built, into the twenty-first century. Alastair had been a hands-on owner who spent two days of the work week in farm kitchens, learning exactly what equipment Saskatchewan farmers needed and using the remaining three days in his office supplying it. With Annie by his side, Warren continued the tradition.

As soon as Zack and I had taken our places, Annie leaned forward and whispered, "You know that Warren and I are trustworthy, so your secret's safe with us. Who trained that blue jay to appear on cue?"

Zack chuckled. "That was Brother Blue Jay's decision," he said. "Brother Blue Jay is a solo act, and Simon got some amazing photos of the sequence of events that culminated in that bird-with-a-message perched on the chuppah."

Annie's brow furrowed with concern. "Did Simon seem all right?" she said. "Social events are still very difficult for him."

"There were no signs of discomfort today," I said. "Simon was relaxed and affable. In fact, he seemed to be having a great time."

Warren exhaled with relief. "You have no idea how much Annie and I welcome that news. For the first time in a very long time, we're truly hopeful about Simon's future."

"He sees Dr. Fidelak twice a week, and that's going well," Annie said. "He's in demand as a photographer, and he loves the work. And, of course, Maeve is the apple of his eye."

Warren covered Annie's hand with his. "Maeve is the apple of all our eyes." A server arrived with a tray and handed us each the drink we had ordered earlier and placed platters of Tuscan antipasto for two and small individual plates and napkins on the table. The antipasto was tempting: three kinds of olives, slices of prosciutto with melon, buttered radishes fresh from the garden, bruschetta, brioche topped with pâté and salami with fresh figs. Mila had assured us that guests who opted for a kosher or vegetarian meal would receive antipasto plates different from ours, but equally delicious.

For several minutes, the Webers, Zack and I were wholly absorbed in sampling the delights on our platters. When I finally looked up, I saw Val and Rainey standing alone.

I pointed them out to the Webers. "There's Val Masluk," I said. "He wrote Steven Brooks's biography. You'll be hearing his name often in the next few weeks."

"Val's an interesting guy," Zack said. "And he was a student of Joanne's. So was Rainey Arcus, the young woman he's with."

"We have two empty chairs. Let's ask them to join us so we can get acquainted," Annie said. "We're sitting with them at dinner, and Ms. Arcus did the pre-interview with Simon for *Charlie D in the Morning*."

"That's wonderful to hear Rainey has projects underway with Charlie and MediaNation now," I said.

"She's got hustle. And Simon was very taken with her," Warren said. "But if she's with Mr. Masluk, I guess Simon's out of luck."

"Not necessarily," I said. "Rainey was Val's researcher for the Brooks biography. Val thinks very highly of Rainey professionally, and, of course, they know each other from their time together at the School of Journalism. That said, Zack and I had lunch with Val last week, and we both felt his relationship with Rainey was simply one of friendship with a valued colleague."

An enthusiastic munch of pâté on brioche left a speck above Annie's lip. Warren picked up his napkin and gently removed the morsel. "We must be sure that you're the one to sing Simon's praises to Ms. Arcus, Annie," Warren said. "No one has ever been able to refuse you anything." He raised his hand and beckoned Val and Rainey over.

They welcomed the invitation to join the four of us. "Thanks for taking pity on us," Val said. "Steven Brooks was behind our invitation. And I haven't seen him yet."

"He won't be coming," Zack said. "Something came up that he had to deal with."

Val and Rainey exchanged glances. "We've noticed that Steven hasn't been himself lately," Val said.

"I hope he's getting the help he needs," Rainey said.

"His sisters-in-law are both psychiatrists, so I'm sure they're taking good care of Steven," I said. Neither Zack nor I mentioned the self-serving books Steven had tried to have delivered to the guests.

As soon as I'd made the introductions, Warren turned to Val. "Annie and I are so glad you could join us. We've read all of Steven Brooks's novels — the last two are impressive."

"We pre-ordered the biography you wrote," Annie said. "It just arrived yesterday, and Warren and I like to read to each other before we go to sleep . . . but something tells me this one deserves to be more than a bedtime story."

Val met Annie's eyes. "Thanks for that. On the night before the official publication day, I welcome any and all reassurance. I have a busy month of travel ahead," Val said. "But when life returns to normal, I'll be eager to hear your thoughts about the book and, of course, to get to know you both better."

"And you'll get to meet our daughter, Maeve." Annie dimpled. "Something to look forward to. And Rainey, we're very pleased to meet you too. Simon said that the pre-interview you did with him was informed and sensitive. He finds it painful to talk about his illness. Borderline personality disorder has historically been viewed as difficult to treat, but Simon wanted people to know that with the right therapist, and with emotional support, understanding and patience, it is possible for people to do exactly what Simon is doing — simply get better over time."

Warren was clearly moved by Annie's passion for his son's slow but steady journey back from the darkness. "Charlie D's producer, Kam Chau, sent Annie and me an MP3 of the interview. It really is powerful."

"I wish I'd heard it," I said.

"You'll have your chance," Annie said. "It hasn't been broadcast yet. Charlie D told us the interview will be aired on Thursday as part of their kickoff for the new season."

"I'll look forward to that," I said. "Val, I know you'll be on your book tour by then, so I'm sure Charlie D will be happy to send you an MP3."

"One more reason I'm glad we came today," Val said. "You're making Rainey and me feel very welcome." He turned to the Webers.

"Rainey and I were in Joanne's Politics and the Media seminar fifteen years ago, and recently the Shreves joined me for lunch."

"Joanne and I had gone to the breeder's to help our grandsons choose a new puppy," Zack said. "We got more than we'd bargained for, but that's another story. Anyway, the breeder's acreage was near Val's, and Val invited us to a real Ukrainian lunch. The spread he put out for us was amazing, starting with borscht he'd made himself."

"He was the consummate host," I agreed, "and it was so good to hear about all the changes in his life, and in yours, Rainey. Val couldn't stop singing your praises as a researcher and colleague."

"Writing the Brooks biography was an education for us both," Rainey said. I'd forgotten how husky her voice was. I always thought that it sounded like a voice that wasn't often used. It had been fifteen years since Rainey and I had been face to face, and, except for the confidence with which she wore a dress that was both revealing and flattering, she had changed very little physically. The flowing white gold hair was now smoothed into a sleek chignon, and she wore little if any makeup. Her extraordinary eyes that, for me, always evoked the pellucid beauty of a stone close to the lakeshore, were still riveting. It was a face to remember, and the tilt of Rainey's chin indicated that she was aware of that.

Rainey had been looking closely at my face too. "You haven't changed much at all, Dr. Kilbourn."

"My surname is now Shreve, but please just call me Joanne."

"So much has happened," Rainey said.

"Yes," I said. "So much has happened."

Our words seemed to carry a weight that surprised me, and it seemed to catch Rainey off guard too. She turned from me to the Webers. "I enjoyed the time I spent with Simon," she said.

"He's a very easy person to be with, and I was sorry when the pre-interviews came to an end. There was so much more I wanted to know about him."

Annie and Warren exchanged a quick glance. "Simon's birthday is on Friday," Annie said. "I know this is short notice, but we were thinking of having the Shreves and Charlie D and Mieka to our place for a barbecue. Nothing fancy, just friends having fun together. Val, I realize that you'll be away promoting the book, but Rainey, I know Simon would be pleased if you could join us."

Rainey didn't hesitate. "I'd be delighted."

"Good. Is there anything you can't or choose not to eat?"

Val grinned. "I'll answer that," he said. "Rainey will eat everything that's not nailed down."

We all laughed. Angus and his groomsmen had come outside and begun escorting guests inside for dinner. Sawyer introduced himself to Val and Rainey and then beckoned to Warren and Annie. "I have the pleasant task of leading you to your table in the dining room," he said. "I've seen the pasta course — ricotta spinach ravioli — you're in for a feast."

"Please lead the way," Val said.

"Annie and I will join you momentarily," Warren said. As soon as Rainey and Val were out of earshot, Warren touched his wife's cheek. "How long have we been thinking of having friends join us for a barbecue for Simon's birthday?"

Annie glanced at her pretty watch. "About ten minutes," she said.

"You really are my treasure," Warren said, and his gaze was as tender as his words.

* * *

The head table was on a slightly raised platform facing the guests. Those of us sitting at the head table had no tasks until dessert and champagne were served, and it was a pleasure just to sit, chat and, of course, eat.

Our four-course meal was traditional for a Tuscan wedding and, as Sawyer predicted, the meal was a feast. The ricotta-and-baby-spinach ravioli with tomatoes and fresh basil was made in house; the roast goose infused with a blend of fresh and dried fennel was succulent; and the romaine, cannelloni and olive salad was the perfect palate cleanser before the dolce, or dessert — our final course.

When the aunts told us Angus and Leah had chosen strawberry mille feuille as their dessert, I had to consult Chef Google. I learned that the cake had four components: puff pastry, pastry cream, a glaze or fondant and sliced fresh strawberries. The strawberry mille feuille that the bride and groom would cut into was an objet d'art, worthy of inclusion in a flossy travel guide to Tuscany. The cakes for the guests had already been cut into individual portions to be served with Asti Spumante.

When dinner was over, it was time for speeches and Zack spoke first. When he explained that he had been asked to deliver the father of the bride's speech because Steven Brooks was unable to attend, there was hushed silence. Zack knew how to read a room, so when he said that being asked to speak publicly about the joy Leah brought to our family was one of the great privileges of his life, it was clear that he was speaking from the heart, and he mellowed the mood.

After he'd thanked the guests for coming and praised the Drache sisters for giving us all a day to remember, Zack said that with Mila's blessing he was going to talk about the roles she and Leah had played in bringing us together. The "summer is for bad boys" story was fun, and it was well received. More importantly, the story kept the focus exactly where it belonged: on Leah's bright intelligence, her willingness to push the boundaries and her respect for the wise counsel of the aunts she loved.

My husband's words of wisdom for the newlyweds were also personal and relevant. Zack began by saying that for both of us, the joy of any experience was doubled by sharing it, and then he told the story that underscored his point. One morning on my run, I had spotted a group of American avocets in the Wascana Park Bird Sanctuary. Avocets are large, slender shore birds, and with their delicately upturned bills, elegant necks and long and graceful legs, they are fascinating to watch. When I told Zack about the avocets, we agreed that as soon as court was over that afternoon, we would go to the bird sanctuary together.

Zack and I seldom quarreled, but when he returned from court that day, we had a fight that frightened us both with its intensity and cruelty. We both wanted the ugliness to end, but we just didn't seem to know how.

Finally, Zack offered a solution. He said that if an actuary was sitting with us, they would calculate the number of years we have left to see the avocets, and "there would not be enough." When he raised his glass and said, "To Leah and Angus — may they never miss a chance to see the avocets together," there was a collective intake of breath.

Reva and Mila had opted to deliver the speech welcoming Angus to their family together. Their reminiscences of the time they took Angus and Leah to the Metropolitan Opera to see *Nixon in China* was warm and affectionate. They knew opera was not high on Angus's list of pleasures, but Leah loved opera, and Angus had done his homework studying up on the Met's production. Mila said she and Reva were so impressed by Angus's determination to honour something they valued that they bought four third-row seats for a New York Yankees game. That afternoon at Yankee Stadium was, she said, one of the highlights of their summer, and she asked that we raise a glass "to *Nixon in China*, to the Yankees and to Leah and Angus, who realized that we all need to be open to possibilities."

Taylor's toast included a story I hadn't heard. She was eleven our first summer at the lake. On busy Saturdays, Taylor was Leah's assistant at The Point Store. For reasons known only to Taylor, that summer the meat section captured her imagination. The real butchering work (cutting roasts, specifics about steaks and tenderloin) was done to order by a butcher in Regina, but The Point Store ground its own meat and sliced its own cold cuts. Taylor loved to grind meat in the old-fashioned meat grinder, but when she expressed her longing to use the electric meat slicer, Leah sat her down and asked Taylor how she saw her future. Taylor always had a ready answer for that question, and she'd said, "Making art."

"Good," Leah said. "Now, you've seen what the electric meat slicer can do. There is a safeguard, but machines can break down, and you'll need your hands to make art. When you decide you're ready, I'll show you how to use the slicer." Leah made a video when our daughter decided she was ready to use the slicer, and Taylor said that she still watched the video whenever she was unsure about undertaking a new project. Then she held up her hands and said, "Thanks to Leah, all ten of my fingers are right where they're supposed to be. She is a wise woman and a loving one. I'm very grateful to Angus for convincing Leah to become part of our family."

* * *

As best man, Sawyer's was the final speech. When he walked past Zack and me, Sawyer let his hand rest first on my shoulder and then on Zack's. Sawyer adjusted the mic and as he welcomed the guests, Zack and I exchanged the kind of look proud parents might exchange at their son's graduation.

Sawyer began by thanking Zack and me for being there when he needed us and for accepting him into our family as their third son. He went on to say that he had known Leah for fifteen years, and that throughout the years Leah was never less than stellar and she was always forthcoming about the role her aunts played in making certain she could become the woman she wanted to be.

His anecdote about the first time Angus and Leah met was brief but telling. They were fifteen years old. The coach of their high school baseball team decided that the time had come for the team to be open to both girls and boys. After Angus and Sawyer watched the girls tryouts, Angus, impressed by Leah's fastball, said, "That girl will make us all look good. She belongs on our team." Sawyer raised his glass for the final toast. "It took Angus fifteen years to make it official, but Leah and her aunts are now on our team, and they will make us all look good."

* * *

For the bride and groom dance, Leah and Angus chose "Wrapped Up in You," an upbeat number by Garth Brooks that had a bouncy lead guitar line and wicked performances from percussion, fiddlers and mouth harp. High-spirited and exuberant, the song was a joyful shout-out to love, and it set the tone for the evening.

The Scarth Club brought out heaters, unnecessary for those who were dancing up a storm but welcomed by people like the Webers and Zack and me who were content just to kick back and watch the action, and there was plenty of action to watch. Sawyer and Lorelei Mae, the physiotherapist he met during his rehab program, seemed to have eyes only for each other. Simon had taken a break from his duties as photographer to enjoy a slow dance with Rainey. Ernest and Peggy waltzed by, cheek to cheek. Madeleine and Lena, flushed and excited, were dancing with the young men they'd sat with at dinner. Madeleine's young man was a head shorter than her, and Lena's dance partner was at least a head taller — something that would have seemed impossible to overcome when I was their age, but the four of them were too busy having a good time to consider disparities.

When yet another high energy song began, Mieka and Charlie D took a break from dancing and came over to join the Webers and us.

Feigning exhaustion, Charlie D collapsed in a chair. "That trip to the barber today changed my life. Mieka won't let me out of her sight."

Our daughter was clearly in a playful mood. "Charlie, you look great and you smell great — I can't help it, I'm just 'stuck on you.'"

"I know the feeling," Annie said. "Warren's trips to Enzo's always end very happily for us."

"I've been thinking along those lines myself," Mieka said. As soon as the words left her lips, the blush, which had been the bane of Mieka's existence since she was thirteen, started at her neck and rose to her face. "I can't believe I said that out loud. If Madeleine and Lena were here, they'd be mortified."

"But Madeleine and Lena aren't here," Annie said. "They've been dancing with their friends on the grass since the music began, so you can speak freely."

We all laughed, but it occurred to me that I hadn't seen the girls for a while. "Where are the ladies?" I said. "They were out here five minutes ago, but now . . . ?"

Mieka shook her head. "Another life lesson for Annie. For years, children are happiest when they know exactly where their parents are, and then — just like that — they decide that they're ready to venture out on their own. The girls loved every second of the wedding, but as soon as it was over, they made it clear that they were old enough to handle their own social life."

"And fortuitously, the plus-one of one of Leah's bridesmaids is her fifteen-year-old son," I said. "Leah told me that she suggested he bring along a friend. And more good fortune — Madeleine and Lena were seated with the young men at dinner."

Warren's laugh seemed to come from deep within. "Those young men were the lucky ones," he said. "Annie and I are lucky too. We have Maeve. And as perfect as this day has been, it's time we went home to our daughter."

"But before we go," Annie said, "Warren and I have an invitation to extend to Charlie and Mieka. Friday is Simon's birthday, and when Rainey did the pre-interview for Charlie D's show, Simon was struck by her candor and her openness. Joanne assures us that Rainey's relationship with Valentine Masluk is collegial, not romantic, so we asked Rainey if she'd like to celebrate Simon's birthday at a barbecue at our place, and she accepted. Zack and Jo are coming, and it would be great if you could join us too."

Mieka and Charlie D exchanged a quick glance. "Absolutely," Charlie D said. "A barbecue with the six of you is a great way to end the work week."

"Excellent," Warren said. "I know that you two like rack of lamb, because that's what you served us the last time we had dinner together."

"That was at the beginning of summer." Mieka shook her head. "Time just seems to slip away."

"Let's stop time in its tracks, starting with drinks at six on Friday," Warren said. "Early, I know, but some of us have very young children."

"Simon will be so pleased. It's been a long time since he felt that his birthday was worth celebrating," Annie said, and her words were poignant for their truth. From the time Simon was very young, his life had been a struggle against mental illness, but he had survived. Those of us who cared for Simon were, in that now hackneyed phrase, "cautiously optimistic" about the possibility that in Rainey Arcus Simon might find someone with whom he could simply be himself.

After the Webers left, Mieka hugged herself. "I don't know about you, but being with Warren and Annie always gives me warm fuzzies. I'm glad we'll get to spend more time with them this week."

"I am too," Charlie said. "And not just because of the warm fuzzies. Simon wasn't the only one impressed with Rainey's pre-interview work. She's a terrific researcher — that's a skill in itself — but she also knows how to edit information. Rainey's research about borderline personality disorder was extensive, but she didn't simply dump information on my desk. What she gave me was organized, and she knew exactly the information I needed to ask the right questions in the right sequence.

"She pretty much laid out the interview for me. All I had to do was shape the questions so that the audience would get the information they needed to understand not only what Simon had been through, but also the courage it took for him to simply keep on living.

"Our show is getting a lot of high-powered guests, and they have résumés that I need to understand in order to ask the right questions about the projects they'll want to talk about on air. I'd be very pleased if MediaNation hired Rainey as a full-time researcher for our show."

"So what's the problem?" Zack said. "You want Rainey in a position for which she is eminently qualified. Isn't that enough?"

"Normally, it would be, but Kam Chau is uneasy about having Rainey as part of what MediaNation insists that we call 'our team.'"

"Zack and I have come to know and really like your show's producer," I said. "Kam is not a person who would be quick to pass judgment. If he has doubts about Rainey, they're worth considering."

"I agree," Charlie D said. "And I've pressed him about it, but he's reluctant to tell me what the problem is. He and I have a great relationship, but it's all sunshine and lollipops. There are times when Kam and I disagree, but we always talk the problem through, and we come up with a solution we can both live with. Whether or not we hire Rainey as a permanent member of our staff is not a deal-breaker. I'm willing to let this go, but I am puzzled by Kam's recalcitrance. He and I both know we need somebody to take charge of research that clogs our computers with information we can't use. Rainey could eliminate that problem with one hand tied behind her back. I don't question Kam's judgment on this. I simply don't understand it."

When Mieka wrapped herself in one of the shawls the Scarth Club staff had unobtrusively placed beside the chairs of the non-dancers and stood, we followed her lead and moved into the club. One of Leah's bridesmaids spotted us and said that she was on her way outside to tell the dancers that Leah would be tossing her bouquet in a few minutes, and if they wanted to catch the moment, they should come inside.

Mieka turned to me. "Madeleine and Lena will want to see the bouquet toss. Why don't you and I split up and check the private rooms? The men can stay here in case the girls show up."

I found the girls and their young men standing by the table for gifts in the Portrait Room. Madeleine was holding a package wrapped in the kind of brown paper used for mailing.

"We were just trying to decide what to do about this," she said. "When we first saw it, we thought it was from someone who was trying to be eco-friendly, but now we don't know. Looks like it could be weird . . ." She handed the present to me. When I saw the words "For the Father of the Bride" written in Sharpie on the front of the package, I felt a chill. Years in politics had taught me that notes written in Sharpie were generally bad news, but I kept my voice even.

"This is probably just a gag gift," I said, "but, you're right, sometimes those gags are pretty gross. I'll take it out to our car, and your granddad and I can check it out later."

After I threw the package into the back seat of our Volvo, I was inside the club in time to see Gracie Falconer, who for two years had been the point guard on Notre Dame's women's basketball team, catch the bouquet and hand it to Taylor. It was the perfect coda for a day that had been filled with love.

Wednesday was a workday and by ten o'clock, most of the guests had left. The party was over, and I was ready for it to be over. After we said our goodbyes to Mieka, Charlie, the ladies and their young men, Zack said, "Rainey Arcus and Val are over there. I have to tell Val about Rebecca Woodrow's interview with Charlie D on his show tomorrow. I'll advise Val to call Kam Chau before the interview at nine thirty to tell Kam he's aware of the announcement Ms. Woodrow is going to make, and he's shocked and saddened at the pain Ms. Woodrow is suffering, but until he knows the truth about what happened, he believes it's best to say nothing."

"Zack, do you think Val will tell Rainey about this?"

"I'm sure he will. After all, Steven duped her too. As Val's researcher, Rainey should be prepared to react to the questions that will inevitably come her way."

* * *

We left the reception with the Drache sisters. Like us, they were weary but relieved.

"Well, we pulled it off," Mila said. "You have no idea how often my sister and I wanted to call you this week."

"Did something happen?" Zack said.

Nothing we have to talk about now," Reva said. "For the time being, all you have to know is how grateful we were to know you were there if . . ." she hesitated before completing the sentence. "If what we were able to do wasn't enough."

When we pulled into our garage, Zack said. "We both drank sparingly tonight, what would you say to three fingers of Old Pulteney?"

"I'd say, 'where have you been all my life?'"

It was an old joke between us, and we were both smiling when we got out of the Volvo leaving the mystery gift, now forgotten, in the back seat.

CHAPTER EIGHT

When I returned from taking Esme for her run, Zack was sitting on the bed in his silk boxers. I sat down beside him and took his hand. "Trying to decide what to wear to the partners' meeting?"

Zack put his arm around me. "Something like that. I'd give my right nut to skip that meeting, but I have to be there. I can't go into the details, but it's a problem with one of the junior partners that cannot be resolved."

"So the junior partner has to go?" I said.

Zack tightened his arm. "My decision and that of the other partners was unanimous, but Partner X will not leave gracefully."

"Will Partner X fight your decision?"

From the weary resignation in Zack's eyes, I knew the answer before he said a word. Nonetheless, the words came. "There will be a fight, and it will last for a while. That said, the meeting today will be ugly but short. As the senior partner, all I have to do is announce the partners' unanimous decision, and, until the truth sinks in, I will say a dozen times that the decision has been made and that what happens next is in the hands of the lawyers Partner X hires and the lawyer Falconer Shreve chooses to represent us."

I had never stopped worrying about Zack's health, and the tension I felt in his body frightened me. "Your meeting isn't till ten. There's plenty of time for a heavy-duty love sesh to rid ourselves of toxins."

Zack grinned. "You're on."

When he started to remove his boxers, I moved in close. "I can do that," I said. And after a while, I did.

* * *

Ninety minutes later, we were showered, dressed, eating truffle omelets and making a list of what we needed from Pawsitively Purrfect to welcome Scout and placate Esme. The truffles were a gift from Ed and Barry, who, always sensitive to the emotions of others, thought we might be feeling "a little deflated" the day after the wedding and knew a truffle omelet for breakfast would lift our spirits.

The decadent meal helped, and by the time I picked up my car keys, we had a plan. I would drop Zack off at Falconer Shreve, drive to Pawsitively Purrfect to shop for Scout and Esme and then pick up a few groceries. Zack would call when his meeting was finished and, tasks completed, we would drive home and idle the day away.

But life has a way of scrambling plans. After Zack transferred his body from his chair to the car and dismantled his wheelchair he turned, as he always did, to put the pieces of his chair in the back seat. But he suddenly stopped. "Jo, there's a package on the floor back there."

"Right. I'd forgotten about it. Last night, when it was almost time for Leah to throw her bouquet, the girls weren't around. So Mieka and I split up to search. I found Madeleine and Lena in the Portrait Room with the boys they'd been dancing with. The four of them were standing by the table where people had left gifts, and Madeleine was holding that package. The four of them were trying to decide what they should do with it.

"Madeleine said they thought it might be some kind of gag gift, but since some gag gifts were in really bad taste, they didn't want to put the package back on the present table. I agreed, and so I took the package out to our car, tossed it in the back seat and came back in time to see Gracie catch Leah's bouquet."

I picked up the package, handed it to Zack and joined him in the front seat. He put on his reading glasses and read the Sharpie message aloud. "For the Father of the Bride."

"The kids noticed it because of the wrapping," I said. "At first they were impressed because it was environmentally friendly. By the time I arrived, they'd begun to think that the package might contain something inappropriate."

"One way to find out," Zack said, and he began unwrapping the package. It contained two items: one manuscript with the title page *Medusa's Fate* and another bearing the title *The Iron Bed of Procrustes.* Both title pages listed the author's name as Laurel Woodrow.

Zack whistled. "I believe the shit just officially hit the fan. I'll call Patrick O'Keefe. His client should know about this."

"So should Val Masluk," I said. "Reva and Mila should know too. After I drop you off, I'll call Val, and then I'll phone the Drache sisters and tell them I'm on my way."

"Jo, I'm sorry you're having to break this news to Reva and Mila."

"So am I," I said. "But time is not on our side."

* * *

As soon as I pulled into Mila Drache's driveway, I called Val. The call went to voicemail. I told him about Rebecca Woodrow's discovery and that she was going to meet with his publishers and their lawyers that morning at nine thirty.

Mila's bungalow on the corner of Albert Street and Regina Avenue had been lovingly renovated, and it was a gem. Mila had a green thumb, and when spring came, my morning runs always took me by the flowers in the beds surrounding her house. Thanks to Mila's careful planning, there were always plants in bloom.

The sisters were waiting for me inside. I'd dropped the manuscript and the outline into a book bag I'd bought years ago at the Stratford Festival. The three of us sat around a table on the glassed-in front porch. At first we were silent, seemingly absorbed in watching the morning traffic, slowed by the rain, moving steadily along Albert Street.

There was no way to soften the blow, so I told the Drache sisters about discovering the package on the gift table at the Scarth Club and then I took out the manuscripts. Reva picked one up and read the title page. "*Medusa's Fate* . . . and the author is identified as Laurel Woodrow. Steven's name isn't there at all?"

I shook my head. "No, and his name does not appear on the title page of *The Iron Bed of Procrustes*."

It was apparent that both sisters were reeling from the news, but they weren't shrinking from the truth. Mila squared her shoulders. "What comes next?" she said.

"Rebecca Woodrow has a lawyer," I said. "His name is Patrick O'Keefe, and out of professional courtesy and probably friendship, he called Zack yesterday and filled him in. At nine thirty this morning, Ms. Woodrow is meeting with Steven's publishers to reveal that her grandmother, Laurel Woodrow, wrote the two novels that —"

"That Steven published under his own name," Reva said, flatly. Finally, she raised her eyes from the manuscripts and looked directly at me. "Joanne, you and Zack knew all of this, but you kept it to yourselves because you didn't want Leah and Angus's wedding to be ruined by this spoor of ugliness."

"There was no way we could change the outcome. The only thing Zack and I could do was control the timing," I said. "It was a tough decision, but, given the joy that day brought all of us, I think it was the right one."

The Drache sisters exchanged a glance. "It was the right decision," Reva said.

Mila was clearly puzzled. "All this happened years ago," Mila said. "Why is it just coming to light now, on the day the biography is published? What kind of person is Rebecca Woodrow? Is she someone who has a grudge against Steven? Someone who craves the spotlight?"

"According to her lawyer, Ms. Woodrow is intelligent and principled. She graduated from the University of Saskatchewan with distinction last June. Her area of study is Classics, and she'd studied both of Steven's novels in a feminist class she'd audited.

"Rebecca Woodrow didn't know anything about Laurel until her own mother died, last spring. Rebecca was travelling all summer, so she hadn't looked at her mother's papers until last week. When she saw the manuscripts, she recognized the titles and immediately got in touch with Patrick O'Keefe. Zack says he's a good lawyer and a decent human being. Apparently, Patrick O'Keefe knew about the wedding yesterday, and when he asked Ms. Woodrow to wait until today to reveal the truth about the novels, she readily agreed."

"So we owe our perfect day to Ms. Woodrow," Reva said. "Life really does turn on a dime, doesn't it? The wedding was perfect in every way, but my sister and I both had a sleepless night. We were concerned about Steven, and, as it turns out, there was cause for concern. Early this morning, we decided to see if he left behind anything that would give us insight into his state of mind when he decided to leave."

"And we did find something," Mila said. "What we found wasn't a suicide note, but it did point to a direction we could not ignore. Steven kept journals. He was obsessively secretive about them. His need to get away must have been desperate because he left three of his most recent journals behind."

"I feel sick about this, and so does my sister," Reva said. "But we violated a principle that's at the core of our profession. We read Steven's journals. We found nothing that, in and of itself, pointed towards suicide. But the journals reveal elements of a mental state that is characterized by delusions of exaggerated personal importance."

"Megalomania," I said.

"Yes," Mila said softly. "Megalomania. Steven believes that history will recognize his greatness, but for that to happen, he has to protect his legacy. Suicide is a possibility, but, more likely, so is an act of retaliation against a person whom Steven perceives is an enemy."

"We don't want to involve the police," Mila said. "Not yet. But we do need to find Steven for his own sake. He needs help."

"Falconer Shreve has a firm of private investigators that they use frequently. Colby & Associates are discreet, and they're very good. I'll send you their contact information. If you tell Bob Colby that Zack and I recommended his company, he'll take care of you."

Mila went inside and returned with one of the journals. "Steven has written this quotation on the first page of the three journals he left behind: We work in the dark — we do what we can — we give what we have . . . Henry James."

She handed the journal over so I could see the quotation was written in Sharpie, all capital letters, just as the message on the package that contained the copies of Laurel Woodrow's manuscripts had been written. I placed the two messages side by side.

"The printing doesn't match," Reva said. "Steven's letters are carefully formed and have a definite backward tilt. The printing on the package is haphazard." Her hazel eyes widened in bewilderment. "Should I be grateful for that?"

I had no answer for her question, so I simply slipped the manuscripts back into my book bag.

When Reva noticed the words on my tote, she smiled. "'Nothing will come of Nothing.' King Lear's words to Cordelia, the only daughter who truly loved him."

"That particular scene has always moved me," I said. "Cordelia knows that when it comes to love, words mean nothing. But Lear is blind to her honesty, and he turns away from her. The minute I saw that bag in the gift shop at Stratford, I knew I had to have it. I use it often, and it always evokes the memory of the afternoon when I saw Christopher Plummer's performance as Lear."

Mila's eyes widened. "My sister and I saw that production. The three of us might have been in the theatre the same afternoon. I remember the audience leaning towards the stage when Christopher Plummer made his entrance. It was as if they were willing him to be a great Lear," she said.

"And it worked," I said. "Christopher Plummer *was* a great Lear." There was nothing more to say, so I pulled the hood of my slicker up and stepped out into the hard rain.

* * *

Zack was waiting under the portico at the entrance to the building that housed the Falconer Shreve offices. Because his wheelchair is manually driven and he needs both hands to keep moving, I pulled into the loading zone and ran over with an umbrella. After we'd snapped our seat belts, I said, "How did your meeting go?"

"About as badly as I expected," Zack said. "A lot of angst. Partner X had apparently forgotten how to use their inside voice, and my ears are still ringing. When they stomped out with smoke coming out of their ears, the rest of us made some quick decisions. The most significant one is that Maisie will handle Falconer Shreve's case."

"But Maisie's a trial lawyer," I said.

"True, but Partner X is angry enough and deluded enough to take it all the way. Having Maisie acting for Falconer Shreve is a pre-emptive strike. Other lawyers respect her, and many of them wouldn't want to face her in court. Maisie doesn't shy away from getting blood on her hands when she cross-examines a witness, and she never allows a witness, however battered and humiliated they are, to step down from the witness stand until she's certain she has established her case beyond a reasonable doubt."

I took a deep breath. "That does not sound like the Maisie I know. One of my favourite memories of our daughter-in-law is watching her breast-feed both her sons at once. She did it effortlessly, no false moves, so the boys were relaxed and content. When I told her how impressed I was, she laughed it off. 'Piece of cake,' she said. 'Nursing these guys involves the same skill set as lacrosse: cradling, scooping, throwing and catching.'"

Zack chuckled. "Pretty much the same skill set as trial law. How did the meeting with Reva and Mila go?"

"It was excruciating. We can talk about it later."

* * *

After we arrived home, Esme greeted us and I checked the time. "It's eleven o'clock, and Rebecca Woodrow's meeting with the publisher started at nine thirty. By now, decisions will have been made about how to handle Steven Brooks's plagiarism."

Zack gaze was assessing. "How are you doing?"

"I'll be glad when this is finally over," I said. "Showing Reva and Mila the manuscripts was, as Angus would say, 'stabby.'"

Zack's brow furrowed. "I know you've explained this before, but does feeling 'stabby' suggest you've inflicted a wound or received one?"

"In this case, it was both," I said. "But that part's over, and there's more to come. I imagine Patrick will let us know about the interview when he's had time to process everything that happened.

By noon, Patrick O'Keefe still hadn't called and I could see that Zack was uneasy. So was I. "Time for me to focus on the one thing I *can* control," I said. "Lunch. We've been eating pretty high on the hog lately. It's time to be abstemious. There's beef and barley soup in the freezer. Sound okay to you?"

"Sounds more than okay." At that point Zack's phone rang. He checked the caller ID. "Patrick O'Keefe," he told me. After picking up, he listened for less than a minute and said, "I'll be right there."

I frowned. "I wish you didn't have to go out in this weather."

Zack touched my arm. "I only have to go as far as our front door. Patrick's here. Jo, Rebecca Woodrow did not show up in his office for her video meeting. She hasn't called, and Pat thinks she's turned off her phone."

"Take him into the family room so you can talk. Lunch will keep."

"Good, because I'd like you to join us. You're as involved in this whole mess as I am, and I trust your instincts."

Patrick O'Keefe and Zack were in front of the fireplace, drinks in hand, when I came in. They were the picture of success: two confident men who were adept at using their knowledge of the law and of human beings to arrive at workable answers to vexing problems. Now they were faced with a question that seemed unanswerable. Why would Rebecca Woodrow disappear on the morning she was meeting with Steven Brooks's publishers to discuss his plagiarism?

When I came into the family room, the smile Patrick O'Keefe gave me was full wattage. He offered his hand, and I took it. Like my husband, Patrick was a handsome man and a snappy dresser.

His closely fitted lightweight suit and his shirt were the colour of cappuccino, his silk tie and pocket square were rust and beige paisley and his leather loafers were nutmeg brown. "It's great to finally meet you in person, Joanne," he said. "I just wish the circumstances were less fraught."

"We all wish that," I said. "But these are the circumstances we have. Our best hope seems to be to share what we know and see if we can make sense of what's going on."

"Jo's right," Zack said. He glanced at Patrick's empty glass. "Can I freshen your drink?"

"Thanks, but no. I haven't eaten yet today."

"I don't know about you, Patrick," I said, "but I can't think on an empty stomach. Do you like beef and barley soup?"

"Love it," he said.

"Then follow Zack and me to the kitchen — lunch is ready."

When the soup was served, Zack said, "We have a house rule: no serious talk with meals. But if you're strapped for time, we can bend the rule."

Patrick shrugged. "I'm not strapped for time. Rebecca paid me to keep the afternoon free in case she needed advice, so I cleared my schedule. No need to bend the rule on my account. Now, tell me about your son's wedding."

* * *

Pat had a hearty appetite, not only for the soup, black bread and Boursin, but also for news about the wedding. After we'd finished eating, describing Brother Blue Jay's star turn on the chuppah and cleared the table, we took our tea into the family room.

When we'd settled in, Zack said, "Let's start by following Joanne's suggestion that we share information. Jo, can you fill Pat in on how we became involved in this?"

"It started with a message our son-in-law, Charlie Dowhanuik received this past weekend," I said. "Charlie has a morning radio show."

Patrick nodded. "I listen to *Charlie D in the Morning* whenever I can," he said. "Your son-in-law does some great interviews."

"Agreed, and Charlie D received a strange email about his upcoming interview with Valentine Masluk. The email said that, before doing the interview, he should reread Masluk's biography of Steven Brooks from page 329 and on, so he could ask Masluk whether those pages told the whole story. When he called me on Sunday, Charlie was sitting in his car outside the library waiting for our granddaughters, so he didn't have the book at hand.

"Charlie knew we had an advance copy of the biography, and the email had piqued his curiosity, so he asked me if I'd mind taking a quick look at the section that this person who referred to themselves as 329ff had referenced. By the time Madeleine and Lena came back to the car, I'd only had time to leaf through a half-dozen pages. The account of how Steven's debilitating attack of writer's block ended when he came upon the Greek legend of Medusa and wrote *Medusa's Fate* was dramatic, but nothing leapt out at me as earth-shattering. Charlie and I agreed we'd look more closely at the pages 329ff had cited, but Madeleine and Lena's return to the car and my pre-wedding social schedule nudged the activities of 329ff off the radar."

Patrick leaned forward, intent. "But it didn't end there."

"No, it didn't," I said. "Charlie believes that his 'spidey sense' twitches when something crops up that merits further attention.

Publication day for *Steven Brooks: A Biography* is today. Val Masluk will be starting his book tour now, so Charlie D's interview with him was being taped on Sunday, August 28.

"Our son-in-law always sounds laid back on the air, but before the interview, he's a stickler for accuracy when it comes to learning everything he can about the person who will be sitting across from him in the studio," I continued. "After the note from 329ff, Charlie went back to the research package on Steven Brooks and started digging for information about Brooks's activities in the period before and after he seized upon the legend of Medusa to rescue him from his battle with writer's block.

"When he revisited the research, Charlie picked up immediately on the fact that Val had trod lightly on Steven Brooks's life during those years. The response to Brooks's third book had been largely negative, and critics agreed that its failure raised the ante for his next novel. The consensus seemed to be that novel number four would either make or break Steven Brooks's reputation. Brooks must have felt the sands shifting beneath his feet and known he had to produce something that would stop the erosion."

"But he didn't produce anything," Zack said. "Charlie's research revealed that as the years passed and no fourth novel appeared, rumblings about Brooks's prolonged silence began circulating in the writing and publishing community. At first, they were innocent enough, along the lines of 'Whatever happened to Steven Brooks?' Then the speculation took a darker turn. There were rumours that Brooks was finished, that he'd been trying to write but that everything he wrote was shit, and that he was despondent and drinking heavily.

"Joanne and I both read the pages 329ff referenced. Until page 329, the biography is filled with energy and the kinds of details that Jo and I agree drew us into Brooks's world in a way that made us understand how it felt to be him. But there were nine years between the publication of the third novel and the publication of *Medusa*. And in those nine years, Steven Brooks fell into the depths of depression, lost his sense of identity and decided that he had to leave his old life behind and start again. He bought a cabin on Anglin Lake, and it was there that he found peace and regained the confidence that allowed him to write the novel that both critics and readers praised as his best ever."

"Charlie pointed out what was obvious to 329ff but hadn't been obvious to Zack and me," I said. "In the span of those nine years, Steven Brooks disintegrated completely, but he was able to reclaim his life and his reputation. Val devoted only two and half pages to that period.

"And in hindsight, that doesn't make any sense. Zack and I read the novel Val wrote about a tragic time in the lives of Val and the people, including me, who felt they had contributed to that tragedy. Val is a sensitive and gifted writer. He knew that what Brooks went through during those nine years was inherently dramatic and that it revealed the heart and soul of the man whose biography he was writing, and yet he never comes to grips with it."

During lunch Patrick O'Keefe's boyish geniality had warned me to him. But our luncheon companion had morphed once again. The mirth had left his hazel eyes, and, once again, he was the lawyer committed to acting in Rebecca Woodrow's best interests. His tone was civil but determined: "Why would Masluk gloss over those years?"

"Because he didn't know the full story, we suspect," Zack said. "Until Rebecca Woodrow told you about the role her grandmother played in Steven Brooks's life and work, we were all in the dark about him. Val Masluk interviewed Brooks for hundreds of hours, and the picture Brooks painted of himself during those years was of a man broken by his inability to write the book he knew he was capable of writing, but redeemed by a Greek myth he found in a library book. *Medusa's Fate* was Brooks's salvation, and Val's writing about Brooks's life after that novel's phenomenal success is as energetic and detail-filled as the writing in the biography's first 328 pages."

"In pointing Charlie D to the pages that had the power to trap Steven Brooks in his lies, 329ff threw down the gauntlet," I said. "When Charlie called for my opinion about whether he should ask the question, I advised him to talk to Val beforehand, tell him the question was in play but give him the option of not answering."

Patrick O'Keefe's gaze was probing. "Valentine Masluk is lucky to have you on his side," he said.

"Val was a student in a class I co-taught over fourteen years ago."

"Do most of your students retain that kind of connection with you?" Patrick said, and his usually pleasant tenor had a sharpness that smacked distinctly of a lawyer dealing with a recalcitrant witness.

I leaned forward. "Pat, we just ate beef and barley soup together, and we're on the same side in this, so maybe dial back a notch on the trial lawyer approach. To answer your question, most of my relationships with former students are now just a friendly smile and a few words in a public place, but something happened in the Politics and the Media class that was a painful memory for both Val and me. We had not stayed in touch, but when our paths crossed, we both knew we'd been given a chance to reflect, and we welcomed it."

"I apologize, Joanne. Rebecca's failure to show up today was a gut-punch. The case she brought to me was cut-and-dried. She had irrefutable proof that her late grandmother Laurel Woodrow had written the manuscripts that Steven Brooks had published under his own name, and she wanted the public to know the truth. This morning, I woke up believing that by noon, Rebecca would have taken the first steps in the lawsuit she had hired me to bring against Steven Brooks. But now, no one seems to know where Rebecca is, and you've just told me that someone who identifies as 329ff has an interest in revealing the truth about the novelist who wrote *Medusa's Fate*." Patrick cocked his head. "What's the significance of 'ff' anyway?"

"It's used in a citation to refer to a section of a book or article for which no final page numbers can be accurately given."

"So 329ff is signalling that the truth of what Steven did cannot be found in the pages after page 329," Pat said. "Very clever."

"Also very revealing. The citation 'ff' isn't used much anymore," I said.

Pat's eyes widened. "So 329ff is an older person?"

"Or a person who reads old books," I said.

The quick smile my husband gave me was approving. "Moving right along," he said. "Our son-in-law brought us an MP3 of the interview he did with Val. The interview was great, but after it was over and Charlie D did his sign-off, he asked Val about the possible plagiarism, and Val fell apart. He said that he was aware of the rumours out there, but he was not going to exacerbate the situation because he, in his words, 'was responsible for two innocent people losing their lives,' and he was going to do everything in his power to keep that from happening again. At any rate, that part of the interview will not be aired."

"We all know this is far from over," Pat said wearily.

"We can't let it get ahead of us," I said. "We also can't let this grind us down. Time for a break."

Zack raised his arms and stretched. "I'm with you, Jo. Our daughter, Taylor, is an artist. We have a collection of some of her work that we'd be delighted to show you."

"And I'd be delighted to see it," Pat said. "I wasn't at the opening of her show at the Slate Gallery last January, but I did stop by one afternoon to look at her work. I was impressed. The biography at the gallery says that Taylor has been making art since she was four . . . ?"

"We'll start with one of the pieces Taylor drew when she was that age," I said. "It's a work in crayon, but when you look at it you can almost see the hula dancers swaying."

CHAPTER NINE

Showing Patrick O'Keefe how Taylor's art changed as she grew older was a pleasure. The questions he asked were knowledgeable and his enthusiasm was genuine, and we returned to the family room refreshed and ready to deal with the problem at hand.

When Patrick checked his phone and saw that there was still no word from Rebecca Woodrow, he rubbed his temples. "I'm starting to get a very bad feeling," he said. "Rebecca and I agreed that she would keep me apprised of any new development so we could deal with it together. She's smart enough to know that when you're dealing with a situation that is likely to end up in a court of law, it's wise to have a lawyer by your side. The woman I have come to know does not act on impulse."

"Tell us about her," Zack said.

As he began his account of his relationship with Rebecca Woodrow, Patrick spoke with precision. "On Monday, August 22,

Rebecca called for an appointment with me. It had already been an uncharacteristically busy month for us. After my executive assistant, Doug Skerrett, determined that Ms. Woodrow's matter was not pressing, he and Rebecca agreed to a meeting early on Monday, August 29."

"Nine days ago," I said.

Patrick nodded, "But that week-plus was enough for Rebecca to shape her evidence into an airtight case. She came to my office with copies of reviews of Steven Brooks's first three novels. The consensus seemed to be that while Brooks was technically proficient, he lacked the spark of inspiration and originality that would lift him from the ranks of the also-rans to the top of the heap. The third novel was published in 2001 when Steven was forty-four."

"*Medusa's Fate* wasn't published until 2010," Zack said. "Steven must have been getting desperate by then."

"He was," Patrick said. "That's why he purchased the cabin at Anglin Lake. He hoped to find inspiration there." Pat's lips tightened. "And when he met Laurel Woodrow, he must have known that he'd found exactly what he needed."

"So Fortuna spun the wheel," Zack said. "Steven Brooks won, and Laurel Woodrow lost — my God, that poor woman."

"How did Steven Brooks get her manuscripts?" I said.

Patrick's eyes met mine. "He and Laurel were lovers. My client did her homework. Rebecca assumed, correctly, that, as a writer, her grandmother would have been a regular patron of the nearest library, so she got in touch with the branch librarian at Christopher Lake Public Library. The librarian steered her towards Laurel's neighbour and friend, Alma Hall. Ms. Hall had been the Christopher Lake librarian until she retired two years earlier, and she and Laurel Woodrow were close. Ms. Hall was eager to talk with her late friend's granddaughter, so she and Rebecca began FaceTiming.

"Ms. Hall felt responsible, at least in part, for her friend's decision to end her life. She had introduced Laurel to Steven. Laurel had written an as-yet-unpublished novel, and Steven was a well-known writer, so Alma Hall was certain they would enjoy each other's company. They were attracted to each other, and, as Ms. Hall said, the rest is history. Ms. Hall told Rebecca that when Steven offered to 'polish' the manuscript and send it to his agent and publisher for assessment, her grandmother was 'over the moon.' She also said that joy was an emotion Laurel had not often experienced in her life."

"That's a painful assessment," Zack said.

"It is," Patrick agreed. "According to Alma Hall, the life of Rebecca's grandmother was riven by trauma. She was sexually abused by her stepfather from the time she was nine years old until she was thirteen and began to menstruate. When Laurel told her mother what her stepfather was doing, her mother slapped her and called her a lying whore. The five years of continual rape left Laurel with wounds so deep they would never heal.

"Laurel was brilliant. She studied Classics at the University of Toronto, and Rebecca ferreted out Laurel's academic record. She was an outstanding student, but she suffered breakdowns so severe that she had to be hospitalized, and twice she attempted suicide."

"All that agony is at the heart of *Medusa's Fate*," I said.

"It is," Patrick said. "I just finished the book last night. It's a tough read, especially when you know how closely Medusa's life mirrors Laurel's own. Like Medusa, Laurel was a beauty, with thick luxuriant hair. Medusa had been a virgin when Poseidon raped her, and, of course, Laurel had been a virgin when her stepfather began raping her."

"She was nine years old," I said. "How could anyone do that to a child?"

Zack took my hand in his. "Since I was called to the Bar, I must have asked myself that question a thousand times."

"And there's never an answer," Patrick said. "The behaviour of people like Laurel's mother and her stepfather makes it impossible to believe that all is for the best in this best of all possible worlds."

"So much for that sunny view of humankind," Zack said. "After Joanne and I read *Medusa's Fate*, we read the original story. Like the Medusa of Greek mythology, Laurel sought help from a woman who had power over her life. But Laurel's mother refused to listen, and she must have filled her daughter with such self-loathing that Laurel believed that every man with whom she became intimate had a right to abuse her."

"When Medusa went to Athena, the goddess to whom she was loyal, Athena turned her into a monster woman with snake hair and stone eyes who had the power to kill any man who came near her," I said.

"And Laurel ended up marrying a man who was so violent that she feared for her daughter's life and her own," Patrick said. "After she took out a restraining order against her husband, Laurel moved to Anglin Lake. She became the manager of a lodge on the lake and raised her daughter there. Not surprisingly, Laurel's relationship with her own daughter was rocky. When Rebecca's mother left for university in Saskatoon, she never returned to Anglin Lake. Laurel was left with her job at the lodge, her friendship with Alma

Hall and her writing. According to Ms. Hall, Laurel didn't have much, but she had made peace with her life. She was content."

"Then along came Steven Brooks," Zack said. "As her lover, he must have known how vulnerable she was. He used that vulnerability to convince her that he could help her realize her dream of having her novel — a work that reflected the pain of lives like her own — published." Zack's body was tight with rage. "*Medusa's Fate* meant everything to Laurel Woodrow, but Brooks had a more pressing need. *Medusa* was the novel that would rescue him from the ranks of the third-rate writers whose works were relegated first to bookstore's remainders tables and ultimately to the junk heap."

"And so he stole Laurel Woodrow's novel," I said. Suddenly, I understood exactly how the scenario had played out. "Steven Brooks never sent her manuscript to anyone. He told Laurel that it would be weeks before they heard back from his publisher and agent about *Medusa's Fate*, but he was certain it would be published. However, he must have told her that before they could make a long-term commitment to her, the publisher would need to see more of her writing. Steven would have seen the detailed outline for *The Iron Bed of Procrustes* and recognized its potential, but he needed Laurel to complete the manuscript."

Patrick O'Keefe was on his feet, clearly furious. "The three of us in this room have lived long enough to know that people can be vicious and unscrupulous, but what Steven Brooks did is beyond the pale. He urged Laurel Woodrow to finish writing *Procrustes,* and when he had what he needed, he rolled the dice and told Laurel that both his publisher and his agent had deemed *Medusa's Fate* unpublishable — 'a sow's ear that could not be turned into a silk purse.' It was a calculated risk, but Brooks knew the odds were with him. Laurel had put her heart and soul into writing *Medusa,* and Brooks was confident that hearing that her novel had been dismissed with such cruelty would push her over the edge."

"And it did," I said. My stomach was roiling. "This morning, I read a journal entry Steven wrote two days ago. He said that he felt 'no guilt' about *Medusa's Fate* — that what he did was art. He said he had turned a sow's ear into a silk purse —"

Zack's lip curled in derision, and he couldn't keep from interrupting. "There's that sow's ear again," he said. "Sorry, Jo. I'm about ready to put my fist through the wall. Carry on."

"No need to apologize," I said. "I'm about ready to put my first through the wall too. Anyway, when I read that passage aloud to the Drache sisters, they were visibly disturbed. Reva said Steven's journals reveal elements of a mental state that is characterized by delusions of exaggerated personal importance."

"Megalomania," Zack said.

I nodded. "Reva said that Steven believes that history will recognize his greatness, but for that to happen he has to protect his legacy. She said suicide was a possibility, but there was also the danger of an act of retaliation against a person whom Steven perceives as an enemy."

"A person like Rebecca Woodrow," Patrick said, and his voice was heavy with dread.

"We need to find her," I said. "This morning, Mila and Reva were worried sick about Steven's state of mind. They had no way of helping him because they had no idea where he was. Zack, I gave them Bob Colby's contact information and told them to tell Bob that I had recommended that they hire him."

Zack turned to Patrick. "Bob Colby owns a private investigation firm that Falconer Shreve uses. They're good. I'll call him and ask him to assign some of his people to find Rebecca Woodrow. He'll need her contact information, anything relevant from her file, and he'll need a physical description. I don't suppose you have a photo."

Patrick shook his head, "No, but I have a digital photograph of her grandmother, and Rebecca's resemblance to Laurel is remarkable. Rebecca sent a note with the photograph. It read, 'This is the woman for whom we're going to find justice. It's too late to save her life, but we can show that even though she had been shamed and dismissed as worthless, Laurel Woodrow created two exquisite novels that deliver a powerful message. As human beings, we must listen to those in pain and do everything in our power to give them an escape route.'"

"I'll send Colby & Associates a copy of that photograph, and a physical description of Rebecca," Patrick said. "She is so delicate that it looks as if a stiff wind might blow her over, but she's one of the strongest people I've ever met."

Zack and I looked at the photo of Laurel Woodrow. "She's lovely," I said.

"So is Rebecca." Patrick's eyes were troubled. "We can't lose her too."

My heart sank. "No, we can't, and that means we have to move quickly."

"I'll call Debbie Haczkewicz," Zack said. "You're right, Jo, we have to move quickly. Even though we've only known Rebecca to be missing for a few hours, who knows what could have transpired before her meeting this morning."

Zack's call was brief. "Deb's involved in a case that will require her presence for most of the afternoon, but if I can be at Osler Street in fifteen minutes, she'll take it from there. Pat, you should come with me."

After the men left, I made copies of Laurel Woodrow's photograph and of the material Colby & Associates would need and brought it all to our home office. Then I sat at our work table and made a list of everyone who might have information that would lead us to Rebecca Woodrow or Steven Brooks and made a few calls.

Zack was hopeful when he returned from his meeting with Debbie. When he said that Patrick's explanation of the circumstances surrounding Rebecca Woodrow's apparent disappearance convinced Debbie that the police should step in, I felt a wash of relief.

"So we're no longer alone," I said.

Esme had rested her muzzle on Zack's lap, and he was scratching her head. "Ezzie, has Joanne told you that on Saturday, we're picking up your new sidekick?"

"That reminds me, I'd better get to Pawsitively Purrfect tomorrow to pick up everything we need to welcome Scout" — I leaned over so I could look into Esme's dark eyes — "and cushion the blow for our friend here," I said.

Zack frowned, "Do you think Ezzie is going to have a hard time with this?"

"She'll be fine," I said. "She misses Pantera as much as we do, and Esme has always had another dog in her life. When she belonged to Lee Crawford, Lee had Gabby, and Gabby and Esme were littermates."

"Okay," Zack said, "I'm reassured. So did you turn up anything interesting?"

"I don't have much to report, just one very strange incident and one apparent dead end that may actually have opened the door to another possibility.

"After you and Patrick left," I said, "I remembered that on Charlie's last show before the semi-hiatus until Labour Day, he interviewed Rainey Arcus about her work as a researcher, especially on the research methods she used for the upcoming biography of Steven Brooks.

"Patrick told us that Rebecca hadn't come upon her grand-mother's papers until the middle of August, but the rumours that Steven might have plagiarized his novels were already out there, and it occurred to me that Rainey might have had calls from people who were eager to share what they believed would interest her."

"Good call," Zack said.

"That remains to be seen. I spoke with Rainey on the phone, and she said she'd been surprised at the number of people who texted her wanting to meet Val so they could fill him in on some 'interesting facts' about Steven Brooks. She said she'd had so many queries that she'd drawn up a form letter, thanking those who'd reached out for their interest and explaining that it was too late in the publishing process to include additional material.

"It sounded as if I'd exhausted that possibility, so I thanked Rainey for her time, and said goodbye. But Charlie's right about her professionalism. A few minutes later, a copy of the form letter and the list of the people to whom Rainey had sent it arrived in my Inbox. Rebecca Woodrow's name was not on the list, but Alma

Hall's was. When my call to Ms. Hall went to voicemail, I left a message introducing myself, explaining that Rebecca's lawyer had told us about Ms. Hall's relationship with Laurel Woodrow and asking if she and I could arrange a FaceTime session to discuss Rebecca Woodrow's apparent disappearance. I haven't heard back, but Ms. Hall might have something."

Zack shrugged. "She was there from the beginning of Laurel Woodrow's relationship with Steven Brooks until it ended, and she's been in touch with Rebecca recently. You could have hit pay dirt."

"Or I could just be spinning my wheels," I said. "Zack, our son is married to Steven Brooks's daughter. Alma Hall might believe I'm on the side of the enemy."

"That's possible, but Anglin Lake is a six-hour drive from Regina, and Leah and Angus are not celebrities. They're two people who are very dear to our hearts, but I doubt that their wedding was a subject of interest to any of Alma's year-round neighbours."

"You're probably right, but if I don't hear from her by tomorrow night, I'm going to email her again and make certain Ms. Hall knows that our only concern is Rebecca Woodrow."

"Since that is the truth, it shouldn't be too hard to convince her," Zack said.

"True, and Zack, there's one other thing — a very strange incident involving Georgie Kovacs and Steven Brooks. Remember Val Masluk mentioning that Georgie and Steven had been an item years ago, when they were both living in New York?"

"I do," Zack said. "I also remember that when you told Val that Georgie was now married to Nick Kovacs, who'd been my friend and poker buddy for more years than either of us care to remember, we all laughed and agreed that it was best to keep that connection buried." Zack had been watching my face. "I take it the subject is no longer buried."

"No, apparently, the relationship is very much alive for Steven. Zack, when Steven behaved so abysmally at the rehearsal dinner, I was concerned that we might get a repeat performance at the wedding, so I called Georgie and asked her for her take on him. She said that they were 'an item' for less than two months; when she tired of hearing Steven wax eloquent about his grandiose plans, she ended the relationship. The break-up had not been acrimonious, but she hadn't heard from him since."

"Right, case closed," Zack said.

"Apparently not. Zack, Georgie called. After you and Patrick left to talk to Debbie, I sent messages to everyone who might have information about the whereabouts of either Steven Brooks or Rebecca Woodrow, asking them to get in touch with me.

"Georgie called, and she had a tale to tell. The morning of Angus and Leah's wedding, Steven arrived at the Kovacses' house on Winnipeg Street."

"What the hell?" Zack said. "How did he even know where they live?"

"Because Nick Kovacs owns a lighting company. He's not in politics, and he's not a trial lawyer. The Kovacs family doesn't get threats in the middle of the night, so their address and phone number are listed."

"Unlike ours," Zack said. "Does that bother you, Jo?"

I moved closer to him. "There's nothing about our lives I want to change. You're the most exciting man I've ever known. I can live with an unlisted address and phone number."

"Then I can too," Zack said. "And for the record, I've never known a woman who excites me as much as you do. But back to the question of the day. Why was Steven Brooks knocking at the Kovacses' door?"

"He wanted money," I said. "Georgie said it was as if the fifteen years between their break-up and that morning never existed. Steven said, 'I need fifty thousand dollars so I can make a new start,' and after that he just stood there on the front porch waiting. Georgie started to explain that she and Nick had a family and she hadn't been doing any writing since Erik was born, so she wasn't in a position to lend him money."

"How did Steven respond to that?"

"He didn't. Georgie said he just turned on his heel and walked away. She didn't tell us about the visit until today because she didn't want to worry us. But when I left the message that we were eager to receive information concerning the whereabouts of Steven Brooks and Rebecca Woodrow, Georgie knew she had to tell us about Steven's visit."

* * *

Once again, we had done everything we could think of, so Zack and I spent Wednesday evening on the patio overlooking the creek, drinking Constant Comment, reading pleasantly forgettable novels and watching the sun set. There was no point in talking about what lay ahead. We needed a respite from the uncertainty and the fears. We both slept well that night and awoke feeling restored and as ready as we could be for what came next.

* * *

THURSDAY, SEPTEMBER 8, 2022

Zack was going to Falconer Shreve for the morning, and he'd invited me to join him for a tube steak and root beer lunch in Victoria Park, which was close to his office. My only plans for the day were to wait for Alma Hall to return my call and visit Pawsitively Purrfect.

Ms. Hall called not long after Zack left to say that she was free for the next hour and that she liked to see people's faces when she was talking to them. She asked if I was familiar with FaceTime; I said yes, and she said she would call me. Within seconds, Alma Hall and I were on our computer screens, face to face.

I hadn't thought much about Ms. Hall's appearance, but it was a surprise. She was deeply tanned and sharp-featured with platinum hair pulled back into a tight bun, shrewd pale-blue eyes and lipstick and nail polish that matched her very revealing cerise halter top.

"Thanks for arranging the call," I said. "I like your top. It must be warmer at Anglin Lake than it is here in Regina."

"Probably not," Alma said, "but from the Victoria Day weekend to September 22, I'm a short shorts and halter top gal." She had the husky contralto of a two-pack-a-day smoker. "But we're not here to exchange weather reports. In your message, you said you wanted to talk about Rebecca Woodrow. So let's get down to brass tacks. I don't mean to be rude, but what's your interest in this, Ms. Shreve?"

"I have a feeling we may be spending a fair amount of virtual time together," I said, "so please call me Joanne." After I explained our relationship with Steven Brooks and our concern that he and

Rebecca Woodrow had both disappeared, I gave Alma a precis of the discussion Zack and I had with Patrick O'Keefe.

"So what was the upshot of this discussion?" Alma said.

"The police are now involved, and the private investigators my husband's law firm uses are actively searching for both Rebecca and Steven."

Alma took a cigarette from a pack of Benson & Hedges and lit it. Her fingernails were daggers. "What does your new daughter-in-law think of her father?"

"Steven was never a presence in her life," I said.

Alma took a long thoughtful drag and exhaled. "She was lucky."

"She was. Steven Brooks is a complex man."

"A complex man with no moral compass," Alma said. "That can be a deadly combination."

"It was certainly deadly for Laurel Woodrow," I said.

"So you know what happened between Laurel and Steven Brooks."

"I do," I said. "And it makes me sick."

Alma didn't respond. For several unnervingly long beats she simply stared at the screen. "I believe you," she said finally. "Faces don't lie. What Brooks did to Laurel makes me sick too. I knew he was using her. I tried to warn her, but Laurel wouldn't hear a word against him. She was my closest friend, but I came very close to losing her friendship. After she died, I found a novel I'd loaned to her in a stack of books on my front porch. There was a note tucked inside. 'None of this is Steven's fault. He did everything he could do to help me, but the proverb is right: you can't make a silk purse out of a sow's ear. Steven is blameless, and he'll be alone. He will need your friendship, Alma. Reach out to him.'"

"And you did not reach out," I said.

Alma's laugh was short and derisive. "That son-of-a-sea-biscuit was gone the next morning. He'd cleared everything out of his cabin. The property was listed for sale the following weekend." Alma stubbed out her cigarette. "Anglin Lake had nothing more to offer Steven Brooks."

I waited while she lit another cigarette. Neither of us seemed prepared to continue the conversation, but I knew I had to try. "I understand that revisiting these memories is painful for you," I said. "However, I still have one question. Why didn't you speak up when Steven Brooks published *Medusa's Fate* as his own work?"

"I was planning to. I knew I'd need someone to guide me along the path to making the truth public, so I consulted a lawyer in Prince Albert. He listened carefully to everything I said, then he told me I did not have a case. I had no proof that Brooks stole Laurel's manuscript. Brooks had taken every scrap of paper from his cabin before he left Anglin. By the time *Medusa's Fate* was published, Laurel had been dead two years. Her cabin had new owners, and her papers had been sent to a daughter who hadn't acknowledged Laurel's existence in years. I had no idea how to find the daughter, and I was convinced that if she had received her mother's papers, she would have destroyed them.

"With no proof, the lawyer in Prince Albert told me if I decided to go ahead with the case, Brooks's publishers would have a team of lawyers who could keep me in court for years and my legal fees would bankrupt me."

"So I did nothing," she said. "And every morning I woke up hoping and praying that I could find a way to give Laurel the legacy she deserved."

"And then along came Rebecca," I said..

"Yes, along came Rebecca, and she not only had evidence that her grandmother had written both *Medusa's Fate* and *The Iron Bed of Procrustes*, she was going to make the truth public on the day *Steven Brooks: A Biography* was published. And now Rebecca has disappeared."

"Alma, we can't give up now. Rebecca's lawyer, Patrick O'Keefe, said that Rebecca sent him a photograph of her grandmother with a note saying 'this is the woman for whom we're going to find justice.' It's too late to save her life, but we can show that, even though she had been shamed and dismissed as worthless, Laurel Woodrow created two exquisite and powerful novels."

"Which that son-of-a-sea-biscuit claims that he wrote," Alma said. "How can Steven Brooks live with himself?"

When I saw the fire in her eyes, I understood the value of FaceTime. If we'd been in the same room, I would have moved closer to her, but we were separated by over four hundred kilometres. The best I could do was offer her words that seemed right for the moment. "Zack says that Steven is a selfish prick and a snivelling coward who ran away on his daughter's wedding day because he couldn't face the fact that the world would soon know the truth about him: that he's a liar, a thief, a hack and a piece of shit."

Alma's laugh, deep, dry and tobacco-cured, was a wonder. "I like you, Joanne," she said. "But I think your husband and I are birds of a feather."

"I think that too," I said. "Let's stay in touch."

"Wait," Alma said. "I did try to do something to reveal the truth about what happened between Laurel and Steven. I'm ashamed to tell you this because what I did was juvenile and cowardly. I was convinced that Valentine Masluk, Steven's biographer, would reveal the truth. Our library ordered an advance copy and as soon as the book arrived, I read it straight through."

"And you noticed that Steven's biographer devoted scant attention to the years between Steven's disappointing third novel and the publication of *Medusa*."

"I noticed, and I was livid. I was certain Valentine Masluk knew the full story and suppressed it, so I wrote emails to the person who was going to interview Mr. Masluk when the book was released and to the director of the School of Journalism, urging them to force Mr. Masluk to tell the full story."

"So, you were 329ff," I said.

Alma's eyes were wide. "You knew," she said. "Why didn't the interviewer or the director do something?"

"I know you'll find the answer unsatisfactory. I find it unsatisfactory too. The truth is that no one knew what to do. The interviewer is my son-in-law, and he did try to ask Valentine about that time, but Valentine refused to answer the question because he feared if he did Steven Brooks would harm himself. The head of the School of Journalism shared that fear."

Alma lit a fresh Benson & Hedges and inhaled deeply. "Well, hell," she said.

I smiled. "That's exactly what my husband would say."

* * *

It was half past ten when I left the house to go to Pawsitively Purrfect. I was in the mood for a leisurely morning, and that's exactly what I got. I chose a large cart and began my stroll. I stocked up on desiccated liver and a product called P-Nuttier puppy treats. It was new to me, but I'd checked the label and noted that the peanut butter was xylitol-free, and the puppy on the package looked happy, so Scout had his rewards at the ready. I chose new dishes for our Bouviers' food and water, new leashes and collars for both dogs and a Ezee-Sleep calming dog bed for Scout that I hoped would soothe him through his first days with us, and then one for Esme, who might end up in need of a little Ezee-Sleep herself. My final purchase would be kibble for the feral cats that lived in the warehouse district where we once lived; I was deciding whether I could fit three large bags of it into my cart when Kam Chau tapped me on the shoulder. "We really do have to stop meeting like this, Joanne," he said.

"Pawsitively Purrfect does appear to be a magnet for us both," I said. "We're picking up our new puppy on Saturday, and I didn't want Esme to feel left out when Scout gets that snazzy red collar and leash."

"So Scout is the name of the new puppy," Kam said.

"Zack's choice, and we both like it," I said. "How are Feng, Mary and Mr. Grant getting along?"

Kam grinned. "Surprisingly well. Feng was an only cat for five years, so her nose was out of joint for a while, and, of course, Mary and Mr. Grant had to adjust to a new owner, a new home and the presence of the lofty Madame Feng, but the three of them seemed to figure out that nobody was leaving so they might as well make the best of it. Cats are pragmatists."

"I'll text that piece of wisdom to Taylor," I said. "She's a great fan of cat lore. I always enjoy talking to you, Kam, and we never seem to have enough time for a real visit. Brewed Awakening is half a block away. Do you have time for coffee?"

"Absolutely. My treat though. I had a terrific time at Angus and Leah's wedding, and that dinner was one of the best meals I've ever eaten."

"I agree with you about the food," I said. "But the bride's aunts picked up the tab for the wedding and the reception. And I have a question that's been nagging at me, so let's make it Dutch treat."

"Dutch it is." Kam put two of the bags of cat kibble in his cart and slid the third into mine. After we'd paid for our purchases and carried them to our cars, we walked over to Brewed Awakening. The café wasn't crowded, so we waited at the counter till our lattes were ready, split the bill and the tip and found a booth at the back.

When we'd settled in, Kam said, "I don't have any new information on Rebecca Woodrow. Zack asked me to let him know about any developments. But I've heard nothing. Have you?"

"Just conjecture."

"In that case, let's get to your question."

I sipped my Chai latte. "Mmm, good," I said. "Now, my question is about Rainey Arcus. Charlie told Zack and me that you had doubts about signing Rainey on as a permanent member of the production team. He also said you seemed reluctant to explain the reason for your uneasiness about her . . ."

Kam looked sheepish. "That's because I'm not sure my reason makes sense," he said. "I like Rainey, and I'm sure Charlie told you what a great researcher she is."

"He did. He said her research is not only thorough, it's edited. Everything extraneous to the questions he might ask is winnowed out, and the material she gives him is interview ready. But Kam, Charlie also made it clear that he trusts your judgment absolutely. He knows you make solid decisions about the people who will work best with the production team, and he says it's your call."

Kam smiled and handed me a napkin. "There's a tiny latte moustache above your upper lip that you might wish to blot," he said.

I blotted and touched his hand. "Only a true friend would tell me that I have a latte moustache."

"I'm glad I meet one of the criteria for qualifying as a true friend."

"You meet all the criteria," I said. "That's why Zack, Charlie and I all value you. The only reason I'm pressing you about Rainey is because you don't make judgments without a reason, and if there's something Charlie D should know about Rainey, he should know it. Let's start with a simple thing. Is your problem with Rainey a personality clash?"

Kam's headshake was vehement. "No. We get along fine. In fact, our birthdays are the same day, October 23, and last fall, Rainey suggested we take each other out for dinner to celebrate. We went to that restaurant on Albert that is continually undergoing name changes —"

"I know the one you mean. The last time I was there it was the Fainting Goat, but whatever its name, the food has always been good."

"And it was good the night we went there. Rainey made the reservations, and she must have alerted the person taking her reservation to the fact that this was a birthday celebration because there was a horoscope birthday book open to October 23 waiting for us on our table."

"That was inspired," I said.

Kam's eyes brightened at the memory. "That book was not only inspired, it was a godsend.

"Rainey and I were work friends, and we didn't know each other well enough to have a real conversation. We took turns reading to each other about what it means to be born on October 23. Joanne, did you know that Scorpio is the most intense member of the Zodiac, and that those born under the sign are able to see deeply into any given situation and cannot be fooled by the hidden motives of others?"

"I didn't know that," I said. "And our daughter Taylor's birthday is November 11."

"Smack dab in the middle of the sign." Kam's lips formed a fraction of a smile. "In that case, there's a great deal that Taylor's family members should know, for example, those born under the Scorpio sign always know exactly what's going on, and they never forget someone who stood in their way."

"Some of those characteristics really do sound like Taylor, but that last part sounds as if Scorpios are ruthless and our daughter is not ruthless. Neither are you." I hesitated. "Kam, do you think Rainey is ruthless?"

Kam splayed his fingers on the table and regarded them thoughtfully. "I've never seen evidence of that, but I do know she's secretive, and now we're getting to the heart of my 'problem' with Rainey. When I took her home after our birthday dinner, I said that the evening had been fun, and I'd like to do it again. Rainey said that she'd like to spend time together again too, as long as I understood that our relationship could never be intimate."

"A platonic relationship," I said. "And you were okay with that?"

"I was. Particularly since she seemed to suggest she was committed to someone else. After our dinner date, Rainey and I went to a Halloween party together. We both hate costume parties, but the host was someone from MediaNation that we both like, so we went together."

"And the two of you went as . . . ?"

"Lois Lane and Clark Kent covering Woodstock in 1969," Kam said. "It was Rainey's idea, and it was appealing. She and I were both journalists, and the concept of Lois and Clark in 1969 was clever. Rainey found a vintage clothing shop here that offered everything we needed, and we had fun shopping together. We both had work obligations, so we agreed to meet at the restaurant where the party was being held."

I gave Kam an assessing look. "I'm trying to imagine you and Rainey in an acre of mud in upstate New York grooving to Janis Joplin."

"The vintage costumes really did transform us," Kam said. He drew a deep breath. "Joanne, Rainey's appearance that night triggered a memory for me. I'd always had a sense that I'd seen her before or knew her from somewhere, but I could never figure out when or where."

"And that night you remembered," I said.

Kam nodded. "Yes, and that's when my uneasiness started. When I've worked with Rainey, her hair has always been pulled back from her face in a bun or — I don't know much about women's hairstyles — just anchored back somehow. The night we went to the costume party as hippies, Rainey wore her hair loose, and it took my breath away. It's almost waist length, white-blond and thick and shining."

"Rainey wore her hair brushed back but loose when she was in my class," I said. "And her hair really is gorgeous. It always made me think of a fairy tale princess's."

Kam sighed. "It's unforgettable, and as soon as I saw Rainey's hair the night of the costume party, I remembered where I'd seen her before. Do you recall that piece Charlie D did on our show about *The Pen*?"

"Of course, *The Pen* was the book the inmates at Prince Albert wrote. Charlie told us that piece was so well received that you were going to use it again as one of the show's summer 'best ofs.'"

"And we did, and it was a hit again. Rainey came to me with a pitch for a follow-up story about the man teaching the class. She said he had committed heinous crimes, but he was now working to reclaim his life," Kam paused. "Joanne, Rainey is thoroughly professional about her work. If some of the research she presents doesn't work for our show, she accepts the decision. But she was passionate about the story of the inmate trying to reclaim his life. I told her it sounded promising, but that our show doesn't do advocacy. She and I went back and forth about it for a few minutes, but she accepted my decision.

"Rainey had not mentioned a name in her pitch for the man working to reclaim his life, but in the research she gave us on *The Pen*, she identified the man behind the project as Tom Kelsoe. I went to the files and found our predecessor Nationtv's coverage of the Kelsoe trial. In all the footage of Kelsoe entering or exiting the courthouse, Rainey is there, hair flowing, wearing one of those bulky knit jackets."

"A Cowichan sweater," I said.

"Right, and it struck me as odd, which is why her image stuck with me," Kam said. "By the time of Kelsoe's trial, nobody still wore those sweaters. Anyway, in the videos, Rainey seems to be very intent on Kelsoe. In one of the clips, he notices her, smiles and waves."

"He must have recognized her from the class he and I co-taught," I said.

"So there's no mystery there at all," Kam said. "Still, Rainey must have thought highly of him to show up when he was being tried for murder. Did she ever say anything to you about him?"

"No, but that doesn't mean anything," I said. "Fifteen years ago, Rainey spoke only when asked a question, and even then it was agony for her to speak."

Kam's eyes narrowed. "That doesn't sound like the woman I know."

"Rainey has changed," I said. "Val Masluk wrote a novel about the circumstances surrounding the two murders Tom Kelsoe committed. That was a dark time in all our lives, but by the time Val hired Rainey as a researcher, she was strong enough to go to the penitentiary in Prince Albert and interview Kelsoe to get his perspective."

"This is the first I've heard about a novel," Kam said.

"It's just been privately published, and there are only a hundred copies. Val gave both Zack and me a copy. Val calls almost every night. I'll check with him, but I'm sure he wouldn't mind if you read it."

"Jo, do you think I should just let this whole thing go and tell Charlie that I'm fine with hiring Rainey full time?"

"No. Don't do anything. Not yet. Let me follow up on this." I stood. "I should get moving. I'm supposed to meet Zack in Victoria Park for lunch."

"Say hi to him for me. Jo, I'm glad we had this talk."

"So am I." The hug I gave Kam was a warm one, and when it ended, he said, "For further reference in your dealings with Scorpios, always remember that the scorpion is the only creature that will sting itself to death rather than be captured."

CHAPTER TEN

From the time I arrived in Regina, two marriages, four grown children and five grandchildren ago, I had treasured Victoria Park. During Zack's one term as mayor, he had enthusiastically supported any and all efforts to make this park in the centre of our city a place where people could skate together in winter; listen to readings, attend music festivals and watch performance art in spring, summer and autumn; and visit the farmers' market that ringed the park from well before the 24th of May weekend until the snow flew.

The city planners had nailed the concept of making the park a gathering place for us all, regardless of ethnicity, sexual orientation or demographics. But the hope that visitors drawn by the pleasures of the old park would linger downtown and shop in the boutiques and department stores in the area had not come to fruition. Cornwall Centre was now a relic, and many of the storefronts that once housed flourishing shops and restaurants now stood empty.

The moment I saw my husband in shirtsleeves, sitting in his wheelchair near the hot dog stand, the tensions of the day evaporated.

Zack beamed when he saw me. "Ready to get in line and place our order?"

"I am," I said. "I'm starving."

We took our food and drinks back to the bench near the play structure that Zack had claimed by tossing his suit jacket over the seat. When we'd settled in, my husband raised his hot dog. "In the pigeon's words when he finds the hot dog . . ."

"It's 'a celebration in a bun!'" my husband and I said in unison. "Zack, how many times over the summer have Colin and Charlie asked us to read that book to them?"

"Every time we had hot dogs," Zack said. "By the end of summer, Colin and Charlie were reciting the story to us. But now it's time to start the celebration and dig in. We have tube steak with all the trimmings, and these buns have been toasted on the not-entirely-grease-free griddle. Let's not let our meal get cold."

When we'd finished, Zack said, "Are you up for another one?"

"Any other day, I would be," I said. "But Zack, there's a problem that we have to deal with immediately. Early tomorrow evening is Simon's birthday party, and there has been so much going on that I haven't bought his present. Any ideas?"

"I've taken care of it. I thought I told you this, but seemingly not. Last spring, Simon admired that between-seasons jacket I have. He said he could use a jacket like that because most often the pictures he wants are outdoors, and the weather is unpredict-able. So, I called Annie to get Simon's size and Norine ordered the jacket. It's gift-wrapped and in my office."

"Well done," I said. "Norine, really is the best, isn't she?"

"She is, and every time I try to tell her that, she changes the subject."

"That's Norine," I said. "I was so happy to see her really enjoying herself at Angus and Leah's wedding."

"I noticed that too, and I was relieved because, through no fault of her own, Norine's been under a lot of pressure, and it's taken its toll. I can talk about this now, since the problem with Partner X has reached the point of no return."

"That sounds ominous."

"It's not good," Zack conceded. "Nonetheless, it's always best to have everything out in the open so that all concerned know exactly what they're dealing with. Anyway, quite by accident, Norine discovered that Partner X had been dipping into clients' trust funds."

"Couldn't they get disbarred for that?"

"Partner X could and should be disbarred," Zack said. "They have been skimming the trees for over a year — nothing that the Law Society had to be notified about, but several times I've had to advise Partner X to straighten up and fly right. Initially, I was sympathetic because when I was young and started skimming the trees in court, Ned Osler would invite me to stop by his office after work for a glass of Glenfiddich and some gentle but firmly delivered advice. Partner X's defalcation cannot be remedied by Glenfiddich. That, however, is a problem for another time. How was your morning?"

"Informative," I said. "Alma Hall and I FaceTimed. Steven Brooks would be well-advised not to meet Alma in a dark alley. When I told her what you said, about his being a selfish prick and a snivelling coward — and a lying, thieving piece of shit — Alma said that she and you are birds of a feather."

"Should I take that as a compliment?"

"Definitely. Zack, if you ever feel your ire towards Steven Brooks cooling, Alma told me something that should bring it back to a hard boil. The morning after Laurel took her life, Alma found a note Laurel left her, asking Alma to 'reach out' to Steven because he did everything he could to help her and, when she was gone, he would be so alone."

"I take it Alma did not *reach out*," Zack said, and his tone when he spoke the words "reach out" was venomous.

"No, she told me that the 'son-of-a-sea-biscuit' had cleared out his cabin and left Anglin very early the next morning. According to Alma, Steven had what he wanted, and he was getting out while the getting was good."

Zack snorted in disgust. "Alma's right. She and I are birds of a feather. Anything else to report?"

"Yes. Another piece to the puzzle seems to have surfaced, but I don't know where it fits. I ran into Kam Chau at Pawsitively Purrfect. After we finished shopping, we went for coffee and Kam told me something about Rainey Arcus that he finds perplexing. She and Kam share the same birthday, and last fall Rainey suggested they take each other out for dinner to celebrate."

A group of very small children in green and yellow T-shirts were being led to the park's play structure by a young woman whose eyes never left her phone. "Stay away from the big slide," she said, and then, her duty discharged, she continued texting.

Zack was watching me closely. "Take a deep breath," he said. "As a lawyer and the man who loves you, I have to advise you that what you want to say to that negligent young woman will get you in hot water."

"Do you see the name of the daycare centre that employs that negligent young woman? It's written on the children's T-shirts."

"Precious Ducklings," Zack said. "The irony does not escape me."

At that point, a young man, sweaty and breathless, ran up and joined the woman. "Sorry I went AWOL," he said. "I had to take a leak."

"Father Duck to the rescue," Zack said. "A happy ending. So, how did the dinner date go?"

I took the deep breath Zack had suggested and continued. "Kam said they had a great time. When he drove Rainey home, he asked if she was interested in another date. Rainey said that she was interested, but that Kam should know that she was already in a relationship and that she honoured that commitment. Any further dates would have to be simply time shared with a friend. Kam was fine with that, and they did have one other date."

Zack raised his eyebrows. "Just one?"

"Yes, because on that date, Kam had an epiphany that stirred up the unease that he still feels about Rainey. She had invited him to a Halloween costume party, and they decided to go as Clark Kent and Lois Lane covering Woodstock."

Zack snorted, but remained silent. I continued. "When you and I saw Rainey at the wedding, her hair was in a chignon. According to Kam, that's the style she prefers when she's working — pulled back. For the costume party, Rainey wore her hair loose. It was white-gold and almost to her waist. Kam said that he'd always had the sense that he knew Rainey from somewhere, and when he saw her hair that night he remembered where he'd seen her before.

"He had been the cameraman for Nationtv's coverage of the Kelsoe trial. The morning after the costume party, he went to

MediaNation and checked the old videos. In all the footage of Kelsoe entering or exiting the courthouse, Rainey is there, hair down, wearing her Cowichan sweater.

"Rainey had not mentioned a name in her unsuccessful pitch to do a segment about the convict working to reclaim his life, but in the research she gave Charlie D on *The Pen*, she identified the man behind the project as Tom Kelsoe."

Bemused by the vagaries of the human comedy, Zack shrugged. "So, tomorrow night we will be dining with one of the young women who stood outside the courthouse in the rain, holding up a heart-shaped sign imploring us to 'Free Tom Kelsoe'?"

"I'm not certain Rainey went that far, but Kam did say that in one of the clips, Kelsoe recognizes her and smiles and waves."

"Ever the gallant," Zack said.

"Kam asked me if I thought he should let bygones be bygones and tell Charlie he was fine with hiring Rainey as permanent researcher."

My husband's eyes widened. "And . . . ?"

"And I asked him not to do anything until I followed through on the possibility that there was still a connection between Rainey Arcus and Tom Kelsoe."

"We know from Val Masluk's book that Rainey began writing to Kelsoe not long after he was incarcerated, and that, later, she did the research on Kelsoe for *Two Journalists*. Jo, none of that is secret."

"I know, but Zack, I've thought this through. Rainey Arcus was always adamant about keeping her private life private, and the fact that she was willing to *publicly* support Tom Kelsoe is a red flag for me. The media was obsessed with that trial, and the people reporting on the trial represented the media outlets Rainey would be approaching about positions that would advance her career. By looking like a groupie for a murderer, Rainey put her future at risk. Zack, this may seem like a stretch, but I think the person with whom Rainey has a committed relationship is Tom Kelsoe."

"Who, as we speak, is serving a twenty-year sentence at the penitentiary in Prince Albert."

"True, but remember the Saskatchewan cabinet minister who was convicted of murdering his wife?"

"Of course I remember that. I was in my first year at the College of Law, and that trial was topic A for months."

"Well, eleven years after the cabinet minister was sent to the maximum security facility in Edmonton, he and his bride were married in the prison chapel," I said. "Zack, I'm going to call Val and ask him if there's a chance I might be right about the man in Rainey's life."

Zack drew a deep breath and exhaled slowly. "So you're playing a long shot."

"It won't be the first time," I said. I took my husband's left hand in mine and tapped his wedding ring. "And my long shot has never lost a race."

* * *

I called Val's cell from my parking space near Victoria Park. He was in a cab en route to an interview, so he was able to talk. He said the book tour was going well and asked about Rebecca Woodrow. After I told Val that both the police and Colby & Associates were now searching for her, we agreed that all we could do was take comfort from knowing that everything that could be done was being done and hope for the best. Then I shifted topics.

"Do you remember Kam Chau?" I said.

"Of course. He produces Charlie D's show. I didn't spend much time with him, but he seems like a good guy."

"He is a good guy. In some ways, he's a lot like you, Val. He's smart; he's sensitive and he's intuitive. Anyway, I had a conversation with Kam today that left me with a possibility that may lead nowhere, but might answer some vexing questions."

"If I can help, ask away," Val said.

I gave him a precis of my conversation with Kam and then took the plunge. "Val, you worked with Rainey for three years — did she ever say or do anything that would suggest that she is in a committed relationship with Tom Kelsoe?"

When Val remained silent, I said. "Are you still there?"

"Yes, I'm here. Sorry, that question knocked the wind out of me. I'll have to give it some thought, but two things leap out at me. Rainey gave me the 'committed relationship' speech too, and it came out of nowhere. I hadn't asked her for a date or made a move that would suggest I was interested in her romantically, but she still felt the need to establish the boundary. Joanne, she and I worked at my house on the acreage, and she often stayed overnight in the guest room. Close quarters, but in those three years, the only detail that suggested that she even had a relationship at all, other than her insistence that she was in one, was that she was adamant about never working weekends."

"And she never explained why she had to have her weekends free?"

"She never had to," Val said. "Rainey's private life was none of my business. I concluded on the basis of no evidence whatsoever that her lover was married and that weekends were the only times he was free to be with her."

"Nothing else?"

"I don't think he lived in Regina, but that's just a guess," Val said. "A couple of times when the weather was bad, Rainey called to say the highway was a skating rink and she'd be late getting out to my place."

"You and Rainey must have discussed Tom Kelsoe when you were working on *Two Journalists*."

"We talked about Tom Kelsoe a lot," Val said. "Rainey thought the character I created in the first draft was two-dimensional, and that the novel would be stronger if I developed the Kelsoe character more fully."

"Meaning more sympathetically."

"Yes, and she was right. Rainey's research revealed details about Kelsoe's past that I hadn't included in the early draft of the manuscript. When I added those details, the Kelsoe character did become more relatable and less like the devil incarnate."

"From my vantage point, Tom Kelsoe *was* the devil incarnate," I said. "But Rainey was always dedicated to presenting the whole story. Remember that paragraph you all had to write about what you hoped to gain from the Politics and the Media class?"

"I remember that assignment well. We all read each other's submissions. Most of them, including mine, were cookie-cutter generic, but Rainey's submission was specific and articulate. Rainey wrote that her goal was to become a journalist committed to providing Canadians with 'dimensional journalism,' which she defined as 'telling the story behind the story, fully, fairly and accurately.'"

Val took a long pause. "Joanne, all I can say is that Rainey impressed me then, and she still does."

CHAPTER ELEVEN

When Annie and Warren Weber brought Maeve home from the hospital, they knew that their two-storey house with a great room, a winding staircase and a meticulously landscaped backyard with a swimming pool was no longer the right home for them.

The Webers began house-hunting. Nothing seemed quite right until they spotted a listing for a house that, like ours, looked out on Wascana Creek. The owners were not planning to move until August, but the Webers spent most of the summer at their cottage, so they were willing to wait. They had been in the house for a little over a month, and the party to celebrate Simon's birthday would be their first chance to entertain.

Warren always made certain the Webers' guests were picked up and returned home by the family's driver, and it was a thoughtfulness Zack and I welcomed. As a rule, we took turns deciding who would be the designated driver, but it was a pleasure not to have to forgo our pre-dinner martinis.

The gift-wrapped box with the jacket was in Zack's lap when he rolled up the accessibility ramp and rang the Webers' doorbell. The party was a celebration of Simon's birthday, but it was also a belated house-warming, and I was carrying our gift for all the members of the Weber family: a framed portrait of Maeve with her parents right before Leah and Angus's wedding reception.

Getting Maeve Weber, a wiggly eight-month-old girl, to sit quietly on her mother's lap and exchange an adoring gaze with her father who, in C.S. Lewis's memorable phrase, was still "surprised by joy" at the miracle of his daughter, was a challenge, but Simon was up to it. He told me once that the secret to taking a great photograph was, simply, waiting for the right moment. At the reception he had been watching the Webers together, and when that moment arrived, he snapped. The result was a photograph that I knew Annie, Warren and, some day, Maeve would treasure, and I had chosen an antique chased silver frame that Zack and I both felt would complement the photo.

Simon met us at the door. Zack shook Simon's hand and gave him his gift. "Happy birthday," my husband said. "It's been a good year for you, and this next one seems to be off to a promising start." The emotion in Zack's voice was genuine. Simon had been an associate at Falconer Shreve when his last and worst breakdown occurred. Zack and Warren had been friends for years, and Simon, an excellent student whose dream was to practise trial law, had been much sought after when he was called to the Bar. When Simon chose Falconer Shreve, Zack was thrilled, and when, after his hospitalization, Simon came to Zack and said that he and his therapist agreed that the high stress level of trial law would always work against Simon's recovery, my husband wholeheartedly supported his decision.

In an uncharacteristically boyish gesture, Simon held the gift-box to his ear and shook it. "This sounds promising," he said. "I've been concerned that I might have overdone all those pointed hints, Zack."

Zack grinned. "Time will tell," he said. "But rest assured, all those pointed hints reached their mark."

Newly minted mothers acquire a useful skill. Like ninjas, they can suddenly appear from nowhere, and immediately assess the situation. Annie Weber materialized with Maeve, demure in a rosebud pink eyelet sundress, in arms. When the baby spotted her big brother, she was ebullient.

"Look, Maevey, more presents!" Simon grinned. "It's my lucky day."

I handed Maeve and Annie the gift-wrapped photograph. "This is a house-warming present," I said to the baby. "Would you like to help mommy unwrap it?"

Maeve looked up at her mother. When Annie nodded, Maeve pulled at the paper, and with Annie's help revealed what was inside.

When she saw the photograph, Annie's voice was soft with pleasure. "Warren is going to treasure this — we all will."

I'd been watching Maeve. As she examined the photograph, her small face was pinched with concentration.

"Simon took the picture," Annie said to her. "So he was behind his camera."

Her mother's explanation seemed to cut no ice with Maeve. She pointed to the spot between Warren and Annie and her brow furrowed.

It was a stand-off, but Zack was smooth. "Don't fret, Maeve. I'll take as many pictures of you and Simon with your mum and dad as you want."

Simon was clearly delighted by Maeve's apparent assertion that no photograph of the Weber family was complete unless he was a part of it. "The way my baby sister just stood up for me may well be the best birthday present I'll ever receive," he said.

Annie smiled. "She definitely has a mind of her own."

Zack was thoughtful. "Annie, neither you nor Warren is exactly a pushover," he said.

"The nut doesn't fall far from the tree?" Annie said, jogging the baby on her hip and eliciting a burble and smile.

"Something like that," Zack said equitably. "Time to join the others, I can smell the charcoal."

* * *

Simon made Zack and me martinis and, drinks in hand, we followed Annie and him to the party.

Warren, Mieka, Charlie D and Rainey were clearly in high spirits.

"Warren just gave us blow-by-blow instructions on how to slow grill a rack of lamb," Charlie said. "The chef at the Scarth Club has advice that offers us all words to live by." He turned to his wife. "Mieka, you're the culinary expert in the Dowhanuik family . . ."

Charlie and our daughter had known each other since they shared laundry hamper–bassinets at political events when they were weeks old, and when her husband passed the ball, Mieka was quick on the uptake. "The chef says, 'Remember always that a fast roast is a lamb's enemy.'"

When Rainey turned to greet Zack and me, she was relaxed and radiant. "This is such a great party," she said. "It's been a long time since I laughed so much." She had come a long way from being the withdrawn young woman who sought refuge in her oversized Cowichan sweater, and I found myself hoping that my long-shot theory would not pay off.

"Zack and I are glad for this chance to get to know you better," I said. "We've both read Val Masluk's novel, *Two Journalists*. It's terrific, and his praise for you in the acknowledgements is wholehearted."

"He's overly generous," Rainey said. "I'm a researcher; I just did what I was hired to do."

"Val and I have kept in touch while he's on the tour," I said. "When I mentioned that we'd be seeing you tonight, he said that *Two Journalists* is a stronger book because of your work."

Zack was skilled at steering a conversation towards a destination that he believed would be profitable. "Jo tells me that you urged Val to give the Tom Kelsoe character depth by showing how his life was driven by the pain he experienced as a child," he said. "As a lawyer, I recognize the need to place the charges against my clients into context. To reach a just verdict, jurors need to understand how my clients were shaped by their past experiences. Val heeded your suggestions, and now readers are free to make their own judgments."

Charlie leaned forward and held his hand up in a "halt" gesture. "Time to rewind the tape," he said. "Where's all this talk about a novel coming from? My interview with Valentine Masluk aired Monday. It was long — twenty minutes long to be exact — and in those twenty minutes, there was nary a mention of a novel."

"*Two Journalists* was privately published, and there are only a hundred copies," Rainey said.

Charlie was incredulous. "I don't get this at all," he said. "Jo and Zack say the book's great. Why isn't it available to the public?"

"I agree," Rainey said. "But Val is the one you have to convince."

"Oh, I will," Charlie said. "Jo, will you be my backup? Val says that you saved his life. He'll listen to you."

"You've never needed a backup, Charlie," I said. "But I will speak with Val. *Two Journalists* deals with a subject that needs to be talked about — our obligation to acknowledge the needs of others and do what we can to meet those needs. More and more, it feels as if we're living in the world of 'The Second Coming.'"

"A world where 'The best lack all conviction, while the worst / Are full of passionate intensity,'" Warren said, and his powerful bass resonated with the certainty of a person who sees the world for what it is. When Annie looked at Warren questioningly, he took her hand. "'The Second Coming' is a poem written by William Butler Yeats. We can read it together and talk about it before we go to bed."

Annie's eyes took the measure of the rest of our small group, and she was quick to explain. "Warren always says he and I complete each other's education. I finished high school, but that was the end of my formal schooling. I found a job at Wheelz, the biker bar that I was managing when Warren and I met, and I was content. But Warren opened the door to another world for me."

"And Annie opened the door to another world for me," Warren said. "And that world is a garden of delights."

"One of the best parts of our day comes when we're ready for bed and we read a poem together and talk about what it means," Annie said. "It's exciting — like watching a bud turn into a flower."

When my glance shifted away from the Webers to Rainey Arcus, I was taken aback by the longing in her eyes. She had always been zealous about guarding her emotions but, at that moment, what I saw in her eyes was real. She wanted the kind of love the Webers had.

* * *

When Halima Ahmed brought out Simon's birthday cake, she did it while expertly balancing Maeve on her hip.

"Yes, it's cake time," Halima said to the baby. "And then Simon gets to open his presents and you can help him, and then you and I are going to say goodnight to everyone and have our singing before bedtime." Halima adjusted the dusky pink silk hijab that I knew was Annie's favourite. "This is a special occasion for all of us." Few words, but in Halima's low musical voice, they conveyed a truth that was a source of joy for both the Weber family and her. They belonged together. They were family.

The circumstances that brought the Webers and Halima together were serendipitous. For over twenty years, Halima had been the housekeeper for Mike Braeden and his late wife, Sylvie, then his second wife, Patti. The Braedens and the Webers were neighbours, and when Halima, a nervous driver, asked Annie if they could grocery shop together, the two women became friends. After Mike Braeden decided that the house on University Park Road held too many memories for him and he was ready to join the old friends who had moved to Victoria, he told Halima that the retirement fund he had set up was more than ample to cover a very comfortable retirement for her.

When Halima told Annie that she was grateful for the retirement fund, but that she wasn't ready to stop working, Annie swooped in. She asked Halima to move in with the Webers and help with the new baby they were expecting. Within a week, Halima had moved into her self-contained first-floor suite, and within two weeks, she and the Webers knew they'd all found their happily-ever-after.

After Simon blew out his candles and we had cake, Halima took charge of the task of bringing presents from the gift pile to Simon with his baby sister. The first gift they brought was the one Maeve, herself, had created. Simon took great care with opening her gift, and when the super-sized, finger-painted poster board birthday card emerged from beneath the wrapping paper, he was wowed. "Maeve, you've just knocked my socks off," he said. "This is spectacular!"

As indeed, it was. Simon's sister was not a minimalist. Her work was bold and very busy. Heavy blots of primary colours had been combined in whorls of non-toxic easy-clean paint, dragged across the poster board by tiny hands, with "I love you — from Maeve" written in red crayon at the card's centre.

The presents from the rest of us paled in comparison with the painting, but Simon was pleased with everything. Charlie and Mieka had given him two pairs of Italian leather driving gloves. The pairs were identical, a gentle nod to Simon's proclivity to lose one of his gloves. Annie and Warren had given Simon a one-of-a-kind hand-spun wool watch cap made by a knitter in Corner Brook. The blue of the cap was the exact shade of blue of the Weber's other gift to their son, a new Range Rover. The between-seasons jacket we gave Simon was a hit, but the real hit of the evening was Rainey's gift, the book of horoscopes. She presented it with pizzazz. "On my last birthday, I had dinner with a friend who shares my birthday," she said. "When I made the reservations, I mentioned that this was a double celebration. A copy of this book was on the table when my friend and I arrived. He and I didn't know each other well, but we read our birthday horoscope to each other and that seemed to break the ice. Simon, the book is open at the horoscope for those born on September 9. May I read it aloud?"

Simon looked dubious. "I'm not sure that's a good idea," he said.

"I think we'd all enjoy hearing it. I read it before you picked me up. It's very favourable, and, in a lot of places, I think it might be right on target."

"All right, but if you read mine, I get to read yours."

"Absolutely. Turnabout is fair play," Rainey said. "Now, here's what your horoscope says. Virgos born today are family oriented. You have a way with you that makes you desirable to others. Strong and confident, you are a person people look up to.

"You have a natural ability to notice the detail that others might miss, and you use that natural ability to create. You are highly motivated, and although you may not have essential goals in place, you will find success in attaining most of your dreams.

"You love your family and want one of your own. However, you are slow to commit, but you will find the right partner eventually. Take your time. Only fools rush in."

When she finished, Rainey moved towards her place beside Simon, but he was already on his feet applauding her, and soon we all joined in.

Simon read Rainey's October 23 birthday horoscope. I remembered many of the comments from what Kam told me. Simon read the line about Scorpio being the most intense member of the Zodiac, but he omitted the reference to Scorpios born on October 23 never forgetting anyone who stands in their way, and I was relieved. The rest of the horoscope was very favourable, and Simon also finished to applause.

The public reading of horoscopes had caught on. By the time Simon was back in his place, Mieka was already on her feet. "I'd like to read Charlie's horoscope," she said.

"And I'd like to read Mieka's," Charlie said. "But no pre-reading for us. We're ready for a walk on the wild side. And because Mieka's birthday is on the 11th, that's the day before mine, I get to read first."

"Actually, I get to read first," Annie said. "Warren's birthday is the same day as Mieka's, and he was blowing out candles on September 11 long before she was."

Maeve had begun to flag as the grown-ups continued to read horoscopes. We had come to Warren Weber's reading of Annie's horoscope, which was respectful and loving; as soon as he finished, Halima brought their daughter around to say goodnight to everyone.

Inspired by the little one, it seemed we all had stories to tell about caregiving, and the conversation moved from children to pets. When Simon noticed that Rainey hadn't said anything, he asked her if she'd ever had a cat or a dog. She shook her head, and said, "I never felt the need." On that enigmatic note, the conversation shifted to other topics.

It was a good party, but like all good things, the evening came to an end. Simon would be driving Rainey to her apartment, so when the Weber's driver arrived to take Mieka, Charlie, Zack and me home, we all said our goodnights. Before our car pulled away, I turned to wave goodbye. Warren, Annie and Simon were beaming, but Rainey looked as if she were close to tears.

***

As usual, Esme was waiting at the front window to welcome us home. Zack leaned over to give her a pat and said, "Only one more day until Scout comes home," and then he held his hand out to me. The fact that I always carried a baggie of desiccated liver in my purse delighted Zack, and he counted on it being there. I handed him the liver; he gave it to Esme, and the three of us headed for the bedroom.

But not, as it turned out, to get ready for bed. Zack pushed his chair to the place by the window where we often talked at the end of the day and motioned me to join him. When I settled into the rocking chair that faced him, Zack said, "What's bothering you?"

I didn't attempt to brush off the question. "Rainey Arcus," I said. "She took such delight in everything tonight. It was as if everything that happened was something she was experiencing for the first time."

"I was struck by that too," Zack said. "I don't think Rainey has had much companionship in her life. From what you've told me, she's come a long way from the painfully shy girl hiding inside her Cowichan sweater."

"She *has* come a long way. Rainey set a goal for herself, and she reached that goal. And I'm certain that she did everything on her own."

"It can't have been easy for her," Zack said.

"I'm sure it wasn't. Just as I'm sure that it wasn't easy for you. I know that when you were in law school, you had mentors and you found the four people who eventually became your law partners and closest friends. But when you hit law school, you had already breezed through grade school, high school and university, and you did it all on your own. You are a self-made man."

"And Rainey is a self-made woman," Zack said. "She had a dream, and she became the person she needed to be to realize that dream."

"And there's the rub. Tonight, when Annie and Warren were talking about the pleasure they take in talking about poetry together, there was real longing in Rainey's eyes, and I wondered about the price Rainey paid to realize her dream of becoming a 'dimensional' journalist. A colleague of mine in the political science department told me once that the priest who prepared her for her first communion said, 'Take whatever you want from life. Take it, but be prepared to pay for it.'"

Zack grimaced. "A brutal lesson, but one we all have to learn. Often by the time we learn it, it's too late to change course because we still have to pay that debt. Jo, how old would your friend have been when the priest told her that?"

"Probably seven or eight."

"Whoa! That priest played hardball. But your friend remembered the lesson. Did knowing that we have to pay for what we take make her life easier?"

"I don't know, but I do know that Solange had some difficult decisions to make along the way, and she had no regrets."

"And you think that tonight when Rainey saw the joy all of us find in our relationships, she began to experience regret?"

"Yes, that's exactly what I think." When my phone rang, I saw that my caller was Alma Hall.

"I have good news," she said. "FaceTime me. I'm at home."

Zack's look was questioning. "It's Alma. She wants me to FaceTime her. Come to the office with me. It's time you met her."

"I'm looking forward to it. Lead the way."

* * *

Alma's bubble-gum pink halter revealed even more of her deeply tanned cleavage than its cerise predecessor had. With her platinum blond chignon and the graceful plume of smoke from her cigarette drifting lazily from her pink lips, there was no denying that Alma Hall was a knockout.

"Zack's with me," I said. "Is that all right with you?"

"It's perfect," she said, "because I also have a guest. Rebecca Woodrow is here with me, and she's eager to talk to you."

* * *

The digital photograph of Laurel Woodrow revealed her delicate Dresden doll beauty. Her granddaughter had the same porcelain complexion, shining black hair and a graceful mouth, but there was determination in the set of Rebecca's jaw, and her cobalt blue eyes were knowing.

"Thank you both for everything you've done to help me," she said. "My lawyer, Patrick O'Keefe, and I are both very grateful. The last couple of days have been difficult, and I'm very tired, but I wanted you to see that I'm fine and to tell you and Alma exactly what's happened since the morning of Wednesday, September 8.

"I went to the gym for my usual 7 a.m. workout. After I'd showered and changed into the outfit I'd planned to wear for my video meeting with Steven Brooks's publishers and their lawyers, I returned to the gym parking lot. When I opened the door to my car, there was a shot.

"The neighbourhood where my gym is located is deserted at that time of morning. I was certain that the person who shot at me would try again, but I thought I might deter them by driving into a more densely populated area. I headed downtown and drove around side streets until I was relatively certain no one was following me. I have university friends in Saskatoon, but as my mind cleared, I realized I might put my friends in jeopardy, so I kept driving north.

"By the time I arrived in Prince Albert, I was hungry and exhausted. I checked into a hotel, ordered lunch from room service then took a long nap. As soon as I woke up, I went down to the lobby to get directions to the nearest bookstore. I purchased a copy of the Steven Brooks biography, and then I picked up some toiletries and enough clothing to get me through the next day.

"After I'd finished the book, I knew I needed to be with Alma. So here I am.

"I've talked to Patrick, and we've made some plans. Tomorrow morning, I'm flying back to Regina. I won't need a car in Toronto, and Alma has invited me to stay with her whenever I need a break from the big city, so I'm leaving my car with her.

"After I talk to the police, I'll meet with Brooks's publishers and their lawyers. I'm taking the Monday evening flight to Toronto, and Joanne and Zack, I'm hoping we can have brunch, lunch or whatever before I leave. Thanks to you three and Patrick, when I arrive in Toronto, I can move into the digs I've already rented and start the classes for which I've already registered."

Rebecca's voice broke. "I apologize for the tears," she said. "I really am tired, and the last two days have been a nightmare.

"Thank you all so much for everything you did for me — a stranger. Steven's biography showed me the face of evil. I needed to see other faces. I'm glad the four of us were together. Goodnight."

Alma rotated the screen towards her. "I'll say goodnight as well. It's been a long day, but in my opinion, it's been a very good day."

"Couldn't have been better," Zack said. "Thanks for letting Joanne and me be a part of it."

CHAPTER TWELVE

SATURDAY, SEPTEMBER 10, 2022

As promised, the weekend weather was sunny but with a bracing nip of chill in the air, a reminder, if we needed one, that it was time to unpack warm socks and woollen sweaters.

Zack and I arrived at the acreage at a shade after nine, but by then, Maisie, Peter and the boys had been at Neil's for close to an hour, and Maisie said that Neil had used that time to teach Charlie and Colin what they needed to know to help Goldie become the best dog she could be.

After our puppies had a romp with their remaining littermates, Neil reminded us that the next few days were the time when Goldie and Scout learned what their lives would be like with their new families, so we should spend plenty of time with them. The twins were holding Goldie as if she were spun gold, and Zack was beaming as Scout licked every millimetre of his face. I took Neil aside and whispered, "Look at them. Don't worry about Goldie and Scout, they're in loving hands."

"Thanks," Neil said. "That will make it easier to say goodbye."

* * *

Margaret McCallum had been silent but clearly proud as she watched her son give Goldie to the boys and Scout to us. When two cars pulled up outside, Margaret said, "More new owners. Puppy pickup day is always busy." She had been watching her son's face closely as he said goodbye to Goldie and Scout. "It's also a very emotional day." She came over to me. "Joanne, I should give Neil a hand, so I wonder if you could do us a favour. I was just about to take a loaf of sourdough next door. Bread's at its best when it's just come out of the oven, and Valentine's place is on your way back to the highway. Would you mind dropping the bread off?"

"Of course not. But I thought Val would be on his book tour for another two weeks."

"He will be. The bread is for Valentine's friend. He's staying there while Valentine is away. I just want to be neighbourly. Valentine has supper with us every so often, and he always brings wine. Neil says he thought only people on television had wine with their dinner." Margaret chuckled. "He likes to tease me."

"My sons like to tease me too," I said.

"Then we're both lucky. Now I'd better get that bread while it still has that good 'just baked' smell."

* * *

Margaret had given Zack and me a loaf of our own, so heading to the car, Zack had the bread on his lap, and I carried Scout. It was a pretty terrific moment, and we were both still glowing as I pulled into Val's driveway.

When I knocked at the door and no one answered, I tried again. When there was still no response, I gave up on handing Val's friend the bread when it still had that "just baked" smell and began looking for a place where I could simply leave it. At that point, the door opened, and I was facing Steven Brooks.

In the past few years, the word "surreal" has been used so often it has lost its meaning, but seeing the man whose fate we had all been agonizing over standing in the doorway of the farmhouse where only days ago Zack and I had enjoyed a Ukrainian feast with Val Masluk was surreal. Neither Steven nor I moved. Seemingly we were rooted motionless, in our respective spots, with Steven staring at his sourdough loaf, and me staring at Steven.

He looked terrible, pale, exhausted and beaten down. "Leave me alone," he said, and he tried to close the door. Like the travelling salesman in the old jokes, I stuck my foot out to keep the door open. "Steven, you need help," I said. "We can't drive away and leave you alone when you're like this."

"I'm always alone. That's how I create," he said. "Don't tell anyone where I am. That's a warning."

Steven's warning frightened me, but it also angered me. We had all been catering to this "son of a sea biscuit" for far too long. I straightened my spine, squared my shoulders and plunged in. "Steven, our son and your daughter are now husband and wife," I said. "Like it or not, that makes us family. That's our car in the driveway. Zack's in that car, and he's almost certainly recognized you already."

"Then it's already too late for me," Steven said. "What happens next is your fault." This time, I was savvy enough to pull my foot away, and Steven slammed the door shut and slid the lock.

I was trembling when I got back to the Volvo. Scout was out of his travel kennel and onto Zack's lap. When he spotted me, my husband's grin was sheepish. "Scout woke up, and you were chatting with Val's friend. I didn't want Scout to feel alone, so I sprang him."

When he looked more closely at my face, Zack's smile faded. "Jo, what's wrong?"

"The friend staying at Val's place is Steven Brooks. Steven said that if I told anyone where he was, I would be responsible for what happens next."

Zack's lips were tight with anger. "What the hell? Jo, you're looking a little shaky. Why don't you get into the back seat with us. You can hold Scout, and I can hold you."

I was more than a little shaky, but the warm strength of my husband's arms and the smell of puppy breath worked their magic, and after five minutes of coddling, I was restored. "Thank you both," I said. "I'm ready to drive now, and it's time we went home and introduced Scout and Esme."

* * *

Introducing Scout to Esme proved to be remarkably uncomplicated. Bouviers are a giant breed, and at the dog park, small dogs always gave Esme a wide berth. Scout's mother belonged to Neil, so Scout was accustomed to full-grown Bouviers. After following Esme around for a while, Scout stood in front of the footrest of Zack's wheelchair and within seconds, he was on Zack's lap.

"Should we divvy up the list of who needs to be told that Steven has been found?" I said. "I can tell Mila and Reva. They're worried sick. They'll want to know where he is. I'll tell them I promised Steven I wouldn't reveal his whereabouts, but knowing that he's in a safe place will be a relief for his sisters-in-law."

Zack adjusted Scout's position on his lap and took out his phone. "I'll call Debbie and Bob," he said. "Debbie won't be happy that she can't question Steven Brooks, but Rebecca did some nimble stick-handling on that point. Her argument that Steven was too absorbed in his legacy to take a shot at her was persuasive. And Rebecca's safety has to remain our priority until we work out what's going on."

"Until then, I guess we all just stay put and hope for an outcome we can live with," I said. "It's still nice enough to sit outside, so let's take our books to the patio and watch the dogs frolic." As it turned out, the dogs were not in a frolicking mood. Esme was content to flop down next to me and watch Scout sniff around. Scout decided Zack's lap was more interesting than sniffing, so it wasn't long before he was back where he felt he belonged, and Zack could not stop smiling.

Over the summer, Zack and I had discovered Richard Russo's novels. The works were not new, but they were new to us, and they had riveting characters, solid plots and enough clever dialogue to keep us sharing lines. The afternoon passed so peacefully that it was almost possible to believe that, once again, God was in His heaven and all was right with the world.

When martini time arrived, we decided we were too lazy to cook, so we ordered a pizza from the Copper Kettle and made plans for the next day. There was church in the morning, and Mieka and Charlie had invited us over to a barbecue to celebrate Mieka's birthday.

Our third event for Sunday was more in the nature of a project. From the moment Neil McCallum decided we needed a dog and Scout was ours, Zack had become determined to master the art of walking Scout while he, himself, remained in his wheelchair. He'd already checked out a number of YouTube videos that would show us what we needed to do.

We were both excited about the idea. Zack had never been crazy about the fact that I walked the dogs alone, early in the morning when there weren't many people around if I needed help, and I was in favour of any activity that had Zack filling his lungs with fresh air and keeping his blood pressure down.

* * *

Angus and Leah's red Subaru pulled in just as the pizza van pulled away. The newlyweds looked rested, refreshed, radiant and very happy.

"Perfect timing," Zack said. "And out of habit, I ordered an extra-large pie."

"And it's Leah's favourite: feta, spinach and black olives. We even have a bottle of Sauvignon Blanc that's very nice with it."

"No wine for me, thanks," Leah said. "But rest assured, not a sliver of that extra-large pie will be wasted."

* * *

Angus apologized for having to eat and run, but they were planning to stop by to see Leah's aunts before they went back to their own place, and Sawyer and Lorelei were taking them to Mercury Cafe and Grill for breakfast the next morning.

Angus and Leah may have been rushed, but they had time to fill us in on the latest from Lawyers Bay. Magoo's had added a Veggie Grill Burger to their menu. Leah said it was tasty, but Angus, who had once eaten a thirty-six-ounce ribeye in our presence, was sticking to red meat. The Point Store had already changed the vinyl tablecloths in Coffee Row from their summer checked blue-and-white to an autumnal pumpkin shade. Morris's aged yellow retriever's rear end had "gone kerflooey," but Morris was hauling his old dog around in a wagon and Morris and Endzone were both content.

Before they left, our son and our new daughter-in-law got down on the floor to snuggle with Esme and Scout. More moments to treasure.

Zack and I stood on the front porch and watched until the red Subaru disappeared. "That was a nice surprise," I said.

"Did you notice that Steven Brooks's resurfacing was not mentioned?" Zack said.

I moved closer to him. "I noticed," I said. "And I was relieved. Leah and Angus didn't have long for a honeymoon, they deserve every drop of joy. And there are more good times to come — we'll be together again at Mieka and Charlie's."

"Do you know what I want to do now?" Zack said.

"I don't," I said, "but the day just caught up with me, and I hope whatever you want to do involves minimal physical movement."

Zack was thoughtful. "That's up to you. I want us to sit on the couch and make out."

"Okay with me, but Scout will have to get off your lap," I said. "Do you think he'll be okay with that?"

"Sure," Zack said. "We're both guys, and guys understand that guys have needs."

* * *

Making out had never lost its charm for Zack and me, and as we got ourselves and then the dogs ready for bed, we were both quietly content. Esme flopped into her Ezee-Sleep without urging, but Scout had other ideas. No matter how often Zack placed him on his bed, he jumped out and looked longingly at the footrest on Zack's chair. Finally, I had a thought. I took the bag of P-Nuttier puppy treats off my dresser and handed it to Zack. "Rustle the bag a little," I said. When Zack did, Scout hopped into his bed and waited. Zack took out a treat and that did the trick.

We had finally gotten into bed when my phone rang. I checked the caller ID. "Jill Oziowy," I whispered. "I'll take my phone out to the hall."

Jill was never big on small talk. "You were slow on the pickup. Did I interrupt something?"

"No, we were just giving our new puppy a P-Nuttier treat to encourage him to sleep in his own bed."

Jill snorted. "Jo, sometimes I wonder if you and I even inhabit the same planet. You live in a world of P-Nuttier treats and puppies, and I live in a world of sharks who lust for my job but know squat about exactly what my job entails."

"You appear to have come out of the last crisis intact."

"Appearances can be deceptive, but that's enough about me. I finally scored some answers about a possible connection between Rainey Arcus and Tom Kelsoe. Hang onto your tutu, Jo . . . Rainey and Tom are married."

"Wow, since when?"

"They've been married for five years, but they've been together since she started writing to him shortly after his incarceration. She began visiting him regularly. The prison authorities felt Ms. Arcus brought stability and structure to lover-boy's life, so they encouraged the relationship. Our journalist can't pin down the exact date when Rainey Arcus and Tom Kelsoe were allowed to have PVRs. As a rule, an inmate gets one seventy-two-hour private family visit every other month, but Tom Kelsoe has been such a shining member of the community that he gets a PVR every month, so Tom and his missus have seventy-two hours a month to be conjugal. The prison employee our journalist spoke to said that Tom is an exemplary inmate and that he is certainly a candidate for early probation."

Seemingly there was nothing ahead for Rainey but blue skies. Still, the knowledge that Tom Kelsoe was a candidate for early probation filled me with dread. I had seen what Kelsoe did to Jill Oziowy, and the memory of his sadism made me fearful of the darkness that was ahead for Rainey Arcus.

CHAPTER THIRTEEN

When Esme and I stepped outside to start our morning run, Zack and Scout were already in the backyard. Zack was in his wheelchair and, not surprisingly, Scout was on his master's lap.

I kissed Zack on the top of his head. "You do realize that one day in the not-so-distant future, your lapdog is going to weigh forty kilograms," I said.

Zack was sanguine. "Scout and I have already talked that through, and we've moved along. Tonight's video on walking your dog from your wheelchair focuses on the importance of mutual trust, so we're getting a head start. By the way, there are macadamia nuts on the table for your porridge."

"A bribe," I said. "But when it comes to macadamia nuts, I'm easily bought."

* * *

Adding macadamia nuts makes porridge, that staple of my boarding school life, sublime. While we ate, Esme stayed next to me on the floor, and Scout stayed next to Zack. Perfection.

When he finished eating, Zack pushed his chair back from the table. "Thank you, Jo, Esme and Scout, for this great start to the day."

I was reluctant to puncture my husband's enthusiasm for what came next, but breakfast was over. It was time for serious conversation, and that meant telling Zack about Jill Oziowy's jaw-dropping discovery.

Zack listened attentively as I explained the relationship between Rainey Arcus and Tom Kelsoe. When I finished, Zack was thoughtful. "If a client came to the office with a story that was beyond comprehension but true, Fred C. Harney would see them out and after the office door was closed, he'd say, 'Well, that was certainly a corker,' and then he'd pour himself a drink and take out a pen and legal pad and come up with a way that would make the corker of a story work to our client's advantage." He smiled. "Luckily, we don't have to come up with a way to make this corker palatable to a judge or a jury. As Jill pointed out, Rainey and Tom have broken no laws. We might as well just get on with our day."

"Before I forget, Patrick O'Keefe called to invite us to join Rebecca Woodrow and him tomorrow for an early lunch before she leaves and starts her PhD in Classics at U of T."

Zack's brow furrowed. "What does a PhD in Classics involve?"

"You asked the right person — I just looked it up online. It is a five-year program. The first three years are spent in classes and

227

seminars studying Latin and Greek, reading classics and doing research that will support her dissertation. At the end of the third year, Rebecca will have to demonstrate proficiency in one of those languages and working knowledge of the other. Then she'll have two years to complete and defend her dissertation."

Zack was thoughtful. "A PhD in Classics was Laurel Woodrow's dream, wasn't it?"

"It was, and it's good to know that Rebecca will realize that dream."

"So what does she have at the end of those five years?"

"A PhD in a field that she loves, and the world's her oyster."

"What are her job prospects?"

"The world is a very big oyster. Rebecca will be fine, Zack, and like you, she will love her work."

"Okay," Zack said. "You've allayed my fears about Rebecca's future, so back to the present. Tomorrow morning at nine thirty, she and Patrick will meet with Brooks's publishers and 'other interested parties' to discuss how best to deal with the tangled mess Steven created. They've all agreed that the news needs to be made public immediately, and Rebecca and the publisher are making a brief video statement explaining the situation. Pat said that he and Rebecca would be very happy to have you at the meeting."

"And I will be very happy to be there."

"So I guess before church you talk to Patrick about tomorrow's meeting and I call Kam, Val and the Webers to tell them about Rainey Arcus and Tom Kelsoe. And after church we go to the Dowhanuiks' for a barbecue."

Zack rubbed his hands together. "Good times!"

"Very good times," I said. "So let's remember to give thanks for that when we're in church."

* * *

Over the summer, Zack and I attended church in Fort Qu'Appelle, and there was a real sense of homecoming when we walked into St Paul's Cathedral for the ten thirty service that morning. It was a special day for our family. In addition to being Mieka's thirty-seventh birthday, and the day before Charlie's thirty-seventh, Colin and Charlie, who would be turning six on September 29, would be making their debut as servers.

When Zack and I arrived, the twins, faces shining, copper curls freshly cut and tamed, robes neatly tied, had already taken their places in the processional. The dean of the cathedral encouraged congregants to take pictures of meaningful moments, and the members of our family had their cameras at the ready. Madeleine and Lena, who'd been servers since they were the twins' age, were giving the boys some last-minute coaching as they waited for the processional hymn to begin. As Colin and Charlie passed our pew, Zack was quick to hand his hanky to me. For years, I'd watched our children and now our grandchildren process up the aisle to the altar and seeing them in their white robes always made my eyes fill.

Mieka was sitting beside me, and when I pointed out the line on the church bulletin that read "Flowers on the altar today are the gift of Joanne and Zack Shreve in thanksgiving for their daughter, Mieka," this time it was our daughter's turn to use Zack's hanky. "And they're gerberas," she whispered. "My favourite."

When I looked down the pew at our family and at the altar where, miraculously, Colin and Charlie seemed to be performing the tasks they were given, the text Dean Mike chose for his homily seemed right on point. It was from Psalm 118: "This is the day the Lord has made; let us rejoice and be glad in it."

* * *

The day my late husband, Ian, and I brought Mieka home from the hospital, the snow that had started the weekend before Mieka's birth was much in evidence. This September 11 was more benevolent, and we were able to eat outside. Mieka had been a caterer before she opened her café play centres, and she had prepared a tempting array of salads.

Charlie D was barbecuing a rolled prime rib roast on the spit. I'd recently read that campfire remains from a South African cave suggest that fire control by humans dates back a million years, and the control of fire had important social and behavioural implications, encouraging groups of people to come together for warmth and shared meals. When I looked over at the barbecue where my son-in-law was presiding, I noticed that Zack, Peter, Angus, Charlie and Colin — observing some deep atavistic urging — had come together to watch the slow rotation of the roast on the rotisserie and that even Des, who had just turned two, knew that when meat was cooking, he belonged with the men. When I pointed this out to Maisie, Leah and Mieka, they shook their heads. "It's probably been that way for as long as we've made fire," Maisie said with a wry smile. "And if we were to point that out to our menfolk, they would get huffy."

My single criterion for a successful birthday party is that no one cries. There were no tears at Mieka's party and there was plenty of laughter. The food was great, and Mieka received some thoughtful gifts, including a vintage earthenware vase filled with gerberas from the Webers. Mieka had made matching birthday cakes for herself and Charlie D — who didn't like a big to-do, but whose birthday was the very next day — and she had added Warren's name alongside hers in piped icing. She had been planning to surprise her birthday twin with a cake of his own, but the Webers were at the lake and unable to attend this joint celebration, so we sent snapshots, and Warren said he enjoyed the photos of their cake almost as much as would have enjoyed the real thing.

After "Happy Birthday" had been sung, and even Charlie D had been compelled to blow out his candles, Zack and I were ready to leave. Mieka hugged us both hard and said how much she loved both of us. Now it was Zack who needed a hanky. It had taken a while for Mieka to warm to Zack, and her reasons for being concerned were legitimate. His reputation was daunting. He was a brilliant but ruthless lawyer, a womanizer, a gambler and a person who drank too much and drove too fast. I did not ask him to change, and he did not ask me to change. But we loved each other deeply, and we valued what we had too much to risk it. And so, in changes that were never spoken of and barely perceptible, each of us became what we needed to be to make our marriage work. And for both of us, the almost ten years we'd been together had been the best years of our lives.

Zack was quiet as we drove home, and I knew Mieka's words had moved him. When we pulled into our driveway, he put his arm around me. "It just keeps getting better doesn't it?"

"It does," I agreed.

Lunch had been great, but I knew Zack and I would be hungry again by dinnertime. I took a casserole of macaroni and cheese from the freezer; remembering that we had some very nice late tomatoes in the garden, I knew we would have a good dinner and an easy one. As it turned out, Zack and I would be grateful for that easy dinner, because our lives suddenly went into overdrive.

None of the people I had called that morning about Rainey's marriage to Tom Kelsoe were home, but, except for Val Masluk, they had sent emails responding to my news. As I read the emails it became clear that I was the only one who was rocked by the news that Tom Kelsoe and Rainey Arcus were husband and wife.

Annie Weber's note was long and effusive in its praise for Rainey. Annie wrote that when Simon drove Rainey home after the barbecue, she told him that spending an evening with three couples who found such fulfillment in their marriages convinced her she would be selfish to take up the time Simon could be using to find a partner who would bring him a lifetime of joy. She then enumerated the many gifts Simon could bring to a relationship. Rainey told him that she was married to a man she loved, but she and her husband couldn't be together often, and there were times when she was lonely and that she hoped she and Simon could continue to be friends.

Annie said that she and Warren had been impressed with Rainey's honest explanation of her situation and with the way in which she attempted to convince Simon that he was a man who deserved a woman who could give herself to him completely. Annie said that she and Warren had picked up on Rainey's sadness the night of the party and that they were hoping that they could become Rainey's friends too.

Kam Chau was simply relieved to learn the truth about Rainey's marriage. He wrote that he embraced Jill's recommendation that MediaNation offer Rainey a permanent position as a researcher; he thanked me for passing along the good news and said he'd call Charlie D and give him the go-ahead.

By four thirty, I still had not heard from Val, so I texted him, asking him to phone when he had time. He called just after I'd put the mac and cheese in the oven. He had news of his own, and it was disturbing.

As someone who once earned a living doing live interviews with writers, publishers and other book people, Val had learned how to keep personal emotion out of his public voice, but as soon as I heard him on the phone that afternoon, I knew he was hanging on by a thread. "Joanne, I need your help. Steven Brooks called this morning. He knows he's going down for the third time, but he believes he can save himself. He wanted me to draft a press release that, in his words, will reveal once and for all that Steven Brooks is the true author of *Medusa's Fate* and *The Iron Bed of Procrustes*.

"He didn't dictate what the press release would say, but he told me to write down the points I needed to guide me. One: acknowledge that Brooks worked on the first two novels with another writer. Two: establish that the other writer's contribution was minimal and that Brooks, himself, 'did the lion's share of crafting both novels.' Three: state unequivocally that the other writer died before either *Medusa* or *Procrustes* was published and that, since her input had been negligible, there was no reason to connect her with the published novels."

As Val spoke, I felt sick, because I knew what was coming at Steven and I knew he had no way out. "Val, you didn't write that release, did you?"

"No, of course not. And I tried to tell Steven that issuing that press release would destroy the vestiges of his legacy that still exist. He slammed down the phone and said that he'd do it himself because he always has to do everything himself. I've been trying to get back to him all day, but he isn't answering his phone. I thought Rainey might be able to drive out there, but it's the weekend, and she's always out of town on weekends."

"I know Steven's staying at your place," I said. "Is there someone close by whom Steven would listen to?"

"Steven has long since stopped listening to anybody," Val said.

"Well someone has to get through to him. Val, at nine thirty tomorrow morning, what Steven did will become public. Laurel Woodrow's granddaughter, Rebecca, has already shown the original manuscripts of both novels to Steven's publishers."

Val's sigh was weary. "I guess that's the final nail in the coffin. It was very early when he called — seven o'clock here, so that would have been five o'clock in Saskatchewan. I tried to call him back a few minutes after he hung up on me. I was hoping against hope that he had cooled down. But Steven is no longer capable of cooling down. I had interviews all morning, a reading this afternoon, and I have a live TV interview tonight. I've tried all day to get in touch with Steven, but he won't answer his cell, and when I call the landline at my place, there's no answer.

"Joanne, I know Steven is delusional. For longer than I want to admit, I've known that Steven did not write those novels alone. I gave the years between Steven's third novel and *Medusa's Fate* short shrift because I knew that disclosing the facts about what really happened would destroy him. He did me a great honour by choosing me to be his biographer . . . I had already betrayed two good people, and I couldn't face the consequences of betraying a third."

"I understand," I said. "I know you need help dealing with Steven. Steven's sisters-in-law and his daughter live here in Regina. It's an hour's drive to your place. Any of us would be willing to make the trip, but to be honest, I'm not certain Steven's still at your house.

"On Saturday, Zack and I picked up our new pup from the McCallums'," I said. "Margaret asked me to take a loaf of the bread she'd just made to the 'friend' who was staying at your place, who, of course, turned out to be Steven. He was in terrible shape when I saw him, and desperately afraid of being found. I think it's possible that now that he knows Zack and I saw him at your place, he's no longer there."

"I'm afraid of that too," Val said. "And I know I'm grasping at straws, but it's a relief to know that you're all willing to do what you can." Val sounded defeated, and knowledge of a defeat ahead is something no one wants to carry into a live TV interview. I had seen Val when he was on the edge before, and once was more than enough to make me seize at a possible solution.

"Val, here's an idea. Margaret and Neil McCallum are ten minutes away from your house. Let me call Margaret and ask her to stop by your place after dinner. That will probably be within the hour, so you might know before your interview?"

Val's laugh was short and mirthless. "No such luck," he said. "I'm in the green room right now, waiting to be shepherded into the studio. But it would be good to know, regardless . . . I'll be finished in an hour or so, and I'll call you then. Thanks, Joanne, and please thank Margaret. She's someone else I can always count on."

* * *

As soon as I hung up, I called Margaret McCallum. After telling her how much pleasure Scout was bringing us, I explained the situation and asked if she could check and see if Steven Brooks was still staying at Val's. Margaret didn't hesitate. She said that she and Neil were just about to sit down to dinner, but she'd get back to me as soon as she had news.

And she was as good as her word. Zack and I had just finished our first helping of mac and cheese and were deliberating the wisdom of having another when Margaret called, and she did not sound like herself.

"I think I need a lawyer . . . Could you and Zack help me?"

"Of course. Margaret, what's happened?"

"Val's friend — the one who was staying at his house — is dead. There's blood — so much blood. He has no pulse, and he's cold to the touch. I knocked, but when there was no answer, I tried the door. It was unlocked, and I came in. I was a nurse for over thirty years. I know the man in the chair is dead, but I can't just walk away. I've called a neighbour to go to our place and stay with Neil, and I've called 911, but I don't know what to do next."

"Zack and I will be there as soon as possible. Meanwhile, try not to touch anything, and when the police arrive, ask one of the officers if you could have a cup of tea with plenty of sugar."

"I'll do that." Margaret was beginning to sound more like herself. "It will be better when you and Zack get here."

My husband had pushed his chair closer to me. "What's going on?" he asked as I was hanging up.

"That was Margaret McCallum. Steven Brooks is dead. When she went over to Val's to check, she knocked at the door. There was no response, so she walked in. Margaret said she was a nurse, and she knew immediately that Steven was dead. She's called 911, so the police will be on their way, but she wants help with legal counsel. I told her we'd be there."

"We should be there soon," Zack said. "But when police are investigating a sudden violent death, it's hard to predict how long we'll be there." He paused. "Jo, do you think it was suicide?"

"According to Val, Steven was planning to write a press release acknowledging that a second writer had worked on both *Medusa's Fate* and *The Iron Bed of Procrustes*, but the second writer's contribution had been negligible and since they died before the publication of either novel, Steven saw no reason to acknowledge their minimal involvement in the creation of the works.

"Val said he tried to explain that Rebecca Woodrow had already sent Steven's publishers copies of her grandmother's original manuscripts, but Steven refused to listen. He was convinced his press release would blow the naysayers out of the water — he didn't sound like someone on the brink of ending his own life. Zack, do you think somebody decided to blow Steven out of the water?"

"We'll know soon enough. Crime scenes are always harsh reminders of the cruelties of which we are capable."

* * *

Val Masluk's once welcoming farm kitchen was now a hive of activity. RCMP officers wearing gloves, booties and hair coverings were taking measurements and photographs, bagging evidence and collecting blood samples and fingerprints. Everyone had a job to do, and everyone carried out their tasks purposefully and efficiently.

As the only person in the room who didn't have a job to do, Steven Brooks, slumped over the kitchen table in a pool of his own blood, seemed oddly out of place. Even Margaret McCallum, sipping tea and answering a police officer's questions, was actively involved.

She brightened as she saw us, and I went to her. Margaret explained that I was there to provide moral support, and the police officer pulled up a chair for me and reminded me to let Margaret do the talking.

Zack was not loved by officers of the law, but they did respect him, and when he explained his connection to Steven Brooks, the officer in charge of the investigation began filling him in on what they knew so far.

After twenty minutes, it was clear we had served our purpose and the time had come to let the professionals get on with their work. Margaret had regained her composure but was uncertain if she was ready to drive, so I drove her home in her car. We talked about the plans she and Neil had made for fall, and she said one of them would be to train the new puppy that had come their way after the couple who'd planned to buy her decided to get a divorce.

Margaret mentioned Steven's death only once. She said there'd been a note beside Steven that the police had, at first, assumed was a suicide letter. Margaret said what Steven wrote was a quote from Henry James about writers working in the dark.

When she apologized for not remembering the rest of what James had written, I said, "Steven used that quote before. It's 'We work in the dark — we do what we can — we give what we have.' I agree that it sounds like a suicide note. What caused the police to change their mind?"

"Steven died from *three* gunshot wounds to the head, and the police are searching, but so far they haven't been able to find the gun."

"Margaret, there's not much Zack and I can do on this end, but when the police have taken Steven's body to the forensic pathologist for the autopsy, please give us a call. There's a deep-cleaning service that Zack's firm used a few years ago when there was a violent incident in their offices. The service is very good. If you'll let us know when the time is right, we'll get the cleaners out here."

Margaret sighed. "That's a great relief for me," she said. "I wasn't looking forward to cleaning that room, but I couldn't live with myself if I let Val come home to *that*."

When Zack pulled up behind us at the McCallum's, Margaret and I both went over to the car. Margaret again thanked us both profusely, and we promised to stay in touch.

When I slid into the passenger seat, Zack held out his arms. "How are you doing?"

"I'm okay, and I'm very glad we came out here. Margaret is strong, and she's handling things well, but tonight she walked into a nightmare. I asked her to call us when Steven Brooks's body is taken to the forensic pathologist for the autopsy and the police are finished with the crime scene. I said we'd send out that deep-cleaning company Falconer Shreve used and have them take care of Val's place," I said. "Did you pick up on anything?"

"Not much, except that the missing gun pretty well rules out suicide. That aside, I'm no expert, but even I could see that there's no way Steven would have been able to fire two more shots into his head after the first bullet went in."

"So, whodunnit?"

"I haven't a clue," Zack said. "And that is a problem for the police to solve, not for thee and me."

"Thank heavens because our dance card is filling up quickly. I'm going to call Angus when we're closer to the city and ask him to break the news about Steven to Leah and then invite the aunts to our place so we can tell them what we know. And then there's going to be those massive legal problems you mentioned when the possibility of plagiarism reared its ugly head."

Zack squeezed my knee. "One day at a time," he said.

"Right," I said, "but one more task on this day. I have to call Val and fill him in."

* * *

When I told Val that Steven was dead, his first impulse was to come back to Regina. I told him there were no reasons for him to come back and many reasons he shouldn't. The first was professional. If Val came back to Regina, he would simply be part of the story about Steven's death; but if he carried on with the book tour, he could continue to promote *Steven Brooks: A Biography* at a time when interest in Steven's life would be high.

Val agreed that his best option was to do what was best for the book. He asked me to give Leah and her aunts his condolences and tell them he would be in touch with them very soon. It was a good decision, and I was relieved that he hadn't asked me about the circumstances of Steven's death.

* * *

Reva and Mila Drache were already in the family room when Zack and I came in. So was a tray with ice, six glasses and bottles of both soda and Glenfiddich. After we exchanged greetings with the dogs, Angus poured everyone a drink. There were five customers for Glenfiddich; Leah chose soda.

After Zack and I gave accounts of what we had learned from the police during our time at Valentine Masluk's, there was surprisingly little to say. Reva pointed out that while Jewish law requires that a person be buried within twenty-four hours of death, Steven's life had not been guided by Judaism, so there was no rush to make arrangements. And given the circumstances of Steven's death, Leah and her aunts agreed that whatever service they chose should be private and simple.

CHAPTER FOURTEEN

When Esme and I came back from our morning run, Zack was sitting at the kitchen table. He was wearing one of the beautifully tailored suits that I always thought of as his lawyer clothes. Scout was on my husband's lap, but the evening before had been hell for us both, so I skipped an expression of opprobrium, nuzzled Scout, kissed Zack and poured myself a glass of orange juice.

I was gathering thoughts about how to get through the day when Zack turned his chair towards the hall. "Just after you and Esme started on your run, Norine messaged me saying that Maisie and I have a meeting with Partner X and their lawyer at seven thirty."

"And that's in fifteen minutes. Want me to drive you?"

"Would you mind?"

"Not at all. That gives me fifteen minutes more with you. These days, I take what I can get."

"'These days' are at an end. I'm planning to go back to the office after lunch and take care of everything that needs to be taken care of. Then I'm all yours. We could both use a few days at the lake."

"I could always use a few days at the lake," I said. "So, you go straight from hashing out the exit situation to hashing out some kind of agreement between Rebecca Woodrow and her lawyers and the publishers and their lawyers? Lots of potential for tension there."

"Yeah, but the end is in sight. By the time I meet with Pat, the problem with Partner X will be resolved."

"So the deed is done, and Partner X is now Former Partner X?" I said.

"It *is* done as far as Falconer Shreve is concerned but not as far as — hell, I can say his name now — it's not over as far as Rick Warner is concerned. He refuses to clear out his office."

"I understand," I said. "The big glass desk, all those carefully chosen complementary shades of brown on the walls and in the furnishings, and that asparagus green ceiling. It's a very spiffy setup."

Zack's eyes widened. "You've seen Richard's space?"

"And I've met Richard," I said. "I know he's in Sean Barton's old office. The day I saw him, Richard was one happy guy. He showed me his new digs and said it was the office he had always dreamed of having in the law firm he'd always dreamed of being part of."

"Then he should have kept his sticky fingers out of the clients' funds," Zack said.

"How much did he take?"

"Fifty thousand dollars, and now the firm has to put that money back."

"I gather Richard has not put any of that money aside for a rainy day."

"No. He's a gambler, and gamblers believe the only course open to them on a rainy day is to gamble because winning will make the rain go away."

"First Sean was in that office, and then Richard," I said. "You should get an Elder in to smudge the space before anyone else moves in."

Zack leaned forward. "How exactly does smudging work?"

"Well, it's a ceremony for cleansing people or a place, so there are prayers. The Elder lights a sacred medicine, like sweetgrass, and directs the smoke around the room, praying for the negative energy to leave and for the positive energy to remain."

"Having an Elder smudge that office is not a bad idea," Zack said. "If Richard Warner has to be forcibly evicted, negative energy will not be in short supply. I can think of six young lawyers who deserve to move into that office, but they might be spooked by its history. We now have three Indigenous associates. Explaining the smudging ceremony to their colleagues and helping them understand how the smudging is cleansing would be a boon to us all."

"You have Ernest Beauvais's number."

"I do, and I plan to use it. We need Ernest to hold a smudging ceremony not just in the ill-fated office at Falconer Shreve, but also in Val Masluk's kitchen. When Val gets home, he'll be dealing with his own demons, he doesn't need negative energy adding to his burden."

"You're really a good guy," I said. "Call me when your meeting is over. I'll pick you up, and we can go to the restaurant together."

＊ ＊ ＊

When I got home, I showered and dressed, and then I packed warm clothes for us both and perishables from the fridge, carried everything out to the Volvo and then went back inside to reread *Two Journalists* while I waited on Zack. Georgie was right when she said the novel had the potential to be developed as a six-part series, and I was soon jotting down ideas. When Zack called and said the meeting was almost over, and he'd be ready in fifteen minutes, I changed, freshened my makeup and picked up the car keys. I was on my way, but a blue hatchback was parked behind our Volvo in the driveway, and Rainey Arcus was standing beside it.

"Hi," I said as I made my way over to greet her. "What's up?"

I felt the change in her immediately. The confidence Rainey had shown since we'd been reunited was gone. Like the young woman I'd taught years ago, Rainey seemed chronically unsure. She was looking past me, towards the house, and her gaze was piercing. "Where is he?" she said.

"Zack? He's downtown. He had a meeting, but it's over."

"You're lying," she said. Rainey didn't seem angry. In fact, she didn't seem to be feeling anything. "Val said the meeting was starting at ten thirty, and it's ten thirty now." Her voice rose. "I have to stop that meeting. This can't be happening."

"But thanks to Daylight Savings Time, it has happened," I said. "When Val told you the meeting was at ten thirty, he should have indicated that was Eastern Daylight Time. Saskatchewan is on Central Standard Time, so that's eight thirty here."

"I was supposed to be the one to make the announcement that Steven plagiarized Laurel Woodrow's work."

"I was talking to Val last night. He didn't mention anything about any arrangement."

"He didn't know," Rainey said. "It was *our* plan."

"Yours and Tom's," I said. "Rainey, I know that you and Tom are married."

My words seemed to bounce right off her. Rainey had her own narrative, and she was sticking to it. "If I was the one to announce the plagiarism, MediaNation would see me as the courageous young journalist who revealed the truth. Tom says I could make MediaNation rethink their decision about telling Tom's story fully and fairly."

"Kam Chau told me you wanted to do a piece on Tom Kelsoe working with his fellow inmates to redeem himself. Kam said that the idea had promise, but that *Charlie D in the Morning* doesn't do advocacy."

"Kam Chau could be replaced," Rainey said flatly.

My pulse quickened. "Rainey, I have to go pick up Zack. If I'm not there soon, he'll know something's wrong."

"Tom will be disappointed in me, and that's the worst. He's done everything for me, and I can't do this one small thing for him. That's how he'll see this. Then he'll withdraw his love."

"Rainey, please, just back your car out of the driveway so I can meet Zack?"

"The love Tom and I share is unique. Our love knows all and forgives all."

"Then it can't be withdrawn," I said.

"You're wrong. It can be withdrawn if you fail the other person."

"Does Tom ever fail you?"

Rainey's eyes lost their focus. "You should have known better than to ask me that."

I started to apologize, but Rainey was too quick for me. She slapped me hard across the face, and while I was still reeling, she slapped me again, this time with such force it made my eyes water.

She glared at me and said, "I weighed the worth of Tom Kelsoe's contribution to the world against Kellee Savage's. It was simple, really. He had everything to offer, and Kellee had nothing. An easy choice."

Somehow, I managed to keep my voice steady. "Rainey, I have to leave now."

"Then leave," she said.

"I can't. Your car is parked behind mine. It's blocking me."

"That Jaguar on the street is yours. Drive it."

I hadn't driven Zack's Jaguar in five years, but the tendrils of panic were spreading. I had to get away from Rainey Arcus, so I started towards Zack's car.

As I passed Rainey's hatchback, I glanced in. A dry cleaner's clear plastic bag was on the passenger seat, her Cowichan sweater inside.

My heart was pounding. I turned to check the driveway. Rainey was on her phone with her back to me. When I looked more closely at the plastic bag, I noticed the note pinned to it, a cartoon of a droopy eyed basset with a printed message: "We're sorry. We did our best." And beneath this, a handwritten note read, "Apologies, we couldn't get the bloodstain completely out. We're all sorry about your cat."

At Simon's party, Rainey said she had "never felt the need" for a pet. There had never been a cat, but there was blood. The realization that the blood on Rainey's sweater must be Steven Brooks's was a body blow. For a few seconds, I couldn't move. But Rainey was coming towards me, and she must have known I'd seen the sweater. I ran to the Jaguar and managed to unlock it, but before I could jump in, Rainey was beside me. She grabbed my arm, and for a few seconds we stood face to face. Finally, she said, "I know what you saw, Dr. Kilbourn, and what happens next is on you. You were there when it started."

When she turned away and went back to her car, I jumped in the Jag and floored it.

In the early years of our marriage, I loved driving the Jag. I'd always owned solid, sensible cars, and there was a kick-ass pleasure in sliding into the driver's seat of something sporty. As I started downtown, the prospect of ever again experiencing kick-ass pleasure was inconceivable, but muscle memory is a much-underrated gift, and that day my muscle memory kicked in.

Patrick O'Keefe's office was in the same tower as Falconer Shreve, so I pulled into Zack's parking spot and called 911. I gave them our address and said that if there was a blue hatchback parked in our driveway, the driver should be called in for questioning. If the car wasn't there, the police should find the blue hatchback because the person driving it had murdered Steven Brooks. Then I called Zack and told him I was waiting.

I'd done what I had to do. Suddenly, I was very tired. I slid over to the passenger seat, leaned against the headrest and tried to think through the possible consequences of what I had just done. But the possible consequences were myriad, and my thought processes were muddled, so I gave up.

When Zack arrived five minutes later, he peered in at me quizzically, opened the door on the driver's side and started the process of transferring his body from his chair to the car. When the chair was stowed in the back seat and he was beside me, he looked closely at my face. "Something's happened," he said.

"Yes, it's nothing to do with the kids or the dogs. It's Rainey Arcus. I just found out that she killed Steven." Then I started at the beginning and told my husband everything that had happened from the time I encountered Rainey in the driveway to that moment.

When I was finished, he took my hands in his. "Last night and now this. It's been too much, but, Jo, we'll handle it. Let's go home."

"I'm not ready yet."

"I understand that, but the police will be there, and they'll want to talk to you. I'll be with you and when the police are finished with their questions, we'll go back to being us again. Let's cancel lunch — Rebecca Woodrow has just been through a stressful meeting herself and will understand. We'll take a swim, then I'll make martinis and we'll order in. What are you in the mood for?"

"Fish and chips," I said. "There are days when only grease and salt will do."

"True grit," he said, and he smiled and hugged me hard.

"So the worst is over?" I said.

* * *

I had cautioned my children hundreds of times about making blanket statements of optimism that are catnip to the vengeful fates. And now the vengeful fates had heard my words. They were at the ready, and they pounced.

When we turned onto our street there were at least half a dozen squad cars parked in front of our house. Zack pulled over and for a few minutes we simply tried to take in what was happening. When another squad car pulled up and officers carrying cameras and the paraphernalia that's necessary for investigating a crime scene got out and moved towards Rainey's car, I said, "Why do the police need all this to take Rainey in for questioning?"

"They don't," Zack said. "Debbie's there too. When did you call 911?"

"As soon as I parked at Falconer Shreve."

"So, on the outside, twenty minutes ago. Something else must have happened. We're not getting out of this car. I'm calling Debbie."

He and Debbie talked briefly. Zack's face was unreadable, but the pulse in his neck was beating visibly and after he ended the call, he turned to me and stroked the cheek Rainey had slapped so hard. "That's swollen," he said. "We need to get some ice on that."

I moved closer. "But we're not going inside our house to get the ice."

Zack shook his head. "No, Debbie thinks it's best for us to meet her at Police Headquarters. And then you and I will go straight to Lawyers Bay. It's too cold for a swim there, but I'll make martinis, and I've heard good things about that fish and chips place that opened Labour Day weekend. It's just before the turnoff."

"What about the dogs?"

"I'll call Angus and ask him to bring the dogs out to us. It may be a while. The police are still working on Rainey's car."

"Zack, why are they working on Rainey's car?"

"I'm not sure," my husband said. "Let's go downtown for our meeting with Debbie. As soon as we're there, I'll tell you every-thing I know."

And after we were parked, that's what he did. "There's no way I can gloss this over, Jo, so here's the situation. Try to keep focused on the fact that our neighbour Norma van Velzer has already told the police that you drove off in the Jaguar a few minutes before the incident occurred."

"What incident? Zack, what's going on?"

Zack leaned closer. "Rainey's dead, Joanne. She shot herself, and the police believe the gun she used may be the one she used on Steven Brooks."

"Was it also the gun she attempted to use on Rebecca Woodrow?"

"Forensics will find out the answer to that question. As you know, Rebecca Woodrow is leaving to start a new life today, and she deserves to know who wanted to end her old life.

"Jo, I hate this as much as you will, but Debbie needs to talk to you. You're the only one who knows what happened in the time leading up to Rainey's suicide. What you tell them may give the police the answers they need to other questions."

"You'll come with me when I talk to Debbie, won't you?"

"Of course."

"That's good because I want them to know what happened, but I need support when I have to relive it again."

My husband's voice was deep and reassuring. "Remember that old saw about the longest journey beginning with just a single step?"

"I do, but there's one more thing I need to tell you before I talk to Debbie. When Simon read Rainey's horoscope at his birthday party, he left part of it out. I knew the passage because Kam Chau told me about it when we had coffee. He said the horoscope he and Rainey read together on their shared birthday said that some believe of Scorpios what is true of the scorpion, and the scorpion is the only animal that will poison itself rather than be captured."

CHAPTER FIFTEEN

Debbie Haczkewicz was not just the force's Head of Major Crimes, she was our friend, and that morning her questioning was thorough but her tone was gentle. She knew I was on the edge. When the last question had been answered, she walked us to our car. Debbie was taller than me, and she was powerfully built. When she put her hands on my shoulders, I could feel her strength, and when she said "You'll get through this, Joanne," I believed her.

It was early evening when Angus brought the dogs out and when I saw our son and the dogs, I felt a wash of relief and I knew I'd taken another step on the long journey. But as long journeys often go, it was a case of one step forward and two steps back.

I couldn't shake the memory of Rainey Arcus's parting words to me. I hadn't intended to repeat her words to Zack, but as we got ready for bed, I still felt weighed down by them, so I told him what she'd said.

He was livid. "What the hell did she mean by that? Why should this be on you? Rainey Arcus was the one who killed Steven Brooks and attempted to kill Rebecca Woodrow. And 'when *it* started'? You were just her professor. You did everything you could to include her in the seminar. What did she mean — what is *it*?"

"I think she's referring to what Tom Kelsoe has probably convinced her was a witch hunt. When Kelsoe latched on to Jill Oziowy, I was her friend, and I hated watching him destroy her. When I finally put the pieces together about the role Kelsoe played in the deaths of Kellee Savage and Reid Gallagher, I told Jill. She not only used what we'd learned to publicly humiliate Kelsoe, she gave the police the evidence they needed to charge him with the two murders."

"So for lack of a better word, Kelsoe brainwashed Rainey."

"I'm sure he did," I said. "I should have told Debbie this, and I'd be grateful if you passed it along to her. Rainey's state of mind today was disturbing. She was like a cult follower, and the leader of her cult was Tom Kelsoe. Tom Kelsoe is charismatic, and he creates an alternate reality for the women who become involved with him. I saw it with Jill, and she wasn't a twenty-one-year-old who was painfully insecure. Today, Rainey talked about the unique love she and Tom shared — a love that knows all and forgives all, but can be withdrawn if one of the partners fails the other. It was when I asked her if Tom ever failed her that she slapped my face hard — twice." I touched my cheek gingerly and cringed. "It still hurts," I said.

"Time for lights out," Zack said. "You've had more than enough, and Scout is already in his bed."

"And Esme is in her bed. Zack, I am so grateful."

"So am I," he said, and the next morning when we awoke, we were still in each other's arms.

EPILOGUE

We didn't go back to the city until after Thanksgiving. Our lives were peaceful and comforting at Lawyers Bay. Zack continued to work on Scout's leash training, and Scout was an apt pupil, so the two of us and the two dogs went for plenty of walks.

We agreed that except for the family and close friends, we would keep the outside world outside. Patrick O'Keefe proved to be a thoughtful friend. He funneled all the information he thought I might like to have through Zack.

He sent us the videotape of the statement Rebecca made in her meeting with the publishers. Despite her Victorian cameo delicacy, Rebecca proved to be a skilled and passionate advocate for her grandmother. As she explained the parallels between Laurel Woodrow's life and the life of the mythical Medusa, Rebecca made the agony of the women's lives real: the rapes; the fact that the women to whom they turned for help punished them, eroding their sense of self and making it impossible for them to find love. As she described the way in which Steven Brooks manipulated and betrayed Laurel Woodrow, Rebecca pointed to a final parallel that drove her case home. Medusa was killed as she slept. Her killer, Perseus, beheaded her and then used her head to turn his enemies to stone. Steven Brooks drove Laurel Woodrow to suicide by breaking her heart. Then he used the work that was the product of her mind and her soul to gain fame for himself.

The settlement reached between the publishers and Rebecca Woodrow and her lawyer had an ending worthy of the American short story writer O. Henry.

Steven Brooks left over three million dollars to the Steven Brooks Foundation, an entity that would be devoted to publishing his future works. Since there would be no future works, the foundation could be dissolved. Three million dollars would not be enough to cover lawsuits but it would be enough to cover the settlements, including a settlement with Rebecca Woodrow.

Val Masluk came to Lawyers Bay to tell Zack and me in person that he had given Rainey Arcus the information she needed to make the attempt on Rebecca Woodrow's life and to end Steven Brooks's. He had been trusting her to act as a surrogate, answering any questions that events raised.

Val had never been strong, and he was miserable about the role he, albeit innocently, had played in the events that had transpired. We both liked Val, and we were quick to assure him that we valued our friendship and were looking forward to spending more time together in the future.

And then we talked about his future. Not surprisingly, the Brooks biography was flying off the shelves. Val said it was already going into a second printing, and many prominent people were courting him to consider writing their biographies.

"Any offers you can't refuse?" I said.

Val shook his head. "No, I am not interested. I've come to believe that all biographies can be summed up in the ten words Joe Louis used to sum up his own life. 'I done the best I could with what I had.'"

"He's right," Zack said. "And Joe Louis was one of the greatest and most influential boxers who ever lived."

"I've been reading about him lately. He was really something," Val said.

"So are you going back to broadcasting?" I asked Val.

"I'm not sure. But I do know I'm not giving up writing. I have an idea for a novel. And I owe Rainey Arcus a debt for doing something that may pave my way. She sent *Two Journalists* to the company that published the Brooks biography."

Zack chuckled. "And let me guess: they welcomed you with open arms."

"They're interested in publishing *Two Journalists*. I'll have to talk to everybody who is part of that novel, but I hope it will work out."

"Well, you have my support," I said. "And not just for the novel. Zack and I are in it for whatever comes next."

* * *

Jill Oziowy called to see how I was doing, and she had news of Tom Kelsoe. "I just got off the phone with our reporter in Prince Albert. Her name is Jym with a 'y'," Jill said. "Anyway, Jym is not a fan of Tom Kelsoe's. She says that Tom is playing his wife's tragic demise for all it's worth. According to Jym, Tom is flashing his wedding ring around the way newly engaged women do, but his eye is not on marriage, it's on early parole."

"That man really is a son of a sea biscuit," I said.

"You just hit the fucking nail right on its fucking head," Jill said. "Gotta go, I'm late for a meeting. One of these days I'll surprise you by showing up at the airport with a jumbo pack of Cheezies and a six-pack."

* * *

As it always does, life carried on. There were still difficult patches, but they were becoming fewer and farther between.

On the Friday before the Thanksgiving weekend, I called Margaret McCallum to wish Neil and her a happy holiday. We chatted awhile about light topics, but I noticed she seemed a little down and asked if something was wrong.

"Nothing to worry about," she said. "Just something not turning out the way Neil and I hoped. Remember that puppy in Scout's litter that the couple who'd wanted him couldn't take because they were getting a divorce?"

"I remember," I said. "And Neil and you took him."

"We did, but the couple who wanted him have decided to stay married, and they want their puppy to be part of their new life. I guess we could have said no to them, but they're nice people and they seemed to be counting on starting again with the puppy they'd chosen together."

"And Neil's taking it hard," I said.

"So am I," she said. "We'll be okay. It's just going to take a while."

"I understand, Margaret. I have an idea. We're at our cottage at Lawyers Bay. It's less than an hour's drive from your place. Could you and Neil come here sometime tomorrow for a meal and a visit? I know Zack has been staying in touch with Neil about Scout's progress as the dog of a person in a wheelchair, but I'm sure seeing Zack and Scout together would cheer Neil up."

"I know it would. Is ten in the morning too early for a visit?"

"Not at all. We're early birds, and Zack will be as excited as Neil when he hears you're coming to see Scout and him."

At ten sharp the next day, the McCallums arrived, and Neil and Scout were waiting for them. Neil bounded out of their car, and the men and dog took off.

"Let me grab my camera and get Esme," I said. "This is fun to watch."

It was a bright, crisp, still day, and Zack took Neil down by the Amur maple because he wanted to show him where our bullmastiff, Pantera, was buried. The Amur was at its glorious best, and Margaret and I both took pictures of Neil and Zack chatting quietly as they looked down at the stones that marked Pantera's grave.

We followed the men to the path where Scout and Zack took their walks.

I wanted to get a video of the occasion, so Margaret and I moved to a spot where we could get footage of the three of them approaching us.

All performed perfectly. Neil and Zack chatted as Zack pushed his chair, and Scout trotted along beside them as smartly as a show dog.

When they joined us, I squatted to congratulate Scout. "Well done," I said.

"Congratulations all around," Margaret said. "Now let's look at Joanne's video."

After we'd watched it a few times, Zack said, "Let's go up to the house and watch it on the big screen."

And we started off, but on our way, Neil took me aside. "Do you remember telling me that raising dogs is an important job?"

"I do."

"When we were looking at your old dog's grave, Zack told me how sad he was when your dog died."

"It was the first dog he'd ever had, and Zack really was sad."

"But Zack says he stopped being sad when I gave him Scout. I was happy when you told me I had an important job, but now I know my job really is important. I'm happy and I'm proud." Neil grinned. "It feels good."

"Let's go in and get washed up. There's lots more to see here. And after we've seen everything, we're having lunch. What's your favourite thing to eat?"

"Spaghetti and meatballs."

"That's exactly what we're having."

"So I'm lucky," Neil said. "Happy, proud and lucky. That's three good feelings."

"Three of the best," I said. "Let's hang on to them."

ACKNOWLEDGEMENTS

Thank you to everyone at ECW who guided me through the paths that led me to the novel I hoped to write.

For Emily Schultz, my structural editor, who knew exactly where to point out the good, the bad and the ugly.

Rachel Ironstone, my copy editor, who maintained the standard of excellence that has always marked ECW publications.

Samantha Chin, managing editor, who unerringly chooses the right person for the task and trusts them to do their job.

Michel Vrana, designer, who created cover art for *The Legacy* that draws readers' eyes and reflects the novel's theme.

Jennifer Gallinger, who typeset the interior, and Emily Varsava, my publicist.

And to Carrie Gleason, who proofread the text.

* * *

Words cannot adequately express how grateful I am to all of you who sent cards, letters, flowers, plants, get-well helium balloons or texts telling me that I was in your thoughts and prayers.

This has not been the easiest time of my life, but thanks to you, I have never felt alone.

This lengthy hospital stay has given me time to reflect on the people who give my day-to-day life joy and comfort: Lynn Bell, whose drop-in hospital visits with whimsical gifts have been a joy; Joanne and Lionel Bonneville, for the chickens, the recipes and the memories of our half-century friendship; Cindy Mackenzie, for good talks about books to read and the changing academic life; our next-door neighbours, Ron and Cindy; our family's pharmacist, Wayne Chau, BSP; Dean Mike Sinclair and the congregation of St. Paul's Cathedral, and our much-loved friend of twenty-five years, Jasmina Terzic.

To my kinswoman, Cheryl Freedman, who's saving me a spot next to her at the old lady bench in the Market.

To my husband, Ted, my children and their partners — Hildy and Brett, Max and Carrie, and Nathaniel and Willow — and my grandchildren Madeleine, Lena, Ben, Chesney, Kai, Peyton, and Lexi. I have always known that my family is the greatest gift I will ever receive. In the past challenging months, they have taken care of everything that makes my life worthwhile. I am blessed.

And last but not least, thanks to Ollie, our loving cat.

This book is also available as a Global Certified Accessible™ (GCA) ebook. ECW Press's ebooks are screen reader friendly and are built to meet the needs of those who are unable to read standard print due to blindness, low vision, dyslexia, or a physical disability.

At ECW Press, we want you to enjoy our books in whatever format you like. If you've bought a print copy just send an email to ebook@ecwpress.com and include:

- the book title
- the name of the store where you purchased it
- a screenshot or picture of your order/receipt number and your name
- your preference of file type: PDF (for desktop reading), ePub (for a phone/tablet, Kobo, or Nook), mobi (for Kindle)

A real person will respond to your email with your ebook attached. Please note this offer is only for copies bought for personal use and does not apply to school or library copies.

Thank you for supporting an independently owned Canadian publisher with your purchase!